FIFTEEN

An Iris Wildthyme Anniversary Collection

Edited by Stuart Douglas

Obverse Books
Cover Design © Cody Quijano-Schell
Cover Artwork © Mark Manley
First published October 2013

The Ninnies on Putney Common © Paul Magrs
Gimme Shelter © Eddie Robson
Party Fears Two © Stuart Douglas
Time to Exist © Andy Smillie
Project: Wildthyme © Cavan Scott & Mark Wright
God Engine Rhapsody © Julio Angel Ortiz
The Wildthyme Effect © Nick Campbell
Ouroboros © Neil Chester
In Passing © Nick Wallace
Samsāra © James Manley-Buser
Scream in Blue © Dave Hoskin
Our Tune © Ross Douglas
The Golden Hendecahedron © Cody Quijano-Schell
Iris and the Caliphate © Eric Brown
Mix Her Own Adventure © Patrick Magee
Iris at the V&A © George Mann
Dog Days of Summer © Roy Gill
Iris Wildthyme and Panda © Paul Magrs

The moral rights of the author have been asserted. All characters in this book are fictional. Any resemblance to persons, living or dead, is co-incidental.

All rights reserved. No part of this publication may be reproduced, stored in a retrieval system, or in any form or by any means, without the prior permission in writing of the publisher, nor be otherwise circulated in any form of binding, cover or e-book other than which it is published and without a similar condition including this condition being imposed on the subsequent publisher.

CONTENTS

The Ninnies on Putney Common 5
Gimme Shelter 26
Party Fears Two 33
God Engine Rhapsody 43
Project: Wildthyme 50
Our Tune 74
The Wildthyme Effect 82
Ouroboros 104
In Passing 112
Iris at the V&A 130
The Golden Hendecahedron 142
Samsara 175
Iris and the Caliphate 181
Mix Her Own Adventure 200
Time to Exist 211
Scream in Blue 235
Dog Days of Summer 259

The Ninnies on Putney Common
Paul Magrs

I was shaken out of my rather dull life that night, and it happened on Putney Common.

The first thing was seeing the yellow lights of a bus through the mist as I made my way home. It was parked on the grass, far from any road. Blinds were pulled down on most windows of both decks.

The Number 22 was the bus that ran between our common and the centre of town, but it shouldn't have been parked on a scrubby patch of grass.

It was then I heard an abrupt squawk of female outrage and the thwacking noise of several heavy blows being landed.

There was a lithe, brutal-looking creature with gnarled, purple flesh. It wore not a stitch of clothing but, oddly, that wasn't the most offensive aspect to him. His eyes were the worst thing. Lilac and green, spiralling madly in the hideous rugby ball of his head.

All of this detail I absorbed in a split second.

Then I noticed that it was an elderly lady he was wrestling. Though she was thrashing about madly with her furled brolly, the demon had clambered onto her back and she couldn't land a blow on him. As she whirled around fruitlessly her frizzy white hair stood wildly on end, and her tweedy cape was getting very tangled up.

'You devilish creep! Unclasp me at once! How dare you handle me like an old baggage!'

Her shrieks and bellows were terrifying, but even more so was the laughter of her assailant as it reached my astonished ears.

'Heeee heee heeeeeeee…'

And then, all at once, I realised that I actually knew this woman. I recognised her. But I couldn't recall where from.

Over teacakes at eleven Walter told me how much he was looking forward to this evening's film, *Get Thee Inside Me, Satan*, which was another of his gory horror movies.

I sat through the thing with my hands over my eyes much of the time. It was irreligious and rather rude, I thought.

In the queue at 'Frying Tonight!' we found we were standing behind the old woman – I still didn't know her name! – and she was ordering a battered sausage and a sixpence worth of chips.

'Ah, my dear. This is your gentleman, is it?'

'This is Walter,' I said. 'A work colleague.'

'How do you do,' said Walter, staring through his fogged-up glasses.

'I am Iris Wildthyme, my dears,' said the woman, clutching her steaming supper to her tweedy bosom. 'Transtemporal Adventuress and Righter of Cosmic Wrongs and – yes! – upstanding member of your lending library!'

Then we had to order our fish hurriedly, for we were holding up the queue.

She suddenly fixed me with a frantic glance. 'Don't just stand there gawping, my dear young woman! Won't you help me destroy this wicked fiend?'

With that she used her free hand to scrabble inside her worsted jacket. She liberated something and flung it at me. I, who have never been able even to catch a tennis ball, snatched the device out of the turbid air with ease.

'I've got it!'

'Hurrah!'

'What is it?'

The foul being was attempting to strangle her, with its tapering purple fingers squirming round her wattled neck.

'J-just switch the damned thing on! It's obvious where the button is!'

I fiddled with the metallic device, which looked rather like a garlic press or a tea strainer. Yes, there was the button. I pressed it, quite hard, and almost immediately a fan of sizzling orange light shot into the night.

The effect of this cone of brilliance on the old lady's enemy was both immediate and dramatic. Jerked upwards like a marionette, he quickly loosened his grip on the ungainly lady. She threw him off and whirled her cape like she was a matador.

When I got in, Mother was sitting up in bed, banging her headboard with an orthopaedic shoe.

'You won't be content until I die! I'm only half-alive as it is! Where have you been, Dodie? Just where the devil do you think you've been? I've been lying here starving all day!'

She does it every time. Mother browbeats me into submission. I just have to take one glance at her looking all fragile in bed, or hear her piercing voice castigating me.

'I'm sorry, Mother. I know it's after seven o'clock. But I took a quick route over the Common on my bike and…'

'What?! I've warned you, young lady. There could be maniacs or all sorts hanging about out there! And how come a shortcut made you so late?'

Did I real want to tell her about my run-in with the strange old woman and that devilish creature? Surely not. It would just be more ammunition for her to throw at me.

'I became rather lost, and had a puncture…'

Mother tutted and glowered from under her hairnet. 'Is it sardines on toast again tonight?'

'I'm afraid I don't have much time to prepare anything more tasty…'

'That job of yours will be the death of me!' Mother roared. 'How do you think I feel, Dodie Golightly? Trapped here all day with no one to talk to but spiders and mice?'

Somewhere close by in the early evening obscurity there was a deadly struggle in progress and instantly my whole body was on the alert.

There! The noise came from directly behind me with redoubled force. I whirled about without thinking, and let my bicycle topple to the ground.

I was so astonished by what I saw that I couldn't do anything but stare.

There was a demon in the middle of Putney Common.

'But I have to work, mother. Without my job at the library we'd be out on the street…'

'Pah!' she shouted explosively. 'Go and fetch me these horrible sardines, then. My belly's rumbling like crazy!'

Waiters were calmly going between tables on the café floor. Iris pointed out Jean Paul Sartre and friends sitting in the far corner. I took a little look at them when I went in to use the upstairs loo. They seemed impossibly young, gathered about their messy table, and their gurgle of conversation was very heated and erudite, floating about me as I ascended those stairs in a kind of trance. I was expecting everything to vanish at once in a puff of smoke. All of this – tangible and Parisian and in the past – might dissolve at once like the cream in my coffee.

Iris had already assured me that this would not happen. She puffed on her thin cigar and fluffed out her hair and said, 'You have strayed into my orbit, Dodie Golightly, and that's quite the most thrilling place anyone could be. Every bit of it is real and it's happening RIGHT NOW!'

So there I was, perched on a lavatory upstairs in the famous Café Flore. I almost fainted with the excitement.

'Mother! What's going on?'
'Oh! So you're back, are you?'
Mother was up on her feet in the middle of our living room. The very room that had remained dark, dusty and unused for so long. Now it seemed, within the space of a day, it had been redecorated and titivated within an inch of its life. It was all very snazzy, with white carpet and beanbags and curious Indian wall-hangings. Mother herself was quite different, wearing a sheepskin waistcoat, purple mini-dress and thigh-high white boots.

On top of that, she looked marvellously spry. She was positively beaming. Her hair had been cut beautifully and she looked far healthier than I had ever known her.

'Back? But... where have I been? I was only out for my Thursday night at the flicks with... with...'

I was about to say 'Walter', when Walter himself appeared. He was standing under a curved archway that had been knocked through to our dining room. He was wearing sunglasses and a furry fake tiger skin suit and a silk kipper tie. I blinked hard several times and struggled to take control of myself.

'Mother? Walter? Would you care to explain just what's going on?'

Walter looked as amazed to see me as I did to see him. He gave a nervous giggle: 'Hee heeee,' before stopping himself.

'Mars?' said I, still quite out of puff.

'Hm, yes,' she said. 'It's where I took all those poor specimens that we found in the sausage factory that belonged to your mother and your erstwhile man friend, Walter. Him with the ears.'

'Wait – the whole factory was owned by my Mother… and Walter?'

As I told her the story she sat herself at the cab of the bus and started flicking switches on what I dimly registered as the most extraordinary dashboard I had ever seen. Besides the steering wheel and so on, which you'd expect, there was a bewildering array of clunky dials and displays. She prompted me several times to get on with my account and I had to shout as she revved the engines.

The engines sounded rather different to those of any ordinary bus, too.

Next thing, I was aware that I was telling her all about my difficult relationship with my mother, and Iris instructed me to fetch the brandy bottle. I shucked my coat on the way, laying it on a chaise longue and that's when the bus lurched and I realised we were moving.

Iris was hefting the steering wheel energetically, and I wasn't at all sure I should be plying her with brandy as we surged into the night.

'It's all about the sausage, you see.'

Was I hearing her correctly? She was shouting over the noise of the engine, so I decided that I must have misheard.

'Remember? At 'Frying Tonight!' you and your man-friend ordered haddock, whereas I opted for a battered sausage.' She grimaced at me as if everything should be clear by now. Just then she took a corner very abruptly, wrenching the steering wheel round with surprising vigour.

'So?' I asked.

But Iris knew what she was talking about. That keen mind of hers had analysed that sausage as she nibbled at it walking down the street with Walter and myself. Now she was thundering towards the factory of the suppliers of said sausages, 'Porkers', right across the other side of the city.

'It was a delicious-tasting meat-based product,' my new friend told me, darkly. 'But there was something quite odd about it too. Extra-terrestrial in origin, I think.'

I went a bit woozy then, possibly under the influence of the brandy, but also maybe because of the mass of fog that we rolled into, momentarily, as the road veered towards the Thames embankment. It was a curiously multi-coloured fog that enveloped the bus for some moments.

'I had to dip through the Maelstrom just there,' Iris told me. 'Speed up our journey a little!'

Then the demon was caught in the orange glare. I let out a cry as he started to shrivel. He twisted and blackened into a tattered scrap, and then there was nothing left. That high-pitched, rather terrible laughter accompanied his demise, until the very second that he fizzed out of existence.

The beam snapped off, leaving myself and the old woman alone in the dark fog and the silence.

I jumped when she clapped me on the back. 'I say, well done, my dear. Hand me back my De-Ninnivator would you?'

She could only have meant the metal device, which had become rather warm in my hand, and so I gave it to her at once.

She stowed it away and went about straightening her old-fashioned garments, and placing her trilby back atop her disturbed hairdo. She told me, 'You did an extremely good job just then. I believe you may have saved my life.'

'W-what was that thing?' I stammered.

'Here. Bottoms up. My dear young lady, we can't argue with fate.' Her face looked suddenly very haggard as it stared at me over our brandy balloons. I sipped the spirits cautiously and found them wonderfully warming. Iris went on, 'Only twice before have I defied the will of cosmic karma.' She tutted sorrowfully. 'And never again. The price is much too high. What we must do is listen very carefully to the workings of the universe and learn its intentions. Our roles may be grand or they may be modest…'

'You sound like a mystic,' I said.

She knocked back her drink and then flung off her outdoor cape and hat, letting them land where they would.

'Do I?' Now she was heading for the cab of the bus, dodging through the furniture. 'Well, I have been a student of many exotic philosophies in my time. Long enough to decide they mostly consist of tommyrot. However, I do believe in cosmic karma. And I know that it has picked you out, Dodie Golightly, to help me in my mission.'

'I saw another!' I found myself bursting out as I took receipt of her books. 'In our backyard. He was watching me through the scullery window.'

'Then I fear that the Ninnies have followed you and become fixated on you,' the woman said, looking stern. 'I insist that you allow me to tell you all!'

It was Mother who said, 'It's very simple, Dodie, my love. While you were away, you left a perfectly good man unattended. Now, Walter and I are lovers and we have been for some time. For the full year since you ran away from home, in fact!'

The interior of the bus had been rigged out like a rather smart living room. The seats had been taken away and replaced by some plush, comfortable sofas. There was an escritoire, a coffee table with magazines scattered and a darling Art Deco drinks cabinet. The lighting was muted and came from some chi-chi tassled lamps.

Iris ushered me to the very back of the lower deck, which had been converted into a sort of galley kitchen. She put a pan of milk on to boil, but then there was a muffled explosion from the stovetop and she swore very loudly.

'Booby-trapped. Hmm. No cocoa for us,' she grumped. 'Will brandy do instead, Dodie?'

'I don't drink.'

'Pah,' she said, heading bullishly towards the drinks cabinet. 'You'll need to if you're to be my new assistant and travelling companion.'

And that was how we ended up having the adventure with the existentialists and the Martians in Paris, which was my first real encounter with extra-terrestrials, if you don't count the Ninny I had helped dispatch during my initial meeting with Iris. It turned out that Ninnies were from space as well. Iris claimed that it was Mars that they hailed from, as did the silver-eyed beings who could disguise themselves as figures from public life and the entertainment industry – hence the sinisterly flashing eyes of Mme De Beauvoir, Jacques Brel and Marlene Dietrich, all of whom we chanced upon (quite violently in some cases) during our Parisian sojourn.

'I don't think we want your cocoa, no,' he said at last. 'My duty is to accompany Miss Golightly to her front door and see that she is safely ensconced at home, otherwise her mother will fret.'

Iris gazed at him beadily. 'Miss Golightly has no need of your help this week, Walter. You may go home on your own at once!'

'What?' he gasped.

'I'll be all right, Walter,' I told him.

'But..!'

'No buts!' said Iris heartily, crumpling up her finished chip paper and tossing it to him. 'Find a bin would you, dearie? And say goodnight to Dodie. Come along, Dodie Golightly. We have cocoa to make and work to do!'

And so we left Walter Murch – my erstwhile beau – standing on the corner of the street in a state of utter dismay.

It was my first journey to another planet and all I could think about – as we thundered through the Maelstrom – was that Iris had let slip that my mother had been investing in the sausage factory. She had been in bed with the Ninnies.

'Of course,' Iris barked tetchily. 'Now, be a dear and keep quiet while I bring us in to land. Mars can be rather tricky, since it exists in several hypothetical realities in the same dimensional space during the very same epoch… We might have a bumpy landing…'

Which we did, slightly, but the bus cushioned the impact. A few ornaments fells off shelves and there was a nasty tinkling sound from inside the drinks cabinet.

I was more concerned with pulling open the blinds and chintz curtains and looking at dawn on the red planet.

It was miraculous. We were in the heart of the crimson dustbowl. The sun came up like someone was cracking a golden egg into melting butter and making the most sumptuous and rich birthday cake. I suppose I must have been hungry. My stomach rumbled loudly in the confines of the bus, making Iris laugh.

Still I could hear my mother's voice. 'Now, Walter and I are lovers and we have been for some time. For the full year since you ran away from home, in fact!'

Iris went to the galley kitchen to make coffee and fry up some bacon.

Next day I was on the front desk when I came face to face with the lady from the Common. I remembered at once that I had seen her here in the library several times during the past few weeks. I believed she was new to the area, and rather fond of books about world history, astronomy, the male nude in western art and tales of lurid murder.

'Good morning, my dear!' she bellowed, plopping a carpet bag and a stack of books upon my tidy desk. 'Nice to see you after our little escapade last evening.'

I looked around quickly, to check that no one was listening in. But the library was quiet at that time in the morning. Walter was having his break. Already he had commented on some difference in me today. Said I looked a bit excited. 'Excited about coming to work?' I laughed.

Walter studied me carefully. 'I brought some tea cakes for our elevenses,' he told me.

Now it was almost eleven and here was this strange woman returning her books.

'My dear, I think I owe you an explanation,' she told me. 'About what you saw last night.'

'I saw another!' I found myself bursting out as I took receipt of her books. 'In our backyard. He was watching me through the scullery window.'

'Then I fear that the Ninnies have followed you and become fixated on you,' the woman said, looking stern. 'I insist that you allow me to tell you all!'

It was as if it was colour itself I was hungry for. I was a child of the war, and of the thin, malnourished, black and white years following on from the hostilities. Now I was waking up to colour and magic. This was how I felt.

And we could breathe on Mars! I said, shouldn't we have apparatus? I had watched things on TV about people in space, I had read articles in magazines about how prepared they had to be. Why, they spent millions on keeping men alive when they went out of Earth's atmosphere. But here was Iris, whooshing open the hydraulic doors of the bus, and stepping outside in her woollen cape and Robin Hood hat, swinging her carpet bag, which contained nothing more sophisticated than a flask of hot coffee and some fruitcake wrapped in muslin.

'Come along, my dear,' she prompted me, and we set off on a walk across the arid Martian landscape.

Walter and I had a standing date at the pictures every Thursday. We saw whatever the Roxy was showing and then we had a fish supper on the way home. It wasn't exactly thrilling but it was my bit of social life and I looked forward to it.

We walked through the streets together, warming our hands on our newspaper parcels and Walter seemed rather miffed not to have me on my own. I was relieved. Last time he had kept trying to get me into dark doorways for a kiss and a cuddle and I was fed up of trying to wriggle out of his clutches. I was avoiding telling him that I just didn't see him as a potential suitor.

'I say,' said Iris, chewing a mouthful of hot chips, 'Why not come back to my bus and we can wash our supper down with cocoa or some such, eh?'

'Bus?' frowned Walter.

'Yes, indeed, young man,' said Iris. Walter looked momentarily pleased. It was a long time since anyone had called him that. 'I live aboard a double decker bus. Do you see anything odd about that?'

I dwelt miserably on what might have happened. All the events of the past few days rolled into one phantasmagorical fugue. I sat on a cold bench looking out over the gravy-coloured Thames and sighed heavily. I had been taken out of time, that's what had happened. And there was no fitting me back. But how could such a thing have happened?

'Yoo hoo! Dearie!'

I hadn't even heard the bus pull up at the stop behind me, such was the depth of my introspection. But she had parked and hopped out and now she was bellowing at the startled people in the queue that no, she wasn't in service and no, she wouldn't be taking them anywhere.

Then she was sitting beside me on the bench. 'Good morning, my dear. Well, you'll be glad to know I've been frightfully busy. I've learned a thing or two about this business of the Ninnies and the Sausage Factory. They're splicing the mortal remains of kidnapped alien species with human beings they have been taking prisoner and then…' Suddenly she stopped and frowned at me. 'You're not paying attention. This is the key to the whole nefarious business and you aren't even paying attention. Why is that? What can be on your mind, Dodie Golightly?'

I found a great splurge of anger rising up in my stomach. I rarely felt as strongly as this. 'You've ruined my life!' I shouted at her, and then realised people were looking over and listening.

'Hardly!' she scoffed. 'And tell me, dear. These investments your mother makes and these men who come to sit by her bedside with their ledgers and graphs? Have you thought just what kind of business your mother might be piling her money into?'

And all at once I remembered where I had heard the name 'Porkers' before. Mother's business associates.

'Your mother has her fingers in many pies,' said Iris darkly. 'Come on. I'll buy you a drink.'

20

I hurried downstairs, glad to be out of the old dragon's sight. In the scullery it was freezing and I fumbled with matches, trying to light the gas.

As I stood over the old stove I reflected that Mother in her declining years really was like an old dragon. She lay fuming and smoking in her cave, sitting protectively on her piles of treasure.

I could never have given two hoots about the money. I was here to look after Mother because no one else would. That was all.

The sardines were bubbling in their tomato sauce and the bread was starting to char under the grill. I looked away for an instant and happened to glance out of the scullery window into the yard beyond.

And I'm afraid to say I screamed.

There was a face looking back at me.

A face with madly spiralling, lilac eyes.

'Of course,' Iris barked tetchily. 'Now, be a dear and keep quiet while I bring us in to land. Mars can be rather tricky, since it exists in several hypothetical realities in the same dimensional space during the very same epoch… We might have a bumpy landing…'

'Heee heeee heeeee…!'

Ice was running down my back, even inside my combination garments. I don't know why I was foolish enough to do what I did next. Perhaps my earlier encounter had made me brave.

Walter seemed rather miffed not to have me on my own.

I returned to the kitchen, bolted the door and found Mother's supper on the point of being incinerated. Just in time!

'Fie, demon!' I shouted. 'Avast and avaunt!'

I believe the words I was yelling came from some spooky film I had seen at the pictures. They came to my lips quite unbidden.

There was a kerfuffle in the dark yard, as it pelted away on slimy cobbles. It knocked over bins and set the Alsatian at number seventeen howling.

What if the beastly being had been able to sneak inside?

Another Ninny!

I was sure of it.

She suddenly fixed me with a frantic glance. 'Don't just stand there gawping, my dear young woman! Won't you help me destroy this wicked fiend?'

With that she used her free hand to scrabble inside her worsted jacket. She liberated something and flung it at me. I, who have never been able even to catch a tennis ball, snatched the device out of the turbid air with ease.

'I've got it!'

'Hurrah!'

'What is it?'

The foul being was attempting to strangle her, with its tapering purple fingers squirming round her wattled neck.

The rest of that evening was a strange sort of blur. I remember us pulling up in a very shady street at the back of a dark factory that looked more like a prison. Iris hurtled up to the top deck of her bus, with me following after her, finding her opening a skylight in the very roof of her vehicle. Next thing we were standing on the roof of the bus and she was launching a grappling hook.

We hauled ourselves up over the wall and gazed at the dim buildings below.

She was astonishingly sprightly, for such an old bird. She even had to help me down, as we made our descent into the enclosure. The air smelled sickly sweet and meaty. When we caught our breath and listened, there came the noises of penned animals, from not too far away. The snorting and whickering of creatures kept in sties. I assumed they would be pigs, but what Iris and I found in those barns couldn't quite be described as such.

I remember grasping her arm. 'Oh my god! What are they?'

She was grim-faced. 'Precisely what I was expecting. Someone has been fooling around with nature. How perfectly dreadful.'

She had an expressive, jowly face with heavy bags underneath her hooded eyes. She looked like an ancient creature who had seen everything that was worthwhile, and quite a bit besides.

'That, my dear, was a Ninny.'

'A Ninny?' I repeated, not sure I'd heard correctly.

'Quite. And I am in the process of doing my damndest to ensure that its nefarious kind do not take over the whole human race.'

'I see.'

'Do you?' Suddenly she beamed at me. When she smiled she revealed crooked teeth, but her whole face lit up with youthful glee. 'Jolly good! Well, thanks once more, dearie, and perhaps I'll see you again sometime!'

With that she gave a hop, skip and a jump and scurried across the tussocky grass towards the illuminated double decker.

And I was alone again, with my bike, in the yellowish fog on Putney Common.

It was early evening and the two of us were sitting at a pavement café, having the most delicious coffee I'd ever tasted. I was a child of the war years, of austerity measures and powdered substitutes and, in more recent years, quite used to dishwater coffee in the staffroom at work. This coffee had been heaped with cream and it was strong enough to blow my head off. This was heavenly and for a little while I hardly cared how the bus had managed to transport us here, wherever here was.

'Autumn in St Germain,' Iris told me, lighting up a gnarled-looking cheroot. 'We're on the Left Bank in Paris in the early nineteen-fifties.' She breathed in the delicious air. 'I can smell Gauloises, Chanel, existentialism and garlic. In short – the whiff of sexual, aesthetic and intellectual freedom. And so you see, my dear, you needn't worry your pretty little head off. We can go back and forth just how we please. Time doesn't work as many theorists believe. No part of history is really set in stone and, also, it's never too late to change. And what has changed from yesterday to today can be made to go back again, any way you wish it to. And such meddling isn't forbidden, you know. It's in our gift. Well, in mine, anyway.'

She smiled at me genially, as if she thought me capable of following every word.

'You see? Now we can take our own sweet time in the universe. Now you've been aboard my magic bus.'

Gimme Shelter
Eddie Robson

'See some I.D., please?' said the barman.

Iris Wildthyme laughed. It was laugh that said: What an absurd question! But it was also a laugh that nobody ever did sincerely. She'd been afraid this would happen.

The barman didn't flinch. He simply waited for Iris to comply with his request.

Iris sighed excessively. 'Fine,' she said, and rifled through her bag. She whipped out a tatty wallet, opened it and flashed it at the barman. She went to put it away, but –

'Wait,' said the barman. 'Let me see that properly.'

Iris handed it over.

The barman examined her driver's licence. Not only was it from 2006, and so looked deeply fake here in 1994, the picture on it was manifestly not the woman standing at the bar. Also: 'This says you're 49.' The barman handed it back.

Iris bit her lip, exasperated. 'Oh come on. What's the big deal?'

'You can have a soft drink or you can leave.'

'I'm five hundred and bloody three, I'll have you know!' Iris screamed.

Twenty minutes later, Iris was sitting in the bus shelter slightly down the road, on the opposite side. Idly, she used a key to add a design of her own to the graffiti that had been scratched into its perspex windows. She wished she could get in touch with Panda. He was off dealing with some 'personal business', and in the meantime Iris had opted to spend a couple of hours at one of her top 700 pubs in the universe, *The Starling's Beak* in Little Flympton, and pick up some gin from the off-licence. But the pub had kicked her out and the offy had turned her down.

Iris pulled her army surplus greatcoat tighter around herself, trying to keep out the November cold.

This was the worst regeneration ever.

She'd had trouble with this one from the start. A Zaksyn Parasite had tried to rewrite her DNA and the regeneration had very nearly failed. Panda had saved her life, giving the process a push with a shot of rejuvenative serum which she kept in the first aid box with the plasters and Germoline, for exactly this eventuality. But in his haste and desperation, he'd used a bit too much. Iris looked seventeen at most; she was slight, awkward and gangly, and her long blonde hair was frizzy and refused to behave. And although that post-regenerative thing where you were moody and capricious always happened, it didn't usually last for months on end.

'Is this seat taken?' said a voice to her right. She looked up and saw a smirking young man, about the same age Iris now appeared to be. A lank, dark fringe hung over his pale face: under his long black coat she could see a Suede T-shirt. The question he'd asked was sort of meant to be a joke. But the subtext was, he was hoping her boyfriend wasn't going to come back from having a piss in the woods, find some pasty indie kid chatting to his girlfriend, and batter him.

'No,' said Iris, hoping she wasn't going to regret it. Another problem with this regeneration was all the attention from the wrong blokes: kids like this one, she just wanted to pat on the head and say 'Aww, bless,' and most of the older ones made her want to throw up.

Oh well. Someone to talk to. And he was carrying a plastic bag, and it was chinking promisingly. He sat down, a respectful distance from Iris, and reached into the bag. 'I'm Mike,' he said. 'Haven't seen you around here before.' He removed a bottle from the bag and offered it to her: a Bacardi Breezer.

Iris' eyes lit up at its lurid orangeness. She didn't like to admit it, especially not to Panda, but since the regeneration she'd slightly lost her taste for gin. By contrast, the offer of one of those was deeply enticing.

Iris took the bottle from Mike. 'I'm Iris,' she said, 'and no, you haven't.'

'Have you got a bottle opener?' Mike asked.

Iris rolled her eyes. 'Of course,' she said, bringing one from the pocket of her overcoat: it was shaped like the Starship Enterprise. 'I'm not an amateur.' She handed him the opener and he opened one for himself.

They chatted a while. Mike was nice enough. It didn't take him long to admit that he'd seen her failing to get served in the pub and trudging over to the bus shelter, and had bought the drinks because he felt bad for her. He was trying to do a romantic gesture thing. Bless!

'How'd you know I wasn't going to catch a bus?' she asked.

'They stopped the buses here last year,' he replied.

She didn't want to crush his hopes – not yet, anyway – and she quite liked being the mysterious stranger. She let him talk – mostly, about what he was going to do when he got out of this village. He didn't ask her much about herself, but that was all right. She wasn't in the mood anyway. So she heard about Mike's university plans; what he wanted to do on his gap year; and a lot about his band, Downwardly Mobile. 'People are always getting stuck in this place,' he said: they all had big ideas, but somehow they just seemed to give up. Well, that wasn't going to happen to him. He spoke so vividly, Iris swore she could see images of this future floating over his head...

No wait, she could. They were in the perspex of the shelter, like reflections of things that weren't really there.

'What's, er...' She pointed at the images. 'What's going on with those?'

Mike looked at the walls, and it was clear from the look on his face that he was no wiser than she was. And then, all around them, the bus shelter started to rattle.

'Come on!' said Iris, grabbing Mike's hand and pulling him towards the doorway of the shelter – but something blocked their way. A force field? Something like that. Iris and Mike turned back to the shelter and saw the images bouncing between the perspex walls – Mike's future howling around them. And then –

Quiet. The images were sucked away. Mike dropped to the ground. Iris examined him: his eyes were open, he was breathing shallowly, he was alive... but lifeless, somehow. Where before he'd been pale, now he seemed grey. And Iris understood, in a moment, that something had been stolen from him. There was something alive in the bus shelter, and it exuded smugness. It knew what it was doing: it had done it before. And by drawing Mike here, she'd unwittingly helped it.

'You wanker!' Iris said to the bus shelter.

The bus shelter responded by making its scratched graffiti swirl and dance before her eyes. It wasn't going to let her go. It would make her talk eventually, and it would steal her future too, like it had stolen Mike's, and so many before it. It sensed her future might be particularly long and rich and delicious. It was only a matter of time: she may as well talk.

So she talked. She talked about how she was going to become the thing that destroyed this creature.

And it couldn't stop her. She talked about how she would get inside it, rip it to pieces and throw its cruel, miserable soul to the wind. It had eaten the dreams of all the people who'd sat here – it was too late to give those back – but she'd stop it ever doing this to anyone again.

It worked quite well.

Cracks spread across the perspex, distorting the graffiti, rendering its messages illegible. The entire shelter shuddered. Iris leapt on top of Mike, sheltering them both with her coat, as the entire shelter collapsed on them – not with a shatter, as glass would have made, but with a huge creak.

Iris and Mike slowly, cautiously sat up and looked at the destruction around them. Mike still looked pretty grim. Had the creature been destroyed along with the shelter, or had it escaped? She couldn't be sure. But for now, it didn't matter. She glanced down the road: a few drinkers from *The Starling's Beak* had popped out to see what the noise was.

'Iris...?' Mike asked, weakly. 'What did you do?'

'It's OK,' she said, absent-mindedly patting him on the head. 'We're fine.'

And then, a bus arrived.

'What the hell happened here?' asked Panda, leaning out of the window as he put the handbrake on.

Iris helped Mike to his feet. 'I'm sorry, Panda,' she said. 'I didn't pick up any gin.'

'Typical,' said Panda. 'Who's the boy?'

'His name's Mike,' Iris replied as she helped the dazed, emptied-out Mike to board the bus. 'And something's stolen all his dreams. So we're taking him to find some more.'

Mike was given no choice in the matter.

Party Fears Two

Stuart Douglas

When the big bloodhound comes bounding in the door, Brenda Soobie, divine songstress and that year's smash Vegas sensation, scratches him distractedly under the chin and tries to feed him clumps of tiny salmon canapés which she smushes in her hand and moulds into balls.

'Hey gang,' she shouts through, 'anyone lost a pooch?' but it's a distance from the reception area to the public rooms of the rented mansion and nobody hears her. The dog pulls at the hem of her long, pale green gown and she's forced to shoo it away. 'Even if little Timmy has fallen down the well, that's no excuse to *savage* my new dress, honey. June would be *furious!*' And she laughs and opens the door, gesturing for the dog to be on its way.

She watches it run down the street for a moment, until she's sure it knows where it's going, then strolls back inside, blowing smoke rings and chatting on an iPhone that shouldn't really be around in that long, hot summer of 1967.

Maurice Newbury is inside, already slightly glassy-eyed but assuring his friend George that 'Veronica simply has a head cold, nothing more sinister than that'. She smiles at George as she passes and he raises his glass to her with a tiny, resigned shrug. Maurice does tend to the melancholy at times, but he's always been very fortunate in his friends.

As she walks across the smoke filled room, she makes out Panda standing on a table shouting at someone. She catches the words 'odious Tory shit' and then a brief glimpse of Jeremy scooping the little animal up before billowing clouds of incense and hashish fumes cover the scene again. Not to worry, she thinks, those two could take care of themselves in any company.

Cody is there, of course, dancing with a balloon in one hand and his rather hunky husband's arm in the other. She should know the balloon's name, but it eludes her for the moment. Perhaps that silly Jenny's mixing her drinks too strong again?

She laughs at herself. There was a time – and would be again in the future – when she could knock back gin as strong as paint-stripper and then be looking for a half pint chaser to follow. Still, the pretty little Sentient's name remains stubbornly on the tip of her tongue, so she makes sure not to catch the eye of any of *that* group. There's nothing so awkward as not knowing the same of someone you're talking to. She still blushes to her core when she brings to mind the time she'd kept calling that little piano player Elvis John.

The crash of breaking glass is just loud enough to be heard over the sound of Cilla and Dusty doing 'View to a Kill' as a duet on the lawn outside, and since nobody else seems all that interested, she wanders over in the approximate direction of the noise, stepping over a slightly the worse for wear Dogberry on the way. 'Hello, Isaiah,' she says. He looks up. 'Have I ever told you your skin is the exact colour of the Turkish coffee they once served in the Shah's court?' he asks in his sometimes quaint and old fashioned, but generally quite offensive, way, and she smiles and continues to pick her way across the room.

A group that she mentally labels the Beardies are leaning against the wall, idly stroking Fester the cat and swapping stories of terrible conventions they've been to. The one with the Welsh accent is telling a story about his first gig, but the American one interrupts as he remembers another Californian tale. The oldest one breaks in to top them all, barely able to get the story out for laughing. Brenda hears the words 'Elric', 'Jack Trevor Story' and 'New Worlds' before the trio roar with delight and drown out the rest. The whole exchange makes her laugh and she's still laughing when she reaches the broken window and discovers a boy – a man really – holding a flat cap in one hand and rubbing a burgeoning lump on his head with the other.

'Tinker, honey,' Brenda says with delight. There's something quite attractive in the way the newcomer colours as she looks him over. When she squeezes one of his biceps and murmurs, 'aren't you getting big?' she wonders if he's about to explode, but he's made of sterner stuff, it seems.

'You're needed, Miss Soobie!' he exclaims breathlessly. 'The Guv says to tell you that he's a fish out of water over here. He's got no authority in the States, he says, and doesn't know the people. He needs a local, he says.' The concern is clear on the earnest young man's face. 'The safety of the world itself is at stake, he said to say!'

Brenda moves her hand along Tinker's arm and takes his in her own. 'Tinker, babe, I'm no local. I just flew into Vegas three weeks ago. This is actually my very first party here, baby. I don't know *anyone,*' she concludes implausibly, waving an arm around behind her at the mass of party guests.

Tinker tries to speak, but she runs a finger along his lips, and his words are reduced to a stammer then cease altogether. He stands unmoving as she leans in and kisses him then, as though coming to his senses, pushes her angrily away and, with a final, parting glare, climbs back through the broken window and disappears into the warm Vegas evening. Brenda shrugs with amusement. 'Always going off half-cocked,' she says to herself, with the smallest of sighs.

Going to see Tinker has led her to the far end of the room. The double French doors to the garden have been left wide open to allow 'fresh' air to enter, but amidst the smells of barbecue, perfume and gunpowder, the clouds of narcotic smoke and the cacophony of chatter and music there seems little space left for anything as prosaic as actual air.

She spots Kelly talking with the quiet poet chap, but they're too engrossed in their conversation to notice her. Hilary's outside, wind-milling his arms in animated debate with Cav and Stew and both the Phils, and behind them a whole flock of her dearest friends are relaxing by the pool. As she stops for a second to take it all in, Other Ian does some sort of complicated dive off the top board and enters the water with barely a splash. Senor 105 looks up briefly, then goes back to showing Jay and Lawrence how to make paper aeroplanes, which makes Brenda smile. Noel and Marlene are draped across loungers, smoking from long holders and posing while their skinny pal - Scott is it? - takes their photograph. A big bugger in a tatty black robe and what appears to be a hat made from a goat skull (bloody weirdo!) stands in what few shadows there are and shifts uncomfortably in the LA heat. He's a big old unit, Brenda considers with a frown. She waves gaily across the grass anyway, and the giant figure cautiously raises a hand and allows it to move awkwardly back and forward for a brief moment. Must be a goth or one of those emo kids, Brenda considers. Something teenage and rebellious, anyway.

A waiter flits by and she takes the opportunity to scoop up a martini. Not a second too soon as it turns out. She's barely got the glass to her lips when a Rolls Royce flies over the back wall of the garden, crashing into the short spiky grass of the lawn and carving a long comma of dirt as it skids to a shuddering halt a few feet from the swimming pool. A few guests scatter in panic but the general attitude, Brenda is delighted to see, is one of polite interest. Steve and Original Ian and the others gathered round a small black and white tv set up on the porch barely break off from their open-mouthed viewing for long enough even to acknowledge the newcomer.

As hostess this option isn't open to Brenda, of course. *Once more into the breach* she thinks and hastens to the car, reaching it just as the driver's door opens. 'I wondered when you'd turn up,' she purrs at the tall, hawk-like figure which emerges.

'Miss Soobie,' he replies politely, bowing from the waist. Seen in profile, Brenda is reminded, as she always is, of a Roman Emperor, a face with not a pound of excess fat, the skin taut across sharp bones. He stands extremely erect, with square shoulders and – if she remembers correctly – a bum you could bounce pennies off. There's no denying it – he sends a shiver down her thighs.

But damn it, this is my party, she decides, mentally shaking herself down. She taps one heel impatiently on the tiles. 'Don't say another word.' She holds a hand up in front of his face to reinforce the command, before continuing. 'Like I told the dog and lovely Tinker, I don't care where the hell little Timmy has got himself metaphorically stuck this time. Brenda Soobie's Magical Expanding Mini-Van is not available for hire this evening! I've been in town for *three weeks*; I'm throwing a party in order to *get* to know people, not because I already do!'

His mouth is opening and closing, but he's not actually saying anything, she's pleased to see. She presses home her advantage before he unleashes that velvety tongue of his. Pleasant though it would be, she's no interest tonight in a repeat of Vienna in ninety-six. 'Now get yourself a drink, petal,' she says, deliberately turning away from him as she speaks, 'and relax.' Whether he takes her advice or not, she can't say. He probably will, though, she thinks. For all his very proper Englishness and precise formality, he had been a bit of a player in his early days, and she knows there's still a smidgen of pulp playboy in his character, even now.

She looks round for someone else to chat to. A group she doesn't recognise are sitting on beanbags nearby, passing round a short, stubby cigarette, from the end of which curls seductive, sedative smoke. The tallest – a pale, thin man incongruously dressed in full evening regalia – has white hair and pink eyes of all things. He falls silent as Brenda makes her way round them, but watches her carefully. One of the others, however, is talking as though his life depended on it. '-and then there's that episode where June Brown is a witness. Obviously she also turns up in The Time-' he says in a Scottish accent until the third member of the party, a shorter, quite sexy chap with a shaved head and twinkling, kind eyes which, for some reason, make her think 'nice serial killer', cheerfully tells him to shut up. 'Nobody's going to get most of your references anyway,' he says with a grin.

She laughs at that, though she's no idea what's he talking about, and then laughs again at lovely Mark painting the erstwhile Miss Clarissa Miller and her new, portly policeman husband. There's something wondrous about being surrounded by all these friends, she realises, like standing in a shower of warm rain on a spring morning. It's something which she wants to cherish, she thinks. She stands still in the centre of the party and let's all the chatter fall away. Julie's obviously taken over DJ duties – she can hear what's definitely an 80s compilation cd pumping from the speakers - but that fades away too until it seems to her that everything is silent and all of her guests still, frozen in a single magical moment of delight. She spins slowly in a circle, the hem of her gown swishing just above the damp tiles, the tip of her cigarette a firefly in the darkness. Some of her drink washes up the side of the shallow glass and slips over the edge. It falls in slow motion, one large drop of gin, towards the ground…

…and with a monumental sound, like a herd of elephants hard at it, the back wall of the garden explodes into pieces of individual brick, which fly off to one side as a big red Routemaster bus to Putney Common makes its entrance to the party. Suddenly, as though a switch has been thrown, everything is noisy and busy and full of life again. Even for so metropolitan a crowd as this, this is something worth investigating. And besides, one or two of the guests have already recognised the two figures even now stumbling down the bus stairs and half-falling into the garden.

Iris and Paul wave celebratory glasses in the air and shout 'cheers' at the sky as they make their unsteady way towards Brenda. 'Where's old Sexy got to?' Iris asks, scanning the crowd through squinting eyes. 'Never mind,' she continues, throwing one arm round Paul's shoulder and poking Brenda in the ribs with the other. 'Never mind, chuck, we don't need him. Someone find him, though, and tell him to stop worrying. Me and Pauly boy saved the day tell him! Sent those Ninnies spinning back to wherever they came from. Dreadful breach of the laws of time, mind. Not—' She sways a little and holds on more tightly to her companion, who grins with drunken good humour and blinks at her through his glasses. 'Not that I care one way or the other, but Brenda love, Brenda... I never thought *you* had the gumption. Fancy phoning me up and getting me to do your job for you, just so you can throw a big booze-up! And I thought you were the more sensible me.' She finishes her drink, then Paul's, then takes him by the hand. 'Come on, chuck, let's go and find Jeremy and Panda – they're bound to be together. Thick as thieves those two, thick as thieves.'

And they head off, around the pool and into the house, with the bus chuntering contentedly behind them, all their friends and family around them and the people they love up ahead. Brenda takes a moment, then shouts 'wait for me!' and runs after them.

God Engine Rhapsody

Julio Angel Ortiz

At the last amusement park in the universe, Iris contemplated her fate.

It had been innocent enough, the desire to bring Franco to the ultimate amusement park left in the current iteration of the universe. She'd always liked the shows. They'd travelled together for several months, and every so often she'd mention it as somewhere fun to go. And now it looked like being the place that would very likely serve as their tomb.

The universe had a delicious sense of irony. Or was the right word 'humour'? Not that it mattered. Pretty soon, these sentient coffee makers would do their work, and she and Franco would be dead.

She risked a glance over at him, and was relieved to find that he was still breathing. Iris could see the scaly surface of his chest slowly rising, then descending in a ragged rhythm. The fact that his tail was severed and lying across the room didn't worry her as much. She knew he would just grow a new one.

If they lived through this.

She hung upside-down, suspended by a cord tied to her foot which led up to a vaulted ceiling, in the shabby remains of an ancient amusement ride, complete with rusted boats and dry, cracked faux-canal. The speakers, however, were neither cracked nor ancient, and continued to blast out what Iris suspected was the least accurate and most annoying song in recorded history. It was certainly not a small world, for one thing. It had taken the Bus days to get here. Had it not been for the deadly coffee makers threatening to douse her in their acidic grinds, Iris would have put an end to the sonic misery a while ago.

'So, you thought you could interfere in our business, eh?' muttered the lead coffee maker, its lid flapping in time to the synthesised voice. 'I told you before, Iris; your involvement is bad for business. Leave us be and we'll continue to allow you to move about freely in this temporal zone.'

Iris mustered as much dignity as someone tied upside-down could, and brushed away the lock of crimson that streaked through her platinum hair. She was grateful she'd opted for the gravity-defying treatment at her last salon appointment.

'Listen, Mugs,' she began, her tone measured, her American accent less pronounced than usual. 'I thought that we had agreed to keep out of each other's way as long as you stopped peddling that ersatz shit you call 'Astro'. Which, by the way, sucks.'

Mugs chuckled. 'And what do you have against Astro?'

'Other than it's highly addictive and contains a time-active ingredient that slowly erodes a person's history the longer they use it? No, I can't think of any reason.'

Were it possible for a coffee making machine to frown, Iris would have sworn Mugs had just done so. His voice rose slightly.

'The Maker has directed us to increase shipments by thirty-four percent.'

'And did you ever wonder why?'

Mugs said nothing.

Iris' eyes flitted about the room. She had to keep him talking.

'Increasing the shipments by thirty-four percent,' she said, 'puts the galaxy at a tipping point. Considering how addictive Astro is, and how quickly it's draining people's temporal energy, increasing at just that percentage will create a critical mass in seven months, at which point most people will simply vanish, leaving behind a massive temporal sinkhole which will collapse the galaxy into a giant God Engine. At least, that's according to the Mueller-Jung theory.'

'What are you going on about?' Mugs asked. He leaned in. 'You've lost it, haven't you? I've left you up there too long with all that blood rushing to your head.'

'Nah,' Iris said. 'I'm exactly where I need to be.' And then she head-butted him.

Mugs stumbled back, crying out in pain. As he did, he accidentally let out some spittle from the acidic coffee grounds churning within him.

Which then struck the cord holding Iris up.

Ten seconds later, as she was scrambling to get up and rubbing her head, Iris cursed her inability to put her arms down fast enough to cushion her landing.

She kicked one of the other coffee makers into Mugs, sending both flying. She then cart wheeled away, just as several strands of coffee grinds sizzled past her lightning-bolt earrings. A moment later she was at Franco's side, who stirred and groaned.

'Oh,' he muttered.

'Now you decide to come to?' Iris said, exasperated.

'What-?' he began, then turned aside and saw the coffee makers rushing towards them, steam whistling from their spouts in evanescent rage. 'Oh, it's one of those days, is it?'

Iris hurried a still dazed Franco to his feet. 'Yeah, something like that.'

They headed for the exit, repeated sizzling sounds being aimed in their direction, barely audible above the cacophony of park music.

As they were about to leave, Iris paused long enough to reach into her thigh-high boots, pull out a dagger, and throw it at the speakers, which promptly exploded. The music ground to a halt.

'Shut up!' Iris cried.

'And that's how we escaped the living coffee makers?' Franco asked later, obviously amused.

'Yes, you could say that,' Iris said, half-smiling. She stood by the window, which let in a dull, flat light. Iris turned towards him, before letting her gaze fall to the floor. 'We made it to the shuttlecraft and took off. It wasn't until we were in orbit that I realised that the data I had been fed was somewhat… inaccurate.'

'How so?'

'Their… 'Maker'… had bumped up production of Astro months before. The tipping point wasn't thirty-four percent. It was actually twenty-seven.'

Silence. Then, 'What did that mean?'

'It meant that the tipping point had already been reached, and that I was too late. While in orbit, I saw… I saw the temporal shockwave beginning to rip apart the galaxy.'

He frowned, shaking his head. 'I don't understand.'

'The God Engine was activated while we were in orbit,' Iris said, pulling her long hair into a ponytail. 'It fired off earlier than I was expecting, and we got caught in the danger zone. I couldn't anticipate the consequences.'

'Which were…?'

'Getting stuck inside the God Engine. Getting stuck inside a series of collapsing para-realities that can shift like a dream.' Iris sighed and pinched the bridge of her nose. 'How many times are we going to have this conversation, Franco?'

They sat on a bench in winter.

'I don't know why you're saying that,' Franco said. 'I've never met you before in my life.'

'Oh, you have,' Iris said. 'The Death Miners of Agapas, the Dreamsmiths of Heralda, and Supremo's Massive Mirror of Manipulation… none of these ring any bells?'

'Supremo's what now?'

Iris harrumphed in frustration. 'Franco, listen. I'm sorry. I really am. But my, I don't know… my special relationship with Time is keeping me grounded in here. But your personal history is acting as a battery for the God Engine bubble we're in. Which is why you can't remember whenever we shift.'

'Like when?'

Franco was holding a baby. His baby.

'Do you know how many times I've seen you holding that child? But it's not real so don't get attached to it.'

Franco was left slack jawed. 'How dare you-'

Iris shushed him. 'Listen… each new iteration means it'll get harder to reach you. But you need to let go. It's the only way I can break out and stop the Maker from unleashing this travesty on the entire universe.'

'What are you saying?' Franco asked.

'You're going to have to die, Franco.'

They were on a beach, under a grey sky.

Franco was kneeling on the sand, hands holding onto damp clumps.

'I… I noticed that last bit,' he said.

Iris, standing next to him, stared out at the sea. The gun in her hand was black and scratched and heavy looking. Nothing like her usual little pink pistol, Franco considered idly.

'Yes. It means I'm getting through to you.'

'But I don't want to-'

'I know.'

'This God Engine. Is it really-'

'Bad? Yeah. A galaxy-sized engine of destruction rarely gets put to good use.'

Franco nodded, staring down at the sand. 'Okay. Do it. Do what you have to.'

Iris frowned. 'I don't want to.' She aimed the gun towards Franco's head. 'I'll see you again in the next life.'

Iris pulled the trigger.

The cork plugged into the barrel popped out and dangled from its string.

'Bang,' Iris said.

Reality shifted and there was no cork, no string, only a gun firing.

Franco had time to think '*Why am I crashing into the stars—*' and then everything went white.

The shuttlecraft hurtled through space, towards the multi-hued nebula. From her pilot's seat, Iris looked over at the severed tail strapped into the co-pilot's chair.

'Soon enough, Franco,' she said, 'you'll be good as new. Now hurry up and grow back.'

The elongated stump slumped over, as if in response.

Project: Wildthyme

Cavan Scott and Mark Wright

'Oracle?'

The computer responded to Matthewman's voice in its usual clipped – if rather sexy - tones.

'Yes, Professor Matthewman? How may I be of assistance?'

Matthewman removed his glasses and rubbed the bridge of his nose. He could feel one of his headaches coming on. Absently, he popped the cap of a tub of painkillers and swallowed a couple of tablets without water. It was funny. His department had decoded alien algorithms, retro-engineered extra-terrestrial weapons, even created a 3D printer that could perfectly replicate a slab of prime steak, but they still couldn't produce a drug that touched his migraines.

'Professor?'

Matthewman sighed.

'Sorry Oracle. I want you to run the scans again.'

'On which spectrum?'

'On every spectrum known to man – and even those we've not heard of yet. None of this makes sense and I want to know why.'

'Professor, may I remind you that you have repeated this procedure thirty-seven times previously…'

'Yes, yes, Oracle, I'm aware of that…'

'And the results have been identical on every occasion.'

'Humour me will you, there's a nice supercomputer?'

There was a pause as though Oracle was trying to think of a response. Matthewman sat back, his chair creaking in the silence of the pokey cupboard that was laughingly called his office in the mobile base. Oracle was probably the most sophisticated computer system on the planet, able to hack into any system from a nation's defence grid to a simple PVR. Capable of a billion different processes every second, she had been crafted from the finest xenotech ever to wash up on Planet Earth. But *could* she think?

When, for that matter, did he start thinking of it as her? He'd been working here for too long. Yeah? Like he could change that. What was it they said? You don't leave the Forge, the Forge leaves you.

Usually with a bullet in your head or your insides scrambled by a stolen Martian sonic beam.

'Commencing analysis,' Oracle informed him with a beep.

'Thank you, Oracle,' he replied, absently wondering who had given their voice to the supercomputer in the first place and whether they were half as hot in the flesh.

Yup, definitely worked here too long, Paddy mate. Need to get out more. Soon you'll be thinking about yourself in the third person.

He watched the progress bar fill on the screen in front of him, his eyes flicking up to the camera feed from the quarantine unit where the creature was being held.

'What are you?' he whispered, leaning forward, his eyes narrowing as he stared at the figure strapped to the medi-slab.

'I am this facility's operating system,' replied Oracle without the slightest hint of irony. 'I am Oracle.'

Matthewman didn't even bother to respond.

Another beep. The scan was complete. A second while Oracle crunched the numbers and then…

'Displaying results,' Oracle announced somewhat redundantly as data scrolled down the main screen.

Matthewman felt the muscles in his jaw tighten as he ran his hands roughly through his tousled, dirty-blonde hair.

The same results. The exact same results.

The impossible results.

Snatching up a sleek tablet computer, Matthewman stood, sending his chair crashing into the wall. Throwing the hood of his environment suit over his head even before his office door whispered open, Matthewman marched down the temporary base's corridor to the quarantine unit. Above him, rain hammered against the base's polycarbide roof, but the storm outside paled into insignificance compared to his own mood. This was beyond a joke. If the Director didn't get results soon, Matthewman's head would be decorating the Crichton Building's battlements.

He didn't acknowledge the two hulking guards in Department C4 uniforms who were standing motionless on either side of the door – the door that refused to open as he paused expectantly.

'Oracle, let me in.'

'Please confirm your identity.'

Matthewman tried to keep his temper in check. 'Oracle, this is ridiculous. You know who I am.'

'I'd do as she says, sir,' said one of the lugs with pulse-rifles, leaning in conspiratorially. Hutchison, was that his name?

'Or what? You'll have to shoot me?'

'More or less, sir.'

Matthewman gritted his teeth. Damned protocol. Damned squaddies.

'Professor Patrick Matthewman, facility scientific officer, requesting access to the prisoner.'

'Commencing DNA Sequencing Scan.'

Matthewman' skin tingled as the sensor swept over him, the hairs on the back of his neck bristling.

'You are Patrick Gordon Matthewman,' Oracle reported a second later, running her patented stating-the-bleeding-obvious protocol. 'Access to quarantine unit granted.'

'Well done, sir.' Hutchison gave him a patronising wink as the doors opened. For a second, Matthewman considered giving the squaddie a slap but, not wanting to end up in intensive care, slipped inside the room instead.

He waited for the door to shut before he spoke to the impossible creature lying prone on the medi-slab, a life form like nothing he had ever seen.

'What are you?' he hissed, still struggling to keep his frustration under control.

'WHAT ARE YOU!' he yelled, losing the self-same battle a nano-second later.

The thing on the bed turned its head to face him.

'What am I?' it repeated, its face an unreadable mask. 'I'm spitting feathers, that's what I am!'

Panda was having a day of it.

It had begun promisingly enough. He had risen bright and early, around 3pm celestial omnibus time, and had been informed by Iris that they were hunting aliens. Nothing new there. Most days with Iris Wildthyme involved at least several implausible things after supper, numerous slobbering monstrosities, an awful lot of running (not the easiest for a panda with very little legs) and a dash of mortal danger. Of course, the sheer amount of lovely booze they consumed along the way took the edge off and, although he would never admit it to the addled harridan, Panda wouldn't have it any other way. Iris Wildthyme, self-proclaimed Transtemporal Adventuress, was his life. She'd probably be the death of him too, but she was worth it, even if she did have ghastly taste in hats. And husbands. And wives. And, well, just about everything.

It turned out that today's monstrosities they were chasing weren't slobbering at all. The complete opposite in fact. Iris was pursuing the infamous Kitty Snax Flying Circus, a band of glamorous lust vampires from the Sybarite Continuum. Panda had always hoped they'd tackle the nimble nympho-nosferatists and it appeared his prayers had been answered. Yes, the six-foot, pneumatic astro-amazonians drove their victims into a destructive frenzy of animalistic ardour, but the future the cosmos was at stake. He'd take the bullet. The sinister sex-bombs needed to be brought down.

Of course, he had been slightly bemused when the bus deposited them in Weston Super Mare on a particularly wet Tuesday in late October.

'The Flying Circus has come here to sate their terrible thirst?' he'd asked as they trudged along the rain-lashed Grand Pier, Iris' sonic corkscrew buzzing furiously. 'I've not seen a soul under the age of sixty-two.'

'Aye, well, Winston's Fish Bar does a lovely O.A.P special on Tuesdays. Best mushy peas this side of Slarvia. And they chuck in bread and butter for nowt.'

'How generous. Even so, I thought these so-called wicked witches of wantonness might have found somewhere a little more glamorous.'

'Like Skeggie, you mean?'

'Exactly.'

'Well, busty butchering beggars can't be choosers.' A septuagenarian in a Ford Cortina blared her horn as Iris clattered across the road towards Weston's prize-winning 14-hole Crazy Golf course.

'They're here, I just know it,' she concluded, stopping in front of a miniature wooden windmill that had seen better years, let alone days.

'How?' the increasingly bedraggled Panda asked in the vain hope that he'd get a satisfactory response.

'Me operation scar's itching,' she replied, as if that answered everything.

'Empirical proof then,' Panda sighed, rolling his beads. 'Can we at least call off the search for a second so I can get some sugared doughnuts?'

'After the last time?' Iris scoffed. 'You had sticky fur for weeks. Seven cycles in that Laundromat in Morecambe it took to get you clean.'

'Mmmmm,' said Panda, the spin cycle still a painful memory. 'The dratted machine ate my best cravat.'

'There you go then,' said Iris, slamming the corkscrew back into her handbag. 'You just listen to your Auntie Iris. Back in a jiffy.'

'Now where are you going,' Panda had asked despondently as she had tottered off down towards the Tropicana.

'Need to make a phone call,' she'd called back over a leopard-skin-smothered shoulder. 'You stay put, sunshine.'

'Sunshine?' Panda had sniffed, trying to shelter beneath the bridge on the seventh hole, 'In Weston Super Mud? Chance would be a fine thing. I'll probably catch pneumonia first.'

Of course, he hadn't caught pneumonia. There wasn't time for that. Ten minutes later he'd heard a blast of compressed air from behind the hook-a-duck booth, then a stab of pain in his pert posterior. Everything had gone a bit squiffy after that.

And here he was, trussed up on some fancy-pants bed-thing, Bernie Clifton knows where, with only the sound of machines that go beep for company.

Oh, and the angry looking gent in the white bio-safety suit. The angry looking gent in the white bio-safety suit who was currently shouting at him.

'Calm down, dear,' Panda said, as the chap's face started to resemble a particularly flushed beetroot behind his protective visor, 'you'll have an aneurysm. Or at least give yourself worry lines. Why don't you nip down the offie, get some Plymouths, and we can talk this through. Mano a pando.'

'Worry lines? The thing on the medi-slab warns me against worry lines?'

'There's no need to resort to name calling. It's bad enough that you abducted me before I could get my paws on four doughnuts for a pound and have me tied to a bed with probes tucked snugly where no probe has any business to be. As I told that nice lady who strapped me in, I am known as Panda. And you are?'

'Matthewman,' the flustered man said, rubbing the back of his neck through the suit. 'Chief scientist Matthewman.'

'Well, I would say it's a pleasure, but mater told me never to lie. Why have you brought me here?'

'To find out what you are, of course. How you work?'

'How I work?' spluttered Panda. 'I'm not some snotty nosed child's toy. I don't roll along on wheels, you know!'

'But you look like a toy, if it wasn't for all the walking and whining...'

'Whining? I've never been so insulted in all my life! I'll let the toy comment slide for now, but whining? I am the personification of the stiff upper lip. Who do you think it was who advised Churchill to 'Keep Buggering On' in the first place? Who told Horatio what to string up on the masts of the *Victory*? If it wasn't for me, the fleet would have gone to Trafalgar with 'Oh well chaps, worse things happen at sea' flapping at them from the flagship. I may be a lot of things – lady's man, wit, raconteur – but whinger? Not on your nelly.'

'Have you finished?' Matthewman sighed, with the look of a man who had already been beaten and was running headfirst towards being broken.

'I've hardly even started, young fella-me-lad!'

'Okay, well before you do, shall I let you know what's going to happen?'

'I wish you would. I am still somewhat in the dark about what's happening.'

'What's happening is that we've drawn a blank. We've scanned you with everything we have. Xrays, infrared, DNA sequencing, deep tissue analysis. But there's nothing. You have no internal organs. No vital signs. No spark of life at all…'

'Well, that's just charming isn't it…'

'All you have is stuffing, as far as we can tell.' He thumbed one final control on the medi-slab, 'Without taking more invasive measures, of course.'

Panda didn't like the sound of that. In fact, he said so, using those exact words.

'At this point, I don't care what you like or not. All I know is that we received an anonymous tip that a walking teddy bear was wandering Weston-Super-Mare…'

'Bear?' Panda bellowed. 'Call me that one more time and I'll give you a punch up the hooter you won't forget for a very long time. Or I would, if I could move.'

'Bear. Panda. Whatever. You're an anomaly and my boss doesn't like anomalies. Makes you wonder if he looks in the mirror when he shaves.'

'So what?' Panda said, struggling against his restraints. 'That's it? You're going to start slicing me up without a by your leave?'

'Not exactly slice,' said Matthewman. 'More like fricassee.'

'You barbarian!' Panda exclaimed, 'I'll be informing I.U.P.A.C about this, mark my words.'

'I-what?' Matthewman asked, a frown crossing his world-beaten brow.

'The Intergalactic Union of Pan-Dimensional Assistants and Companions. I'm a founder member I'll have you know.'

'You're a nutter, that's what you are,' Matthewman tutted, shaking his head before appearing to address the ceiling. 'Oracle, send in the surgical unit. Have them bring the molecular scrubber.'

'Acknowledged,' intoned a voice that Panda would have considered particularly slinky if the situation hadn't been so absurdly grim.

'It's been nice talking to you, *Panda*,' Matthewman said, turning and shuffling back to the door. 'I doubt it's something we'll be able to do again.'

'Oh very melodramatic,' Panda scoffed, filling his tone with as much bravado as he could muster. 'I suppose that's supposed to put the fear of God into me, is it? To give me the willies? Well, let me tell you…'

Matthewman disappeared through the doors, leaving Panda alone in the soon-to-become operating room.

'… it worked perfectly. Bugger.'

His head flopped back onto the brushed metal table with the soft thud of polyester against steel.

A second later, the door hissed open again. Rubber booted feet stomped into the room, wheels squealing as something cumbersome was wheeled in. Panda craned his head up to see several bio-suited thugs manoeuvring a scandalously sinister piece of equipment into place at the foot of the bed. It looked like a metal tree on wheels, appendages flowering up from a central column like spindly branches, each ending in a malicious looking needle. Or knife. Or drill. It didn't take somebody of Panda's magnificent intellect to work out his position in the macabre equation that was being written.

'I'm really quite unremarkable,' said Panda, laughing nervously, as the suited figures busied themselves around him. Their visors were blank, the rhythmic hissing of their regulated breathing only adding to the sinister air that pervaded the chamber. 'I wouldn't bother if I were you. Waste of time. Why don't we go and get chips instead. My treat. I'll even throw in a saveloy if you like?'

'Is everything ready?' a voice crackled into the room. It was Matthewman. One of the faceless figures gave a thumbs up sign to a wall mounted camera.

'Oh I see,' said Panda indignantly. 'Removing yourself from the scene of the crime. What's the matter…'

'…the sight of stuffing makes you faint?'

Matthewman didn't take his eyes off the screen. 'Let's just get on with it, shall we?'

He was standing in the small operations centre located in one of the tube-like corridors that snaked around this temporary facility. Screens cast a sickly glow on the various technicians ready to offer support, computer consoles beeping away merrily. At the door, stood the hulking figure of Captain Donbavand, his head of security. Why did brick-wall shaped squaddies like that always make him feel like chucking the towel in to go and work in a shop?

Matthewman pinched the bridge of his nose. 'Power up systems…'

'…we have a green board to proceed. Everybody stand by.'

If Panda's beads could widen in horror, they would have as the gruesome apparatus powered up with a whine. Every arm began to stretch forward, needles glinting, blades slashing, drills screaming into life.

'I must have been a very naughty Panda in another life!' Panda said, pulling at his restraints. It was no good, he was stuck fast.

Closer and closer the deadly implements came. 'The inquisition had better manners than you lot!' he shouted defiantly at the line of faceless visors, waiting like sentinels, like vultures. 'Iris, if I ever see you again, I'll bloody well kill you!'

Panda turned his head away from the horrible mechanical vista, tensing against the first bite of steel on fur.

But it never came.

Matthewman looked around frantically as, one by one, the screens in the operations centre blinked off. All around, the whine of power dulled to nothing, plunging the room into darkness.

'What the hell is going on?' shouted Matthewman.

'All the power is out,' said one of the technicians, stabbing frantically at buttons on the console.

His eyes acclimatising to the dark, Matthewman glanced across at the wall-like shadow of the soldier.

'Captain?'

'All units, report in,' Donbavand said into his radio mic. 'All units.' The comm unit crackled in response.

'Sir, this is Sanford. I'm with Hutchison in sector 3…'

'… proceeding to sector 2. The power's out everywhere.'

Sanford and Hutchison stalked cautiously through a polycarbide tunnel, their boots thudding ominously in the darkness. 'Make your way to the quarantine unit,' Captain Donbavand squawked over Sanford's comm.

'Can't see a thing,' said Hutchison, squinting into the blackness ahead, pulse rifle up and ready.

'Keep your comm channel open,' said Donbavand

'Acknowledged,' confirmed Sanford, creeping after Hutchison.

'What are we going to do, this is all messed up,' complained Hutchison.

'We're not going to panic, all right?' Sanford said reassuringly.' He unclipped a torch from his belt and shone it into the darkness up ahead. We're trained for any eventuality,' he said, sweeping it around in an arc, turning to face the way they had come. 'For king…'

'…and country?' purred a voice that sounded like honey dripping down a blackboard.

Sanford gasped, then relaxed as his torch picked out the blank visor of a C4 bio-suit. 'Thank god for that, I thought for a second…'

He moved the torch beam down the newcomer's suit, his eyes narrowing as he looked at the boots.

'Those heels are a bit high, aren't they?'

The figure didn't move, just stood there looking at the two soldiers. It was only then that Sanford registered the thing that his mind had been waving frantically and trying to tell him for the last five seconds. The bio-suit looked like a standard issue C4 model, except… 'Leopard print?'

'Hello tiger,' purred the voice behind the helmet.

'Sanford?' barked Captain Donbavand into the comm unit. 'Come in. Hutchison? Respond.' Static filled the air. 'I've lost them,' he relayed to Matthewman.

'This is all we need. The director will have my balls for this,' said Matthewman wearily, running a hand through his hair.

'Sir,' one of the technicians shouted, 'I've got partial power.' A screen was glowing dimly, casting a small pool of light into the room. Matthewman peered over her shoulder at the screen. It showed the security feed from one of the tunnels.

'Well that's useful,' he complained.

'Sorry sir,' the technician apologised.

'I want to see the quarantine… wait!'

On the screen, a flash of movement. A flash of movement; a figure sprinting past. Was it... Yes, a bio suit. But...

'Leopard print?' he murmured. Around Matthewman, the technicians glanced at each other, all thinking the same thing about their boss. 'Leopard print!' he said louder, a note of alarm entering his voice. 'I was right!'

Matthewman turned and dashed for the door, which slid open. 'Captain, we have a Code Jezebel. Stay here!' Before Donbavand could protest, Matthewman had vanished into the silent base.

'It couldn't be, could it?' Matthewman muttered feverishly as he dashed through the deserted tunnels. He didn't need to see where he was going to know the way. Fear gripped at his heart. And something else. Elation? They'd been after this one for years, another of the Director's pet projects. He'd had his suspicions with the toy creature, but this confirmed it...

'After all these years,' he cackled to himself, turning a corner. 'This is it. The big one!'

Matthewman didn't even pause to check on the two unconscious guards at the door to the quarantine room. He darted through the open door, skidding to halt at the sight that greeted him.

''bout time,' said a voice, muffled by a helmet visor.

The bear-creature was still secured to the bio-bed, staring balefully in Matthewman's direction. The molecular scrubber had come to a halt, blades and needles centimetres from the bear's body. The five scientists he'd sent in to perform the procedure were collapsed on the floor, their sleeping bodies arranged in a neat clock-face pattern around the bed.

But it was the figure standing at the head of the bio-bed that interested Matthewman. A tall figure, wearing a bio-suit. A leopard-print patterned bio-suit. The arms were crossed, and although the face was obscured by a helmet visor, Matthewman knew the eyes beneath the helmet were burning with anger and glaring accusingly at him.

'It's right bloody rude to keep guests waiting,' growled the voice.

'Are they dead?' Matthewman asked, glancing at his team.

'What do you take me for?' the figure replied.

'I can't tell without seeing your face.

'Oh.' The figure's arms dropped in disappointment. 'I was going for terrible and mysterious.'

'Not in that suit, dear,' said Panda.

'Cheeky. But you might be right, love. Hang on.' The feral-suited figure reached up and pulled the helmet off. Blonde - bordering on incandescent - hair spilled out in every direction, framing a strikingly attractive angular face. Eyes that danced with energy and mischief looked straight at Matthewman, but there was no smile. Just a flat frown that dripped with foreboding.

'You don't have to worry about your little friends here. Chloroform-based perfume. It's a knockout every time. They'll wake up with a banging head, that's all.'

'But who are you?' Matthewman asked, although he already knew the answer.

'The name's Wildthyme. Iris Wildthyme.' Matthewman's heart nearly skipped a beat. It *was* her. 'And you sunbeam, have got a lot of explaining to do.'

'Yes,' said Panda. 'And I'll be wanting compensation.'

'Explaining what?' asked Matthewman, attempting to keep the tremor from his voice.

'Explaining why you go around snatching innocent panda's off the street, pump 'em full of drugs and try to gut them like a mackerel on a slab?'

Panda sighed. 'Lovely imagery there, Iris.'

'I'm just doing my job,' began Matthewman.

Iris sucked in a breath. 'That the best you've got?'

Matthewman licked his dry lips. 'It's what we do. Watch the skies, investigate the unexplained-'

'Scavenge whatever alien flotsam washes up on Earth,' Iris cut in, her distaste obvious.

'For the good of the human race.'

'Who are you trying to kid. I know all about you lot,' said Iris, heels clicking as she stepped around the bio-slab, and over one of the sleeping scientists. 'Department C4. The Forge!'

'The nickname never quite goes away.'

'For King and bleeding country.' Iris rolled her eyes. 'I've had run-ins with your mob before. The Forge has always had its fingers stuck in some pretty nasty pies.' She was standing right next to Matthewman now. He winced as she prodded a bony digit into his chest. 'And it stops. Now. Comprende?'

'It's not that simple, protested Matthewman. 'There's so much to discover, to investigate…'

'To cut open?' Jab! 'Tear apart?' Jab! 'Blast to bits?' Jab!

'Yes… I mean no!' Matthewman was gabbling. 'But look at you! You're magnificent.'

'Well,' said Iris, flummoxed for a second. She trussed her wild hair back into some semblance of shape. 'It's nice of you to notice, chuck.'

Panda's head flopped back. 'Give me strength.'

'I've read the files about you. All the others, always obsessed with Lazarus…' Iris snorted with derision. 'But you. It was always about Iris Wildthyme for me.'

Iris sighed and looked to the floor. 'Like that, is it?'

Matthewman was confused. 'Like what?'

'I always knew you'd be coming for me one day. When I felt me operation scar itching in Weston, I knew this was it. The Forge was getting nearer.'

'What?!' spluttered Panda. 'I thought these cut price Mulder and Scullys were after me?'

'Afraid not, Panda love.' Iris looked sheepishly back at Panda. 'All it took was one little call.'

'You set me up! Of all the low down, underhanded…'

'They'd have found me sooner or later. I thought if this lot were investigating you…'

'You'd be free to investigate us,' realised Matthewman.

Iris' eyes narrowed.

'Aye. Have a shuftie at the entire operation.'

'Oh the treachery,' wailed Panda. 'The betrayal. I will never forgive you for this Iris Wildthyme!'

'I'll buy you a Nandos to say sorry.'

Panda didn't even blink. 'Done!'

Matthewman looked from one to the other, not quite knowing what to say. Iris broke the silence. 'Go on then, go and get your doohickey.'

'My what?'

'A syringe, lovey, a syringe.'

Matthewman glanced to the medical trolley sitting a few feet away. 'But…'

'Look,' said Iris. 'I'm cutting you a deal. I've just barged in here and disabled all your fancy-shmancy security counter measures, so odds are I can walk out just as easily. But that isn't going to satisfy you and that Director of yours, is it?'

'Iris…' There was a warning tone in Panda's voice.

'The Forge will always be looking out for me and his nibs. So, here's the halfway house, a once in a lifetime deal – I'll give you a phial of my blood, and then me and Panda are out the front door. Savvy?'

'But Iris, you mad old harridan!' protested Panda. 'Just one drop of your blood could change the evolutionary path of the human race!'

Matthewman wasn't listening. He stumbled across to the trolley, hands shaking as he prepped a syringe. Was this really happening? Was Iris Wildthyme offering him the holy grail of xeno-research?

'Oh you can worry about stuff like that too much, Panda, love. What does it matter?'

'On your head be it. Don't say I didn't warn you!'

'Ready, chuck?' Iris turned to Matthewman and undid the seal around the glove of her bio-suit. Matthewman nodded, barely able to contain his excitement as she pulled off the glove to reveal a slender hand, the nails perfectly manicured and painted deep scarlet. 'Right then. Be gentle, lovey.'

Gently, almost reverentially, Matthewman found a vein and slid the needle slowly into the skin. Iris winced once, and then the thick blood was flowing into the syringe. As it swirled into the receptacle, Matthewman could have sworn there were flecks of gold glowing within the deep scarlet fluid, but then it was gone.

'There,' said Iris with satisfaction as Matthewman pulled the needle away. 'Happy now?'

'Oh yes!' Matthewman held the phial up, a grin spreading across his face. This was it, his moment, what he'd worked towards for all those years. Now, Abberton would have to listen to him. Now, he was going places.

'If you're quite done,' Panda grumbled, 'could you please release me from this death trap.'

'Ah, stop your skriking,' said Iris, walking over to free Panda from his restraints with a blast from her corkscrew.

'About time. Now, can we leave? I have a hot date with a bucket of gin.'

Iris scooped Panda up from the bed as, behind them, Matthewman rushed over to a bank of consoles set against the far wall. It was as if he'd forgotten about Iris and Panda.

'Einstein seems happy,' observed Panda as Iris carried him towards the door, holding him close.

'He'll be bloody ecstatic in a jiffy,' she chuckled.

'What do you mean?'

'Wait and see.'

'Oracle, initiate scan of xeno-biomass,' Matthewman said with quavering voice as he prepared a data-slide with a smear of Iris' blood. With a click, the sample was pushed into a slot on the console.

'Scanning,' intoned Oracle, echoing from above. Matthewman's eyes shone with anticipation.

Iris paused as the door opened, a hum of power beginning to throb around the room. She chuckled, turning to watch Matthewman rubbing his hands with glee, watery eyes dancing over the readouts.

'This is incredible,' he breathed.

'Oh no,' Iris whispered. 'The incredible bit is coming right up.'

As if on cue, the murmur increased in pitch, the dead lights around the room flaring into life, one after the other.

'Scanning,' intoned Oracle. 'Scanning. Scanning. Scanning. Scanning.' With each word, the normally husky computer became ever more high pitched. 'Scanning. Scanning. Scanning.'

Lights danced across every console in the room, the arms of the molecular scrubber going haywire, the entire unit spinning on its wheels. Matthewman's face went from triumphant excitement to sheer terror in the blink of an eye.

'What's happening?' he cried out, turning in desperation to Iris and Panda. 'What have you done?'

'The thought had crossed my mind too,' shouted Panda over the rising throb of energy.

Iris strode into the centre of the room with the poise of Dolly Parton on show night. She turned a complete circle before fixing Matthewman with the Iris-Wildthyme glare. '*I* happened.'

Suddenly, the increasing whine cut out and Oracle spoke again: 'Wildthyme's Law, Rule Number One,' boomed the computer, the hint of a northern accent creeping in at the edges. 'Blood is thicker than water, so watch it. Sunshine.'

With a final flourish, the bank of consoles exploded in a neat sequence, one after the other, sparks flying everywhere. Matthewman flung himself to the floor as the lights erupted into clouds of cascading glass, one of the arms of the molecular scrubber narrowly missing him, before it too was consumed in flames.

And in the eye of this storm of chaos stood Iris Wildthyme, her best friend Panda clutched in her arms. She stepped through the flames, and peered up at the camera set high into the wall.

'I know you're watching, Nimrod, lovey. You've been after me for long enough, and I knew you were going to catch up with me sooner or later. Some fellas just send flowers, you know. But enough is enough. One drop of my blood was enough to fritz your remote systems, but the damage will be localised - although Oracle'll be speaking funny for a while I reckon. Next time, I won't be so lenient, got it? Consider yourself on notice – Project: Wildthyme is cancelled. Effective right bloody now.'

Iris stared up at the camera. The camera stared back.

'I have absolutely no idea what just happened,' said Panda, cutting through the tension. 'But I think I enjoyed it.'

'Never a dull moment with Iris Wildthyme.' Iris laughed and started to walk towards the door.

'Wait! You can't leave!' Matthewman had picked himself up from the floor and staggered after them. 'Please!'

'You watch us, sunbeam,' Iris called over her shoulder, heels clicking on the metal floor plating.

'But you can't!'

'You're lucky I'm not suing!' retorted Panda as he and Iris disappeared through the door, which hissed forlornly shut after them.

Matthewman sank to his knees amid the debris, smoke curling around his head. 'What do I do now?' he asked, looking up to the ceiling.

But there was no answer.

Our Tune

Ross Douglas

**MIAOW Situation room.
Earth Date: Aug 15 2015**

'What in the name of blazes did you do that for?' asked the officer in the over-starched uniform, rubbing his cheek as a palm shaped welt began to appear on his face.

'Because my dear man...' Iris slurred. 'I've had quite enough of your impeuwed... Impeuwedince... Impeud... bloody cheek.'

Swaying gently, Iris continued. 'I will not be accused of being a doddering tart hell-bent on pissing everyone's life away. I am fully in control of all my mental faculties.'

Without spilling a drop from her glass, Iris spun around and half fell, half slumped into a swivel chair. Her voice, no longer mocking, became serious.

'And because, unless you have a better idea of how to make peace with a horde of the most vicious and ruthless killers ever known, we are wasting time!' she bellowed.

'Very well,' said the senior officer. 'Begin the broadcast.'

A young Ensign in front of a large bank of buttons and blinking lights flicked a switch. From speakers around the room the sound of extremely loud thrash metal poured out.

Iris sat tapping her feet to a beat not employed in the music and conducting an invisible orchestra with her hands. Impressively, her right hand swooped and swung with the same gusto as the left despite the presence of most of a pint glass of gin. The senior officer and everyone else in the room covered their ears and grimaced in pain as the music thundered from the speakers.

Sheepishly, the Ensign twisted a dial and lowered the volume. 'Sorry sir,' he said as the music dwindled to a more reasonable level.

The senior officer spoke. 'Any response from the lead craft?'

'Negative sir.'

Iris, still conducting the orchestra playing in her head, looked over at the Ensign. 'Give them a minute to listen to it.'

The Ensign glanced quickly from his superior officer to the woman who appeared to have taken command of proceedings, then adjusted another dial. As he waited he took a longer look at Iris. In any company, she was striking.

Her hair was so dark it felt like looking into a black hole, and to the Ensign it had much the same effect. He could feel himself being pulled towards her as though by some irresistible force. Her ruby red lips, he realised, matched the calf hugging, Cuban heeled and highly polished riding boots and knee length leather coat she wore. The Ensign knew he was looking at clothes that never looked better on anyone, ever. She was a gorgeous vision in fifty shades of red. He began to groan audibly.

'Any response?' said Iris throwing a wink and blowing a kiss at him.

'Incoming message' he said, swallowing hard as he flicked several switches and increased the volume from the speakers. The hideous metallic screeching cut off and was replaced by a feminine, if definitely robotic, voice.

'People of Earth… We word not translatable accept your word not translatable invitation and propose the word not translatable gathering take place on Saturn's moon, Iapetus, at the word not translatable temple of The Lord of the Clock. A word not translatable temple fitting for the word not translatable representative you have chosen.'

'I love a good party,' Iris grinned.

Saturn's Temple.
Earth Date Aug 16 2015.

The temple had been hastily decorated by the sort of woman who decorates village halls. A 'Happy

Birthday' banner hung above a tattered DJ setup. Partially inflated helium balloons hung limply over a dozen fold out chairs. A buffet table was pushed against one of the walls. A small, sad selection of rapidly curling egg mayonnaise sandwiches, half-filled bowls of crisps, and cocktail sausages on sticks covered about a quarter of the table's surface.

Although vast in size, the temple actually had very little room in which to move. Other than the single table of food, crates of wines and spirits were stacked high and deep behind a bar made of a dozen empty beer crates and three railway sleepers. Iris was propped up against it, drinking from a martini glass and smoking a Cuban cigar.

A disembodied voice echoed from the speakers at the sides of the DJ table just as a grainy image began to appear on the screens of the karaoke machine. The voice of the senior officer from MIAOW headquarters filled the room, albeit a little faintly.

'Earth Base to Saturn Party come in, over. Is this thing on? Earth Base to Saturn Party come in, over... Oh for the love of God. The Americans wouldn't have this trouble. They'd be in their amazing control room, supercomputers whirring away in the background and people darting around sorting things out. What do I get? Three useless idiots not capable of dishing out slop in the canteen and the technological equivalent of a broken +Commodore 64.' He sighed. 'Earth Base to Saturn Party come in, over.'

If she was being honest with herself, Iris had never really thought it would come to this. But here she was, standing in the temple of Saturn with sufficient beers, spirits and lagers to slake the thirst of several hundred troops, and enough buffet food to satisfy one moderately peckish sparrow. She glanced at the image of a large spacecraft on the screen of the karaoke machine. It appeared it was about to land outside the temple.

Bringing with it several of the universe's most brutal – and thirsty - killers.

'I hear you, love,' she said, finishing off her drink. 'Let's get this show on the road.'

**A Space Dock somewhere on the outskirts of the Nebulon Constellation.
Earth Time Aug 14 2015**

Iris stared at her cards intently and focused on winning the pot with nothing more than a pair of Omegas, a squarnishellian goundarg, an Eight of Hearts, a Chronian Sept, a thrimp of quendalls and Mrs Bun the Baker's Wife. Quite a good hand, but beatable. Especially if you happen to know that there is no version of multidimensional poker in which Mrs Bun the Baker's Wife is a legitimate part of the deck.

Her bluff had been strong. Very strong. She had spent the last day concentrating on a hand that was almost unbeatable. That was the trick to winning the game, after all. Let the other players tune psychically into a hand chosen by you. It helped if you actually had the hand you were thinking of, but it wasn't essential, so long as your will was stronger than everyone else's.

She had it all figured out. She was about to win...well she wasn't sure exactly how much but definitely loads.

Unless, of course, someone at the table just happened to have the perfect hand. But the odds of that were so unbelievably enormous that Iris felt completely safe with her bluff. Despite the fact she had no money with which to pay her debts, should she lose. Nobody was going to call against the hand she was projecting furiously at her opponents.

'Call' said the Naxian across the table.

Unexpectedly – and unpleasantly - she realised she was about to be killed.

And not in a nice way. Killed in such a manner that even a serial killer working in a slaughter house would feel his gorge rise a little. The assembled aliens across the table liked to make an example of their victims.

The dealer asked the players to turn their cards over. All eyes were focused upon Iris. Looks only got you so far. She smiled broadly and did her best not to look like she was about to flee, despite every sinew, nerve and muscle in her body telling her to get the hell out of there as soon as possible. Of all her many incarnations, she considered briefly, this one did seem to get into the most scrapes.

'Gentlemen...' she began, the wobble in her voice betraying her slightly. 'I realise I have made a serious error of judgement, and am possibly moments away from death. If I can be so bold as to assume something about you all for a second, I'd say you were all gambling men…'

And that was how the whole affair started.

Iris bet each of the players around the table that within a single day she could not only get them, but also every member of their respective crews, more drunk than they could imagine. And all she would need to do so was one of their communicators and a tape recorder.

For a moment it was touch and go. One of the gamblers raised a lethal looking blade and, in a panic, Iris raised the stakes. She need to offer her opponents something fun.

'Tell you what, people. How about this? It's two days to my birthday and I promise you that I'll throw a party where not only will I get you and all your crewmembers so drunk you'll forget your own species but I'll have MIAOW pay for it.'

The gamblers took the bet. Well, they would, wouldn't they? Nobody liked MIAOW.

One of the gamblers handed Iris a communicator, which she set to broadcast in the direction of MIAOW headquarters. Next, she pulled a small device from her pocket and fiddled with it until music began playing. She prodded some buttons on the front until the 'music' resembled the screams of a billion tortured souls, then linked the device to the communicator and sent the broadcast on its way.

Five minutes later she received an urgent message from MIAOW informing her that she was needed on an issue of some urgency. A previously unknown race of multidimensional beings was headed towards Earth with the sole intention of destroying every life form on it. Her services were needed to communicate with them and negotiate on behalf of MIAOW. It seemed they had asked for her by name.

After another couple of minutes recording something into a tape recorder and telling one of the gamblers when to play it, Iris jumped in the Bus and set the destination for MIAOW headquarters, Earth.

A bet was a bet, after all.

The Wildthyme Effect

Nick Campbell

There had been a bookshop in St Michael's Street for as long as anyone in Oxford could remember; even, had anyone thought to ask him, the Senior Censor of Magdalen College, who was ninety years old if he was a day. Everybody knew of it, but few had ever been inside. Optimistic bibliophiles circled in vain for a browse. For weeks at a time there was so sign of life behind the curtains, and the bow windows were lined with dust, not in heaps but mountain ranges. Dig around a little, though, and you would probably find someone who knew someone who had been taught by someone who had bought something there, at least. The bookshop traded in antiquarian materials so rare they might be apocryphal, and its operations were obscure, but no-one liked to ask too many questions. The talk in the Head of the River was that it was owned and run an eccentric ex-colonel who had been at Ghazni in 1839 but subsequently done alright for himself, but gossip had it wrong for once. Anybody who knew anyone who had... well, you get the idea - could tell you the owner was a woman. A most extraordinary woman.

It wasn't a constant concern of Iris Wildthyme's, of course. There were long periods where she forgot she even owned the place. But she had a taste for being talked about, for being that mysterious woman walking up the street in her sensible shoes, curls shining like a cluster of lilac, invited to soirees and receptions, rarely accepting. When this wish arose in her - to be somewhere she was (to stretch a definition) known - she scooped up a stack of folios and ephemera and swept back into town.

She said nothing of this to her new companion Timmy when they arrived there, that morning in June. She took him to a coffeehouse, turned a few heads, and let him work it out for himself.

To begin with, he felt self-conscious. As a young man who liked to wear dresses, Timmy had developed something of a sixth sense. He could sense eyes upon them as they walked up the High Street, and he was slightly nonplussed when he saw it was not his trendy London outfit but his older companion who was garnering attention. Iris laughed childishly at his expression, as the dimensions of her aura became apparent.

There was business to see to, of course. The shop came in useful as a source of ready cash for Iris, who in this incarnation was especially proud to be a woman of means. She was prone to sudden longings for property, perhaps sublimating an indistinct yearning for a home. To avoid awkward conversations, she would only see customers by appointment, so she had letters to respond to, diaries to consult.

Timmy was content to keep out of her way and bask in the city's golden serenity. There was something about English summer sunlight that made the most ancient, dusty corners of the city seem clean and new, for some reason recalling a particular summer in 1998, revising his GCSE's in the garden. Falling in love with the head boy whose eyebrows met so beautifully, feeling the surface of the physical world shift, suggesting new patterns. It had been easy enough to give up on that idealism, though he couldn't say when it had happened. Since meeting Iris, though, the feeling was in reach again. Sometimes, it was necessary to getting along with her.

They had had a wild time of it since he had come aboard the Number 22. They had only just spent three hectic days trapped in a garden centre with a carnivorous form of vegetable life. Somewhere in the modern day, he was working in a shoe shop, unaware that Iris was speeding toward his life: from the vantage point of 1862 it was like being on the ground floor of a house, hearing someone moving about upstairs. Timmy hadn't got his head around it yet.

One evening, Iris took him for a chop in a place out in Cowley where no-one she knew had a residence. She poured him a large red wine and asked if he had noticed a certain girl visiting the shop that afternoon. She had come with her friend, an older, rather lanky schoolgirl with mousey blonde hair, but this girl was more petite, with short, black hair and eyes to match.

Timmy did remember, because he had thought how odd it was to see children in this austere city of old men, but especially in Iris' shop, which the girls seemed familiar with. There was something about the younger girl: she almost seemed to wear a halo, and her eyes were watchful. Timmy had seen Iris busy with her, tried to hear their conversation and failed.

His curiosity pleased Iris. She started telling him about the girl's mother, Mrs Liddell, who was looking for a new governess for her daughters. The last one had vanished quite mysteriously. 'Into thin air,' were the words Iris used.

Iris went on, saying how something in the self-same thin air was agitating her. It seemed electric with potency, she said.

Timmy tried to reassure her, such phenomena being usual at this time of year. In fact he had even seen summer lightning on their way to dinner. When Iris asked him if it was behaving at all suspiciously, he refused to answer. He was becoming agitated himself, waiting to hear where this was leading. What was it about this girl, this Alice, that Iris was so concerned about?

She toyed with her wineglass. 'You know,' she said, 'I don't think it's healthy, your being so under-occupied. Could lead to anything.' Her smiling cheeks were like two little apples off the tree of forbidden knowledge.

I used to believe some strange things about the bookshop on St Michael's Street. The strange shop that only opened 'by arrangement,' Mama said, meaning it kept its own hours. I pictured them as its stock in trade, bottled behind the counter. I was certain, for years, that the place opened at night only, like certain flowers. A mutual friend disabused me of the notion on my fifteenth birthday. We had been dozing in the meadow, talking, I suppose, of books. Suddenly she rose, saying, 'We shall go to Wildthyme's.'

And there it was, open, and empty but for the proprietor. Music floated through the building, from an adjacent building I presumed. It was an overcast day but the atmosphere in the shop was lightly charged.

Alice was evidently no stranger to the place. She handed over a small volume. (I caught the title: *James and the Giant Peach*.) 'Thank you for the loan of this, Mrs Wildthyme,' she said. 'It was like nothing I've read before.'

'And nobody caught you at it?'

'Oh no,' said Alice. 'I'd never allow that to happen. I do what you say, Mrs Wildthyme.'

'That's right,' said she at the counter sternly. 'Who's your friend?'

'She's called Mariana Hepplewhite and she's my friend,' Alice replied, looking at me. 'May we - might we take a look in your upper room...?'

Iris was seated on a stool behind the counter, with the attitude of Cleopatra, and a cheroot in her right hand. She wore a pair of purple corduroy trousers, a green blouse and a thick, blood red cardigan. I had never seen so much colour on a person. She looked at me as if I were a volume whose authorship must be ascribed.

I said, 'Don't worry about me, Alice. I've the last instalment of Oliver Twist still waiting.' I could see there would be awkward talk otherwise.

Alice went off into the shop. We were left alone. Mrs Wildthyme took a long drag on her cheroot, still unsmiling. 'Mariana...' she said. 'With blackest moss the flowerpots were thickly crusted one and all...'

'That's right,' I managed to say. 'Mama can do the whole thing, you know, with gestures. And In Memoriam, too.'

'What about The Charge of the Light Brigade?'

'Father does that one. He says she mustn't do it herself or she'll become coarse.'

'They sound a right pair,' Mrs Wildthyme said. 'Like a bit of Dickens, do you?'

'Oh, I know it's improper,' I said, in a rush, 'but I adore it.'

'It's his charity work I can't stick,' she replied. 'I like it when people spontaneously combust. That's where his heart is, I think.'

I told her I thought she had expressed it perfectly, though I had no idea what she meant. But it had the desired effect. She smiled.

I am sorry to go on, but every detail seems important. Don't you think?

***

They invented Miss Timothy that night. It was like a dare, with Iris to encourage him, and the better part of a bottle of Tanqueray. He had never had anyone to urge him to such things before.

The next day, a rather nervous figure was received by Mrs Liddell, imperious as a young Victoria. Perhaps because she did not expect to see a shoe salesman from the 21st century in drag, however, Mrs Liddell saw a governess. One with references glittering enough, Timmy felt, to blind Mary Poppins.

Mrs Liddell's empire, the Deanery, was a part of the College itself, an enclave of pale brick around a lawn with a fountain at the centre. The fountain was inert, the quad empty, and the Liddell girls - including Alice - spoke only when addressed. When their heads were bent over their *découpage*, no noise troubled the air.

There was no opportunity to speak privately with the girl and ask what it was that gave her such a constant, secret expression. Timmy longed to confer with Iris, but she had assignations with various people of the city, including a man in town she had tried to contact, for whom she had a commission. Timmy suspected this to be Lewis Carroll, or rather, the Reverend Dodgson, a close neighbour of the Liddells. He dreaded to think what she was asking him for.

One afternoon, filled with restless energy, Timmy proposed an outing to the Cathedral Gardens. The weather, as usual, was very fine, and the atmosphere in the house heavy as the scent of cut lilies. Timmy thought removing Alice from the orbit of her mother might loosen her tongue a little.

Alice invited a friend, Mariana, and they sat in the dazzling sunlight eating liquorice comfits and getting headaches. Timmy's attempts at conversation, though, were met with monosyllables. To keep himself occupied, he brushed out Alice's hair, which stood on end like a little animal's, due to 'little shocks', said Alice.

He was so determined to make conversation that he found himself talking about *Alice in Wonderland*, a book not to be published for three years. He had been thinking so much about it since Iris had first told him that his Alice was *the* Alice that he hadn't thought twice about when the book had actually originated.

Suddenly the girls were looking at him in horror. 'You're not supposed to know about that yet,' said Alice.

'It's between us girls only,' Mariana continued, which at least reassured him he had not disturbed causality, only been rather tactless. 'Surely, Miss Timothy, you are not already acquainted with Mr Dodgson...?'

Timmy was grasping for a suitable response to this innuendo, when Alice interjected, saying that she would certainly have known if they were - that she knew all kinds of things she wasn't meant to - that Miss Timothy had arrived much too recently in town for such an attachment to be formed, and that in any case, she didn't feel her governess was the sort of person who stimulated the Reverend

Dodgson's famously overactive imagination. She managed to maintain an air of innocent seriousness, whilst also implying she was aware that Miss Timothy was not, in fact, Miss Timothy, and not, strictly speaking, a Miss at all.

Timmy blushed deeply, requiring him to fan his face with a glove and mutter about the warm weather - a blatant lie, for the sunlight belied a palpable chill.

Mariana, though older, seemed insensate to Alice's suggestiveness. She launched into a story about Pricks, the Liddell's last governess, who accompanied the girls when they were photographed by Mr Dodgson, even though they were too young to need a chaperone, and Miss Prickett too grown-up to be in his pictures. Though not too pretty, Mr Dodgson had said privately; a remark reported by Alice to Mrs Liddell.

Timmy noted that Miss Prickett was less likely to have been scrobbled by aliens than to be lying low in Brighton, sheltering from Mrs Liddell's wrath.

'But if you haven't spoken with Mr Dodgson,' Mariana said, 'then you must have been reading Alice's letters.' She reached for the last piece of liquorice.

'Hardly, my dear,' Timmy replied, beating her to it. 'I'm just one of the girls.'

After that, they started home. The summer sun had begun to die, and light needled across the twilit sky. He contrived to walk home via the bookshop, a scheme that Alice encouraged.

But the shop was shut when they passed, with as little sign of reopening as if its owner had once more plunged herself into the swirling lights of infinity. Undaunted, Timmy stalked on. Mariana had put an idea into his head.

Iris had not yet gone off. She was, in fact, tramping through a meadow on the other side of town, a furled, pink plastic umbrella in her hand, and her eyes on the heavens. Out in the long grass, the light lay low, as if retreating into the earth.

Now and again, she held the umbrella stiffly ahead of her, like a water dowser, searching for a particular spot. As well as fencing esoteric volumes to enthusiastic dons, Iris had spent this visit to Oxford considering the peculiar weather hanging over the town, coming to some strange conclusions. Unfortunately, since they seemed directly concerned with her business, she had had to keep them to herself.

She stomped this way and that, uncovering nothing of more note than a dead cow beneath a hedge. For a second, she thought it had run into an electric fence; then she remembered the year, and looked up at the perfectly blue sky.

There was an energy abroad in town. Every time she had parked the Bus carefully within her weathered garden walls, she had felt the atmosphere vibrating. After all, time wasn't used to being treated like that, whichever theory of it you ascribed to.

It had never been a problem, and Iris had chosen to wait until it became so.

Thankfully, in relative terms, her last visit had been not too long ago - and yes, here were the bent grasses, the dents in the soil, suggesting the recent presence of a large motor vehicle, four-wheeled, probably red.

Well, something had happened. Some catalyst. And not in her garden. So, was it -

She held out the umbrella. It jolted in her hand like a twig in water.

As she stood there, half satisfied and half perturbed, three dim shapes sat up in the dusk. Their eyes glinted and their fur stood on end. She peered at them, trying to fit this new detail into her picture of events. The cat trotted over to her and grinned, and she was distracted for a second. Then her instinct reasserted itself, and before the two hares sprung at her, she had her umbrella open. They ricocheted off the PVC, regained their ground, and took after her again.

Away went Iris like the wind, pursued by hares, cats, a bat even. She didn't dare look back, just kept pelting on, as far as her lungs would take her, which was, thankfully, into the city itself. It was dark now, and nippy. She stood beneath a gas lamp, glad of its warm, crackling company, before walking more sedately back to the bookshop for a cocoa. As some sort of a reward for her exertions, a letter awaited her, hand-delivered. A request for a sitting from the Reverend Charles Dodgson. Slightly giddy on success, she congratulated herself on having kept Timmy clear of all bestial threats, not to mention the facts of the matter.

At that moment, Timmy was cursing Iris' name. He had found Alice's letters from Dodgson, and after the nightlights were dimmed, he had taken them to his room. They made curious reading - and he knew whose house he would be visiting in the morning...

We ran away together at midnight.

I needn't tell you how unprepared I was. At fifteen, I hadn't even been on a train by myself. I thought the world was Oxford, interspersed with versions of Llandudno, and hot countries massed with missionaries. I had been brought up to keep a house, bring jam to a rolling boil, interpret the Language of Flowers and, should I have been invited by some young man to comment upon the state of the world's affairs, to change the subject to what tune the band were striking up, and was my new acquaintance already engaged for this dance...?

Iris thought the whole thing was rotten. When I talked about dear Mama, a look of pity stole over her face. It wasn't till she had abducted me that I realised the pity was for me. I didn't understand her, as Tom Tower tolled midnight, as I stepped aboard the Bus, as I accepted a tumbler resembling a pineapple.

I was quite green, in those days, and I look back upon it all with fascination.

Suddenly we were fellow travellers. We were in London, in the future. It looked to me like something out of Dante, men and women dressed in the scantiest of things, running about, up to all sorts, accompanied by Bacchanalian pipes and drums.

'Is this the fall of civilisation?' I asked Iris, nervously. She frowned at me.

'Far from it, my dear. This is the Nineteen-Sixties,' she said. 'Civilisation has rarely improved on this.'

I resolved to show no more fear.

Later that night I had my mind expanded on a street corner in Soho. I knew I was on the brink of something extraordinary that I must grasp with both hands.

It was a pity that at this point a malevolent alien force tried to take control of my mind through a nearby 'phone box. Iris dealt with it magnificently, of course, and later explained that this sort of thing happened quite frequently in that era. I must admit it left me chary of telephonic devices (especially ones that smelled of urine).

Not long after that, the Bus transported us - if you can believe it - to another world entirely, in which we were enlisted by a party of archaeologists to delve beneath the planetary crust in search of a forgotten city. Rather rough going, but fortunately Iris had persuaded me out of my cumbersome Victorian garb and into more practical, 'modern' womenswear. The combination of leather boots and hot pants made me feel like a true voyager beyond my own territory, and we were having an awfully fun subterranean adventure, till we discovered the forgotten city was inhabited by undead robots with ray guns. I screamed till I was dizzy. Fortunately, when I regained consciousness,

Iris and the expedition had sealed them back into their tomb.

I suppose this sounds rather mad. All the worlds beyond ours, the realms within myself, have been swallowed up in the silence of this deathly summer, drawn back into the shadows of memory. The more I try to evoke them, the more they are like an invented language used in secret letters, where the respondent is gone. And the more incomprehensible my wilderness years grow, the more need I have of them.

I wish now I had kept a record of it all, that time of metamorphosis. I would ask Iris about it in any quiet moment snatched between changing cassettes. When the engines were growling and the winds of time rushing by, she would unravel all sorts of stories from her past, reassuring me and urging me onward.

I believe you, of all people, will understand - the lost connection with one's most vital hour. Somehow, it feels a part of me was left behind there. I would stop at nothing to get it back...

'Mr Dodgson,' Iris cooed, 'is that a camera under your hood or are you just pleased to see me?'

She was beginning to get very tired of standing around on the riverbank, and of having nothing to do. It was not like other artists' studios she could recall. Not like popping in and out of Caravaggio's workplace, offering her services. 'I'd make you a lovely Salome, ' she'd said, bringing him a coffee. She had had all those whores to chat to then, drafted in to be made saints. There was no banter with these two girls he was snapping. Huddled together, Alice and Mariana were more like forlorn little ghosts.

There was a flash, and a cloud of vapour, and Dodgson was out from under his veil, considering her remark. 'I am honoured to have you, uh, sit for me, Miss Wildthyme.'

'Likewise,' she said. He had a lovely voice, she thought. She loved his little stammer, and she could tell he was proud of it too, the way he played it up mid-sentence, making you hang on his words. 'I feel quite honoured. I'm hardly typical of your portfolio. I hope you don't plan on capturing me *déshabillé* - much too chilly.'

Dodgson expressed a contrary opinion, actually using the word, 'Contrariwise,' which made her raise an eyebrow. 'Isn't it a perfect day?' He gestured at the gunpowder cloud, shimmering in the eternal sunshine.

'Look at a barometer, Charles,' she said. 'Damp and drizzly, it ought to be. You know, like an ordinary summer in England.'

His gaze was unwavering, and she was actually prickling beneath it. Not exactly professional. Something about those subtle eyes; and then he was so tall and hearty. Not how she had imagined Lewis Carroll at all.

If only the kids would take the hint and leave the two of them alone. Iris was in need of Dodgson's confidence. They would compare photographs together - even this photograph, she thought, when developed in the Reverend's rooms, would tell its own story, especially if he compared it with other recent images of Mariana and Alice together. Yes, that would be very revealing.

'Anyway,' she said, 'what do you make of my proposal?'

'To write your biography, Ma'am,' he said, politely. 'It would require many, ah, interviews. You have seen so much.'

'Ha! You've not heard the half of it!'

'Hmm,' he said, 'but what I've heard suggests your queer, umm, appearance conceals a more transcendental reality.'

Iris was not sure how to take that. She brought herself up sharply. 'Who's been gabbing about my business, then?'

'Word travels,' he murmured. 'I'm a, umm, man of letters, you might say.' His gaze flickered to Mariana.

She followed his glance, but the girl had turned away. Impossible to perceive her now as the blithe thing Iris had first encountered. But had anyone here noticed? Surely not.

But a letter...

'It is funny about this weather,' she resumed. 'It might sound odd, but it's almost as if this sun we've been having is all *underneath* the clouds. Washing about like sand under the sea.'

Dodgson said that, as one who worked with light, that was impossible.

She admitted that it was, if nothing else, new. It was young, making mistakes and learning. Lingering at windows, hiding in lamps, sitting on Alice's shoulder, perhaps, and whispering in her ear. Watching for something...

Dodgson laughed nervously. 'What could, uhm, light look for?"

'Well, whoever released it in the first place,' she replied. 'Someone suitably cracked to get inside. It can send itself out, like a spark. And a cat may look at a king, but it can't operate heavy machinery, can it?'

As though invoked, the woodland creatures stole in silently upon them. The light was falling in rays, but as she'd half-expected, it suddenly grew in strength, like mist clearing between the ground and the sun. She looked to the girls, who were turning their faces like flowers to the light.

For a second, it danced in her eyes, tauntingly. When she could see again, the girls had vanished. She and Dodgson were alone in the silence.

'Hold still, my dear,' he said. 'I want to capture you with just that expression on your face.'

Now he was haloed in cold fire, his long hair all on end, irises hanging in the glow like after-images.

'Those girls...'

'Illusions,' he purred. 'I had to be certain of you. You were only too right, when you spoke of mistakes. The Eminence has lavished too much time on the Dreamchild - Alice, that is. This document - *Alice's Adventures under Ground* - was, um, misleading.' It drew nearer. 'But then it learned the truth about you.'

Iris pouted. 'Really?'

'Perhaps,' Dodgson whispered, 'we all make mistakes.'

Before she could respond, the stillness was broken by a petrol engine.

You see, following one long flight through the maelstrom, we came to a halt in a field beneath a starry sky. I had been upstairs, drowsing on the back seat. I remember slowly descending the steps of the bus. The doors stood open and the breath of night-scented stock was coming in like incense.

'Where has the Bus brought us this time?' I yawned.

'Home,' Iris said.

'Where is that?' I asked, expecting it to be just a name.

'I've had word from my mysterious superiors,' she said, staring out into the darkness. 'They say it's got to stop.'

'I don't understand...'

'I'm meddling with history, you see,' she said. 'Interfering with destiny. That sort of a thing. I wasn't thinking, when I swept you up. I just wanted to open your mind. But they've told me I must return you to your own time.'

'My own time?' I still felt dazed. 'Not mine. I don't belong here now. I'm not the girl I was.'

'We don't have a choice, Mariana,' she said, her face whitening with anger. 'People like us, and the time we've had, they're unlicensed; it doesn't make any of it less real, but -'

I stepped out of the doors. Already the Bus seemed to belong to a dream. It stood in the meadow behind Christ Church. I was deep in clover, cow parsley and long blades of grass.

'It's the night I left, isn't it?' I said.

'To the minute,' she said. A clock was tolling midnight.

'I shan't miss a thing.'

She smiled, extending a hand. 'Remember, keep it dark...'

It was a terrible to-do.

'A letter?' Iris bellowed. 'Which part of keeping our affairs a secret translates as writing about it all to your local Victorian fantasist!'

Mariana was standing at the doors to Iris' bus. Timmy, with his bonnet rakishly askew, was eyeing her nervously. His attempt to challenge Mariana directly had not been an unqualified success.

'I won't tell you again,' she said. 'Get on the bus. This is a rescue.'

'Piss off!'

'Very well, then,' said the young Victorian madam, folding her arms. 'A kidnap. Either way, you're coming with me.'

'You can bloody well think twice about that too.'

'Your mysterious superiors can't hold you accountable if I'm the one at the wheel,' Mariana had explained. 'Mr Dodgson volunteered to keep you occupied while I stole the bus. After that, I had only your... assistant to deal with.'

'Have you seen your pen-pal lately? He seems to have something on his mind.'

This is where Timmy had leapt in. How was Mariana supposed to have known about that? Come to that, what had stopped Iris telling him about Mariana? A guilty conscience?

At this point, Iris had asked if there was anyone there who didn't want her delivered into the hands of alien forces. Timmy said it depended on the alien forces.

'One miscalculation. Selflessly, tidily, bringing *her* back the moment she'd left,' she said, 'seems to have released this erstwhile 'intelligence'. But I know how to handle time things,' she added, running her fingers through her hair-do. 'It's perfectly fine unless you touch yourself.'

Dodgson had smouldered at the words. He was evidently coming aboard, if Iris was. The bat made a swoop for the doorway and was fortunately met by Mariana's boot. Timmy suggested that they should name this phenomenon after her: the Wildthyme Effect. After all, no-one else could have ballsed things up the same way. Mariana called him an uncouth he-she lady, and suggested dropping him somewhere while they headed for Montmartre. She added, 'Don't cause me to use force, dearest.'

That had done it.

'Force?' Iris said, clapping her hands. 'You, use *force*? Smelling salts, that's all you used. Every trip out, you'd scream or faint, and every other minute, it was: ooh, what's this, Iris? What's a computer? What's a corkscrew? Face it: we're not compatible. You're an historical figure,' she said, 'and you like it. I'm ahistorical at best.'

Mariana stepped off the bus. 'Why are you saying this?'

'Because,' said Iris, 'I didn't have to return you to your proper time and place. I didn't have instructions from my mysterious superiors or anyone else's. I brought you back because you belong here - and not with me.'

Back aboard the bus, Timmy pulled a control. The doors slid shut.

Dodgson looked the most alarmed. 'What does this mean for us?' he asked.

Iris watched Mariana carefully. 'It means she's as much a fantasist as your Lewis Carroll,' she said. 'Mariana made me up, romanticised me like Alice. I'm a figment of her imagination.'

Mariana's eyes were wide. 'Yes,' she said. 'I think that must be so.'

Dodgson tumbled to the floor, as though in a faint. The animals danced in a panic. 'Then what will become of me?'

The girl looked at Iris. 'Well?'

'I suppose,' said Iris, 'it's time to deal with the Wildthyme Effect...'

The bookshop in St Michael's Street had existed for a century at least; so said the drinkers in the Bird and Baby, whose interest in literary matters was matched by their love of legend. It had opened daily, even through the Great War, and if that had dented its mystique, it is sometimes better to be liked for what you are than admired for your promise. The news that, following its owner's demise, *Wildthyme's* would be sold up and converted, excited its loyal customers. It tantalised them to think of the shop vanishing, passing into memory; it would become their very own myth.

And what a chance to bag some fabulous item at auction...

After all, it the place would hardly be the same without its owner: that sphinx in men's clothes, who travelled to all points of the globe and had affairs with everyone in the Bloomsbury set. She had been a little touched, some said. They said she would hold conversations with her cat - an ancient, flame-coloured animal - and that she once claimed to have inherited the shop from the Devil herself. But if it had been an infernal place before her, Mariana Hepplewhite had finally made it her own.

So perhaps it was a shame that before the day Mariana's grand-nephew had arranged to visit with a man from London who would estimate everything, a freak electrical fire broke out in the basement. Like a dam bursting, the building was suffused with light, and every item was consumed. Adjacent buildings escaped unscathed, though that cat was never found.

But there are some - who drink alone, perhaps - who say an aura still hangs about the place. They say that anyone spending the night in the house that was *Wildthyme's*, who happens to be awake and with their e-reader switched on, will find it inexplicably filled, with every cockatrice-rare book, manuscript and letter lost in the blaze.

It would make Iris furious if she ever found out but then, she hasn't been seen around town in a while...

Ouroboros

Neil Chester

Sunlight glinted sharply off a shard of broken window, light dancing across my retinas. I blinked to clear my eyes and took a good look at Crosslands Cottage for the first time in years. I kept being drawn back to the cottage, back to the past...

I was shocked at how dilapidated and unloved it looked, windows broken, paint peeling. The garden was overgrown, grass and weeds choking the path, shrubs and trees obscuring the front. Isolated in the woods it looked like a witch's cottage from a fairy tale. I snorted to myself in wry amusement – it wasn't an inappropriate description given the cottage's reputation. Given the things that I had seen, and felt, in its narrow passageways and small rooms.

I felt a pang of guilt then as I looked at the state of the place. In some ways the cottage was my responsibility. Well, Rose's more than mine really – after all, she had once been employed by the owner. The mysterious Iris Wildthyme.

After we'd married in the summer she and I had lived there for a little whilst I had attempted to restart a career interrupted by the war. As I sought a position amongst the local solicitors firms, she'd carried on working for her mistress and I had earned my keep by doing such physical work around the property as was required. I was pleased when success came and we could move to Brighton, and leave that cottage behind us. I had always felt uneasy there, the place had an atmosphere that I found unnerving. And, of course, I *had* seen the ghost.

I felt the same sense of unease now as I levered myself stiffly out of the car, a twinge of arthritis shooting through my knee, and crossed the narrow lane to the front gate. I rested my hand on the old, dry wood. Was I really going to go in? I had to didn't I? Just to see. 'Stupid old fool.' I muttered to myself. 'What would Rose say if she knew you were here?' Why hadn't I told her, when I'd left the house that morning, what I had planned? Was I afraid that she would laugh at me? Or worse, that she'd want to come along?

I'd twice seen the ghost – once on my first visit in 1913 – it was just an indistinct shape then. A blurred figure, pale and fuzzy, glimpsed by a nineteen year old man, barely more than a boy, forced to stay overnight in an unfamiliar cottage after missing the last train home. The old Colonel had told me about the ghost over dinner, after his unusual will was completed and our business concluded. I had been sent by my superior, Mr Forrester, to make a first draft of Colonel Jackson's will which he would then work up into a proper document upon my return to the office. He had claimed at the time that it would be good training for me in my path to becoming a qualified solicitor, although, with hindsight, I suspect that he considered the task of travelling to the old man's cottage a job more suited to a junior clerk than the head of the firm. In the bright sunlight of the following morning I half convinced myself that my imagination had supplied the figure. The atmosphere of the cottage had still disturbed me though and I had left soon after breakfast, bidding the Colonel farewell and setting off through the woods to the train station, glad to leave the place behind.

My second encounter had been three years later. On leave from the terrible war I had made the journey from Brighton to see the old Colonel again. Nervously adjusting my uniform cap I had knocked at the door. And come face to pretty face with the woman who was to be my wife. She had shown me in to the cottage and introduced me to her mistress, the new owner of the cottage, Miss Iris Wildthyme. I thought then for a moment about that strange old woman – her neat, trim figure, her bobbed hair, so black as to be almost purple in the firelight and her dancing, probing green eyes. Sadly my friend, the Colonel, had died the year before and, as per the terms and conditions of the will that I myself had helped to draft for him, Miss Wildthyme had assumed ownership of the cottage. I reflected for a moment that she herself must surely be dead by now. Her age then had been difficult to determine – her face, although largely unlined, could've been anywhere between forty-five and sixty-five – but that had been over forty years ago. We'd never been informed of the old lady's death and the cottage, as far as my contacts could ascertain, still belonged to her. Maybe I'd find her ghost haunting the place too.

On that second visit Miss Wildthyme had insisted that I stayed the night and proved herself to be an excellent hostess. Over a delicious meal, and rather more wine than I was used to, she had told, in a rich and mellifluous voice, a series of improbable tales, including the story of how she had met the Colonel, and saved both his life and his reputation – acts which had caused him, out of duty, to leave her his cottage in his will. It seemed that she had an interest in the paranormal. This was, she explained, why she had been so interested in the Colonel's cottage – she had heard the tales of the ghost and wished to experience the effect first hand. She even showed me some pieces of equipment, that looked like something out of a novel by H.G. Wells, that she said could 'measure disturbance'. Our talk continued long into the night – the old lady was fascinating and outrageous. And, I have to confess,

I was also drawn to Rose, her maid, my eyes always sliding sideways in the hope of catching her glancing at me. Miss Wildthyme noticed our clumsy flirtation, her bright green eyes sharp, but she said nothing.

I reached the door of the dilapidated cottage, having pushed through the overgrown path. Cherry red paint, dry as old skin, flaked under my touch as I pushed hard to force the door open. With a sense of unease I stepped into the darkened hallway. The air was musty – dusty and still – but not redolent of damp and decay as I'd expected. I stumbled, my eyes slowly adjusting to the dim interior. Although it was sunny outside, the dirt on the windows and the overgrown foliage conspired to cut out most of the late afternoon sunshine.

As I walked further into the cottage, nosing into old, familiar rooms, a feeling of melancholy fell over me. The air of abandonment that greeted me in each room was almost palpable – an empty chair by a cold, dead fireplace, a forgotten book, inch thick with dust, floral wallpaper peeling from the wall. As well as melancholy I also felt a familiar sense of apprehension. A feeling of being watched, of something glimpsed just out of the corner of my eye. The feelings I had always had in this cottage, even when it had been bright and lively and full of people. Others had felt it too – not only Rose but also those who had come after us. The couples, and occasional individuals, who had come to live here after Miss Wildthyme had gone travelling, never to return. No tenant had stayed here long.

All of them had spoken of a strange sensations and an occasional glimpsed figure. Had the old woman herself felt it? I was never sure.

I mounted the stairs to the first floor and they creaked under my weight. Memories came flooding back then – fractured, disjointed images and sensations – going to bed after having dinner with Miss Wildthyme, my head swimming with heavy, heady wine and preposterous tales. A sense of sudden cold as I walked along the corridor – a light, a pale, unhealthy green, almost a corridor of light, and a figure – a blurry figure of an old man with his back to me, his grey hair limned with strange emerald highlights. My breathing was harsh and my heart pounding as I remembered the encounter, so long ago now. The touch of the apparition's icy fingers as he turned and reached out for me. A sensation, like electricity, as we touched, and then a pulling, sucking sensation, as if I were being drawn into the corridor of light. Finally the sound of my own scream as I passed out.

My breath caught in my throat as I slowly realised that the green light was not in my memory but was all around me. Here and now. A figure formed in front of me. A young man, smart and neat in an army uniform, his eyes shaded by his cap. There was something familiar about the way he stood, about the way he moved. My mind skittered madly away from the inevitable conclusion…

'He's you.' The deep, familiar voice startled me. Someone moved into my peripheral vision and stood beside me.

Petite and trim, Iris Wildthyme was unchanged by the forty years that had passed since I last saw her. Her dancing green eyes were fixed on the figure as she spoke. 'A time fissure runs through this location. The ghosts aren't really ghosts – they're displaced time images. And this one is you. When you touched the fissure all those years ago a part of you was sucked into it.'

I remembered the days I had spent convalescing at the cottage, feeling weak and drained. During that time Rose and I had grown closer and closer, our love growing as my strength returned. That incident had changed the very shape of my life.

'What should I do?' I croaked, my mouth dry with shock and fear.

'Reach out,' Miss Wildthyme instructed, briskly, 'You *know* what to do. You've done it before…'

Tentatively I raised my hand, reaching out, feeling the cold fingers of the young figure, the young me, touching mine. The shock of electricity ran through me, up my arm, into my brain and I gasped with pain. Suddenly I realised that the 'ghost' I'd first seen as a young man, back in 1913 was also me. Me as I was now, an old man. My whole life, stretching back and forwards along the axis of that cottage. Energy coursed through me, nerve endings tingling. I could barely stand it and the energy overwhelmed me, just as it had so many years ago. Through the blackness clouding the edges of my vision, I saw Miss Wildthyme step forward, a fascinated glint in her eye. Just before I passed out my eyes returned to my own young face, staring at me across the years...

I awoke to the feeling of a hand lightly slapping my face. My eyes flickered open to see the bright eyes of Iris Wildthyme fixed on me through the shadows. The unearthly light of the fissure was gone and we were alone now in the crepuscular gloom of the old cottage. I was slumped against the wall, she crouched in front of me.

'Are you alright?' she asked, her usually brisk tone softened into concern. I nodded, unsure that my dry throat could shape the words.

'Good.' The concern was gone as she stood and consulted the slim device in her hand. 'You've closed the fissure. The energy discharge between the two temporally different versions of yourself overloaded the fissure and closed it.' She gave a small smile, 'Ouroboros.'

'Um, good,' I offered, unsure of much of what she was saying.

'Thank you Michael. I've been waiting forty years to close that time fissure.' With a strength that belied her small frame, she grabbed my hand and hauled me to my feet.

'I must go,' she said, suddenly, 'People to go, places to see. Give my love to Rose.'

And with that, she turned on her heel and disappeared from view...

In Passing

Nick Wallace

The first thing I know is the size of the room.

By rights, it should be some small detail, like a draught on my skin or a distant echo or maybe something right before my eyes as they blink open. But it doesn't work like that at all.

I'm just here, upright, waiting, and immediately aware of the space around me.

The room's big. Massive, really. Two hundred metres long, with towering walls of brick and rendered concrete and floor that's hard and unyielding. This building is, I think, solid; like it's stood forever and forever will.

The only indication that, somewhere, a ceiling exists, is a row of spotlights, blinding in the dark.

Spotlights that weren't there a moment ago.

'That can't be right,' I whisper and slowly turn around.

Other things snap into focus. Random pieces of machinery stand about the room; isolated and tall, their massive gears revolve and pistons glide, driving soundlessly on. I count four of these industrial towers, one in each quarter of the room.

I continue to turn, slowly increasing my awareness, and with each revolution new details appear. Too many details. Too much information. I screw my eyes shut, try to close it all out, but somehow the room keeps on coming, building itself around and inside me, drowning my senses.

I feel dizzy, sick, stumble, clutch my head.

I sink to the floor, and as my knees hit concrete, there's another new sensation. A voice.

'You just need to steady yourself, my dear child,' the voice says.

And I do.

The voice should be a new feature. More detail, more stimulation, overwhelming with proximity, a furnace of sensation. But it's different to everything else. Somehow this is just *other*.

'Steady yourself,' the voice repeats. 'And if you do that, you'll feel fine.'

I open my eyes again. The ground is firm once more, the room around me just background now. I climb to my feet, unsteady, but gaining strength.

There's a hand on my arm, helping me.

I turn to look at my helper and find an old woman staring at me. I blink and she's gone, replaced by a young woman smiling at me, blue eyes masked by a stray blonde curl. I blink. And every time I blink she's someone else. The glamour of an entertainer. The comfort of a grandmother.

'Do stop that,' the voice says. 'I'm starting to feel unwell.'

I blink. The grandmother is a pouting man in a tuxedo.

'Darling,' he says, 'we can go no further till you stop all this.'

I blink again and the man becomes a woman again. The first one again. An old lady, with a long nose and a slightly drawn face. She doesn't change the next time my eyes flutter, and this development prompts a slight smile of relief.

'Who are you?' I croak. 'What is all this?'

'My name,' she says, 'is Iris.' She pulls herself upright and glances around. 'I may need to explain a few things.'

It turns out I'm a spaceship.

A Septima IX generation ship. Commissioned in the early 23rd century and built in the dockyards of the Mars Orbital.

'Warp drives were just the stuff of fantasy back then,' Iris tells me. Her voice is sharp and brittle like a past age, yet full of childlike wonder, all at the same time.

We're walking now, moving through the room. I'm keeping my eyes on her as we go, trying to ignore the way the room keeps on changing. Except 'changing' isn't right. Becoming *more* feels better: more detail, more weight.

'Exploration and colonisation were the business of pioneers,' Iris says. 'A family business. An age gone by.' She pauses. 'All arrogant swines, of course'

'Arrogant?' I ask.

'Even travelling on full burn, the journey to the rimworlds is the work of centuries.'

'Is that where we are?'

Iris doesn't respond to that. She just smiles. She's been smiling a lot, a quiet enjoyment; although of what, I'm not quite sure. The smile is different this time. Before I can ask about that, she breezes on.

'What those few hundred years mean is whoever starts that journey is never going to finish it. It is a legacy mission. One for their children and their children's children. And that is why they're called generation ships.'

'And I'm…?'

'One of them.'

I stop walking and grab hold of Iris' arm, suddenly tired of being led around. I look past her, at the room. Not a room, I suddenly decide, but a hall. A giant hall.

In its corners the machines move silently on, but the rest of the space is now filled with objects that have always been there. A rusting car; an oversized vase of lilies; a collection of spoons; a neatly folded paper napkin; a string of paperclips draped around a cherry tree. On and on, a collection of things, all picked out in the dark by the spotlights above. Somewhere music plays, a sad voice emerging from a hissing turntable, and behind all the clutter, cinefilm flickers over one bare whitewashed wall.

Iris watches me look around. I don't need to ask.

'This is an interface,' Iris says. 'Somewhere we can talk.'

'Is that what it was all about earlier?' I ask. 'When you changed.'

'You saw the future,' she says. 'A host of possible futures.'

'You were different people.'

'I am large,' she asserts. 'I contain multitudes.'

'You were a man.'

'A retirement outfit.' Iris looks at me with sudden steel. 'I'm not as yet convinced it will take well.'

I leave it there. Of all the things that have happened so far, that's one of the least perplexing.

I point at the towers in the corners of the room. 'All this machinery?'

'They're you. All of this is. It's a representation of who you are. '

'If that's me,' I look down to my hands, 'then what's this?'

'That's you as well. The objects are external functions. If you were a human, we'd be calling them motor functions and senses. They're part of you, but separate from *you*.'

From behind her, Iris wheels out a full-length mirror that wasn't there a moment ago. For a moment, there's no image to be seen, and then I'm there. Female, on the cusp of middle age, a mature body but not one wrecked by time. Also, stark naked.

'Bloody hell,' I say, and screw my eyes shut and concentrate. When I open them I'm still there in the mirror, just fully dressed.

Iris nods in approval. 'You're getting the hang of it now.'

And I am. Things are beginning to make sense. The room is a representation of me, my physical form and memories, but this body that I'm walking around in is separate to all that. This body, now fully clothed, is the thought processes, the decision making. I'm a representation of the essential me that runs the show.

'You could have told me about the clothes,' I complain.

'How about a name?' Iris asks.

I think, and like the clothes, in thinking the information comes to me. 'My registration is G7-MXX.'

'That's not a name.'

'Jennifer, then,' I reply and smile. 'For generation ship.'

'Right,' I say. 'You've plugged yourself into my mind, yes? And this space, the interface, is something my unconscious has created for us to talk in?'

Iris gives a stately nod.

'I understand the how,' I tell her, 'but not the why. Why are we talking?'

We're moving through the hall, our footsteps echoing into nothing. The only other sound is the flick and whir of the cinefilm projector.

'How unusual.' Iris stops and picks an ornate china vase up from a thick black base. 'How unusual. Ming dynasty. Ruler of the universe, not the Chinese one. Very rare,' she says. 'You don't get much surviving pottery from fictional worlds any more.' She glances at me. 'What does it represent?'

'Nothing,' I say. 'The stuff about the vase is your thoughts, not mine. It's the stand that's important.'

Iris looks at the vase, then the base it was on. An obsidian block, heavy, immovable. 'A sense of self?' she muses, 'Holding up a precious cargo? Your colonists?'

'You're phrasing that as a question when you already know the answers,' I say. 'You made this happen.'

'I did not,' Iris responds, 'You made it happen. I just gave you the tools.'

'And you're evading,' I snap. 'Why are we talking at all?'

There's a pause, and she looks away. After consideration, Iris replies, 'I was just passing. I thought you might appreciate a chat.' But she doesn't meet my eye when she says it, and I'm not sure if she's lying to protect me or herself.

'No offence,' I say, 'but if I'm Septima IX generation ship, then I've got thirty thousand people to be looking after. Chatting isn't high on the agenda.'

'Maybe you need to relax,' she answers. There's sadness in her eyes as she looks at me. 'Be yourself a little more.'

I pause, something cold creeping across my back. Stupid, I tell myself, because I don't have a back and I don't have a body. This is all just a representation of –

'This is my mind,' I whisper. And suddenly, for the first time, I really feel it.

My skin tingles; I can feel every tiny breath of air across it, moving the invisible strands of hair on its surface.

But there's more than just me. I can see the tiny details of the vase in Iris' hand, the web of thin lines across its veneer and the brushstrokes that form the patterns, and beyond that to the hairs on the brush and the mix of pigment and oils that have gone into the paints, and the skill of the steady hand that drew the paints across the china.

So much detail, so many elements, contrasting and clashing, combining, building, to form that vase. The way form emerges from that maelstrom seems like a possibility so remote it should be almost impossible.

'Yes,' says Iris, 'the basic fact of life is quite impressive if you stop to think about it.'

Everything in the hall has a new sense to it now. The cherry tree is in full blossom; the grain and scratches of the cinefilm carry history and love; the three pillars of silently shifting machinery have more strength than ever; the hissing turntable tells a sad and lonely song.

'Awareness,' I say to Iris. 'This is what it feels like being alive.'

'And that is the point, that is why we're talking.' She lifts her chin once more. 'Just because you've been keeping it a secret, doesn't mean you're not a person. I thought you might like to see what it was really like.'

'I'm a spaceship.'

'You're a series of processes and thought patterns, all accumulated knowledge, with a body which has evolved and grown and changed and decayed. That makes you as alive as anyone else.' She turns and spreads her hands, encompassing the room. 'This is you and was always you. From your first moments at the Mars Orbital, all the way through your test runs and safety checks, embarkations and debarkations, you've been building all this. Priorities, experiences, life.' She takes my hand. 'People can be quite small. They're goal-oriented. Wonderful in what they achieve, but focused. Unless something comes up and tells them it's alive, then they assume it isn't.'

All those sensations make sense now. The end of the process that began with those first waking moments and sudden knowledge of the hall. It's the same, just a thousand million times greater. Knowledge and memory.

'I've never told them,' I say. 'We're...' The tiniest pause as I calculate the number. '...one hundred and eighty-three years out from Mars space. And I've never told them.'

'That's five generations or so who've never thought to ask,' Iris replies.

I smile. 'But it's not like that. We're all working towards the destination. Them and me. There's a world waiting for us.'

But as I say it, I stumble over the words and frown.

'Only…' I look at Iris. 'That feels wrong. That's not it.'

Iris bows her head and wanders away. She doesn't want to speak but wants me to follow, so I do.

Down the corridor, towards the far end, where a reel of film coils on the floor as the chattering projector shines a light and life plays across the whitewashed brickwork in front of it.

We round one of the columns of pistons and gears, all silent fury, focusing on the images.

It's a wooden carriage, with little bays of seats and big windows. The varnish is dirty and the frames are chipped in places, the tables between the seats have ring stains on them, and the fabric on the seats is faded and worn. But the seats are filled with people, men and women, young and old, some laughing, some studious, some holding hands. The camera moves down the aisle, jostled as children run by.

And while the image is faded, every now and then the film vanishes in the glare of sunlight coming through the windows and staccato effect of the world going by.

'A train,' I smile. 'A steam train on a summer's day.'

'Your journey,' Iris says. 'Carrying five generations across space, out to the rim.'

I look at her. 'Why are you sad?'

She stares at me for a moment, then crosses over to the projector. 'Because everything has its time.'

She flicks a switch and a speaker – silent till now – crackles into life.

The images remain the same for a moment, only now with sound I can hear the laughter and the low murmur of conversation and the drum of the wheels. It triggers a memory of some kind, because I can almost taste the smuts in the air, except…

There's something else.

And the people in the carriage can feel it too, a noise rising from nowhere. Almost as one, their heads turn towards the window and the camera follows them, and the carriage rocks as something breaks through alongside the train, pushing air aside, moving fast, sleek and modern. Unstoppable force. And then it's gone.

The projector judders to a halt and we're caught between frames, the passengers looking at each other in panic.

They're frightened and so am I. We're all helpless.

'What was that?' I whisper.

'That was high warp drive,' Iris says.

'High. Warp. Drive?'

'A Septima XXIV colony ship. Passing you on the far side of the Tricorn Nebula.'

As she says this, I remember it. Vaguely, distantly, like a story I was told a long time ago. I remember it and I know that it's true, but I also know that something isn't right about this, about any of this.

'We decided to carry on,' I say.

'Did they ask you?'

'*They* decided, then.'

'And their colonisation mission was completed by others before it even got under way,' Iris says.

You can't keep cinefilm static too long. The heat from the bulb in the projector is already starting to show.

'Bypassed by the speed of technology.' I look around. 'State of the art explorers one minute; stuck in the slow lane the next.'

'There's a lot to said for life in the slow lane,' Iris remarked.

The image begins to brown, bubbles appearing at the edges. More memories, bringing heat and flame with them, my voice changing with their touch. 'They sent a ship out from the colony to intercept. Swaggering in, offering to take anyone who wanted to go with them. They wanted to make everything we'd done redundant.'

'They were just trying to help.' She waves a hand. 'In a rush, as always. Humans are like that.'

'Not all humans,' I insist.

'No,' Iris smiles.

I look back at the projector. Another moment or two and the film will catch fire, beyond repair.

'They decided to carry on.' My back straightens and a smile forms on my face as the thoughts become clear. 'They told them to go back to their colony. That their grand-children would see them in a hundred years' time.'

The projector stutters for a moment, and then the reel plays on, the damaged frame passing out of sight, and with it, the fear vanishes from the passengers' faces.

I stand there, Iris forgotten, just staring at the film playing out.

Things are different now. There's still happiness and laughter, but it's more subdued, with backs straighter and eyes a little older. The edge of courage and anticipation has gone, replaced by a stoicism and certainty in their lives and the way they've chosen to live them.

'It should always be the journey,' Iris says. 'Never the destination.'

I turn and nod, smiling. There are tears on my face. Pride like I've never felt before, and also a deeper realisation.

'What's happening here, Iris?' I ask. 'Because this corridor we're in, I'm not sure, but I think it used to be a room.' I point at the columns of machinery at either end. 'And there used to be another couple of those, but then there were three, and now there's only two. And –'

She takes my hand and squeezes, and the words fade on my lips, because I know what's coming, have known the entire time, and just wasn't making the connections.

Didn't want to make them.

'You are dying, my love.'

Iris moves an object to one side – I don't even notice what – clearing a space on one of the pedestals and sits me down.

I think I should be more shocked than I am. Except…

'It's okay,' I say. 'I knew. Really, I knew.'

Iris explains that this subconscious knowledge is something to do with the interface and how it carved off a portion of me, isolated it from the remainder of my mind. But I'm not interested.

'Why?' I ask, again, and insist: 'An answer this time, please.'

'I thought you might like to talk. Someone to help take your mind off things.' She shifts uncomfortably, looking off to one side. 'We all need someone to talk to as the end approaches.'

And as she starts on about the interface again, I realise something about her. That she doesn't like questions like 'why?'. I can imagine Iris just not seeing the point in them.

Her answer, when it finally emerges, comes down to this. 'I wanted you to know what it was like to be properly alive. And I didn't want that first feeling of yours to be your final one. I didn't want it to be fear.' She looks down at the ground. 'I didn't think that would be terribly fair.'

'I'm not frightened,' I tell her, then frown, trying to remember. 'What is it that's happening?'

'That impossible collision of events which makes things, also takes them away.'

'What's happening?' I repeat, harder this time.

Iris gives a sigh, weighed with sadness and recites: 'A micro-meteorite and a temporary blind spot on your sensors, plus a failed update on your charts and a course correction for a dangerous radiation band.'

'Which means what?'

'You are caught in the gravity field of a neutron star with no possibility of escape.'

I look at the screen. There's a final glimpse of the train's passengers and then the last inch of film flips through the projector and snakes onto the floor, and the passengers are gone, their summer journey replaced by a constant square of white light.

'We've got to get them out,' I say. I get to my feet, glaring at Iris, suddenly angry. 'Why are we wasting time with all this? We've got to help them.'

Iris looks away, and I grab her, turn her back to me. And I realise she's not hidden her face in shame, but sadness.

'But my goodness, you already have, dear,' she says and gives me the kindest smile. 'You knew, you see. In the first moment, you could see it happening, the whole chain of events.'

'The colonists,' I whisper, half-memory, half-deduction. 'High warp drive.'

'They got to you in time to clear your passengers.'

But not me, I realise. Because that's the point. There's no escape for me. The way the room's been closing in.

'My mind,' I say. 'The gravity field is eroding my programming, systems going off line. That's why I can't remember, that's why you're here. You didn't want me alone and afraid in the dark.'

'And are you?' Iris asks. 'Afraid?'

I look at her, uncertain, thinking. It's so hard now. There are thoughts and moments and memories, skirting the edge of my consciousness.

There are things I should remember and know, things I should feel, and they're slipping away, more and more with every passing moment.

That vast breathtaking collision of life is getting smaller and smaller in my vision.

There's a moment of clarity as I realise what the column of machinery is. An engine. One last remaining engine, fighting against the pull of a star.

'I used to sing to them,' I say. 'I don't think I could manage a single note now. But I used to sing, I'm sure of that.'

'Sing to who?' Iris asks.

'The stars,' I smile. 'As we passed by. With the sensors nets and radio scanners and on all the frequencies, I'd sing to them, to tell them how brilliant they were. How massive and clever and beautiful and wonderful they were.' I pause, then whisper once more: 'I used to sing.'

Iris lays a hand on my shoulder. 'And did they ever sing back?'

My cheeks are wet as I look up and smile, thinking back, losing the present. 'Oh, yes,' I say, 'some of them, sometimes. A sound so old you can't begin to imagine.'

'You're crying,' Iris says.

'Am I?' My hand goes to my face and the memory of the tears returns. 'It's not... It's not for me. I don't care about me. It's them. They're gone from me now, I know, but...' I look at Iris and there's a pain that fills my whole body and my voice, born of desperation, deep and full and impossible to escape. 'I wanted to see. I wanted to be there for them, from the start and all the way to the end, and now I'm dying and I'm leaving them all alone and I can't do anything to help. I can't make it right.'

The emotion drains away, and when I speak again, I'm calm once more.

'I just wanted to see them home. I just wanted to be there.'

The spotlights have closed in and beside us the column of machinery is slowing down. A few moments more and it'll be barely moving. A few after that and it'll stop entirely.

'You did the very best you could,' Iris tells me. 'And they loved you for it. They love you still.'

'Do you think?'

She sits down beside me again. 'All those things you wanted to see and be there for… You'll be there. In the triumphs and the disasters, and the births and marriages and the deaths, every memory and word and action, there'll be a part of you. Because they'll remember.'

The silent column gives a resounding bass thump as it stops and Iris looks over her shoulder at it. As she does so, her hand disappears, then the rest of her follows, and I blink.

There's an old woman standing in front of me. She looks familiar somehow, but I can't place the memory.

She says something, but I can't hear it.

I'm looking at this room. It's small and dark, but there's one light on, a tiny star shining on a pedestal that's holding a vase. It's the only thing in the room and the world.

The woman leans in towards me and with her lips at my ear, I can finally make out what she's saying. One word.

Then there's a pedestal and a vase and me and nothing else.

A glint of light that catches its rim, reminding me of something, something I think I should be doing, and I begin to hum.

The light fades and there's the sound of breaking china, but only for a moment and then it's gone. Replaced by a song.

A sound that so old and wise it could break my heart.

And there's nothing for me to do but sing back as the dark rolls in.

Iris at the V&A

George Mann

An exhibition celebrating the life and times of the transtemporal adventuress

CATALOGUE OF EXHIBITS – GALLERY ONE

(With additional margin notes by Art Critic Panda)

Lilith as a young girl in the Clockworks
(circa unknown, artist unknown, oil on canvas)

Here we see one of the only surviving images of Iris as a young girl, around the age of nine. Her white linen dress is streaked with dirt, and her knees and palms are black with mud. It's clear she's been up to no good. Note the expression on her face, glancing nervously back over her shoulder as if worried she might be interrupted at any moment by one of her Aunts. Historians believe the room she is in – which has the appearance of a chamber in a mediaeval British castle – is her room at her Aunts' house, somewhere in the mysterious Clockworks.

The tiny glimpse of black and white fur in the lower left corner of the canvas is thought to represent Iris' long-term companion, Art Critic Panda.

(Don't be taken in by her sweet, innocent appearance. There's something going on behind those eyes. She knew what she was about, even then. We were plotting escape, contemplating running away with a highwayman. She hasn't changed much, in all these years, despite appearances.)

Iris emerging triumphant from the Pyros Mines of Alpharon IX
(circa 1245 Earth Standard, Pierre Du Mench, colour photograph)

A rare candid photograph of Iris, captured in the moments after she'd helped to liberate the Alpharon Cat People from servitude at the hands of the oppressive Mendrites. Note the cigarette dangling from her bottom lip, the victory salute (often mistaken for a rude gesture), and the unidentified Pussy-Girl rubbing itself against her legs.

(Look at that bright red hair and all that black leather. She looks like some sort of lesbian space pirate. Goodness, I'm relieved I've never had the misfortune of running into that incarnation. I imagine it's all 'do this' and 'do that', dashing about firing guns and rubbing people up the wrong way. All a bit butch for me, I'm afraid.)

Still from Murder, She Said
(1961, b&w still from celluloid)

Here we see an older Iris in a train carriage, looking horrified at the sight of an apparent strangulation occurring in a second, passing train. No one quite understands how Iris came to be caught on film in this way, but she soon displaced the original actress who'd been cast to play Agatha Christie's famous sleuth, Miss Marple, and went on to take the lead role in three films. They are now considered classics of their genre, and Iris' performance (attributed under a pseudonym) is considered to be one of the most authentic yet committed to film.

('No one quite understands?' Least of all Iris! She had no idea she was starring in a film. She'd blundered onto the set in that way she blunders into every adventure, and when she saw that strangulation going on, she thought it was real. That's why her performance is so authentic – she was investigating the murder for real. She thought the cameras were there to make a documentary.)

Dancing with 'El Jefe' at a Christmas party
(circa 1973, signed 'Josephine', gouche on board)

One of a number of representations of the mysterious 'El Jefe' on display at the exhibition, this painting depicts him as an older, grey-haired man in a purple silk cape. Iris' relationship with the man remains unclear, but here they are shown to be larking about on the dance floor, smiling merrily as El Jefe swings Iris around in a waltz, while a number of men in army fatigues watch from the nearby tables. The public house has been identified as 'The Witch's Tipple' in Hertfordshire.

(Look at that Dandy! And all of those men in army uniforms. What the Devil are they doing, turning up to a party dressed like that? It beggars belief. I can't fathom why Iris used to knock about with this lot, I really can't. And honestly – look at the quality of this painting. It leaves a lot to be desired.)

Posing with unknown Scottish warlord
(circa 1447, artist unknown, oils on canvas)

Legend has it that, during the Scottish Border Wars with England in the mid-Fifteenth Century, Iris assisted this burly-looking fellow after he'd drunkenly tumbled down a well shaft, having spent the evening celebrating his victory in a small skirmish near Alnwick. The following day she reportedly beat him in a caber-tossing contest, although this may be an apocryphal story.

Here, Iris is depicted as a young, pretty black woman, with gold hoop earrings, a gold lame top and a denim skirt.

(Iris and a man in a kilt? Caber-tossing? Is it just me…?)

Firing a laser pistol at a Tarixion Gas Fiend
(circa 4281 Earth standard, Marlene Dietrich, b&w photograph)

In this famous photograph by Marlene Dietrich, Iris appears as a svelte young woman with long blonde hair, an Amazonian figure and a revealing bodice. The negative has degraded due to poor storage conditions (it was found in a safe-deposit box in a derelict hotel, along with a number of other papers pertaining to Ms. Dietrich's unusual, largely-unrecorded exploits during the second half of the 20th Century). The smudge of pale grey on the left is the Tarixion Gas Fiend mid-transformation, and the young man hiding behind the boulder is Carlos Esteban, a popular Latino R&B star from 2012.

(My, didn't she have nice boobs in those days?)

Relaxing on the number 22
(circa 2010, George Mann, crayons and felt tips)

This impressionistic sketch by the author, George Mann, reportedly shows Iris in a state of repose, having just returned to the bus after a boozy book launch party on Shaftsbury Avenue, London. The girl, sitting on the chaise longue beside Panda, is said to be Elspeth May, a newspaper columnist.

(Good God! What an abomination. For the life of me I cannot understand why such a primitive offering should be considered worthy of this exhibition. Are you sure that's even a girl? I'd certainly think twice before chancing my arm, judging by this monstrosity. Mann should stick to writing – he has no talent for visual art.)

Long Island Party
(circa 1929, Celeste Parker, b&w photograph)

Iris sits at a patio table, deep in conversation with the famous New York dilettante, Gabriel Cross. She's smoking an American cigarette and looks very relaxed. Close by, Art Critic Panda frolics by the side of the heated pool, entertaining the partygoers with a witty tale of his recent exploits.

Legend has it that, hours later, the three of them were gadding about the Manhattan rooftops fighting moss men, gangsters and inter-dimensional monsters.

(That man knew how to drink. I hadn't seen anyone put away as much liquor since those heady days in Montmartre, back in the 1880s, when Toulouse

Lautrec got utterly plastered and somehow ended up stuck at the top of a tree after wrestling a boa constrictor.

The really shocking thing, however, was the fact that – pissed as he was – Gabriel Cross ended up donning a load of bondage gear, driving us to Manhattan in a strange coal-powered car and then swinging from the rooftops like he thought he was Tarzan. Still, it was a fun night, from what I can remember. Apart from getting shot at, that is.)

The crab nebula, seen against the aftermath of the explosion of the Bathory outpost
(circa 2399 Earth standard, artist unknown, watercolour)

The Bathory outpost was a human deep space staging post for the vast colony fleets that would/will leave Earth in the late 23rd Century, used as a refuelling station and monitoring post for nearly one hundred years.

This painting shows the perspective from one of the station's escape pods, following the cataclysmic explosion that tore the outpost apart. To this day, the nature of the explosion remains unclear, but responsibility has been claimed by at least two anti-colonial terrorist groups.

If you look carefully, to the right hand side of the explosion you can just make out the number 22 bus amongst the debris.

(Anti-colonial terrorist groups, eh? Oh, the injustice! That's not how it happened at all. They were lovely fellas, up there on that station, and they welcomed us with open arms. Iris got the party started, as usual, and they were very grateful for the company, I can tell you. She shook them right out of the doldrums. It all went wrong, however, when she offered to make them a vegetable biryani. Somehow she managed to leave the gas on, and that, coupled with an electrical fault in the life support system, was what did for the Bathory outpost. Terrorist groups, indeed!)

In the Egyptian wing of the British Museum
(circa 1969, Romola Jones, b&w photograph)

Here we see Iris in her young, athletic persona once more, this time posing with her friend and sometimes-companion, Romola Jones. These two women, being outwardly of a similar age, were popular faces about town in the late 1960s and early 1970s, often seen at parties with the Beatles, Marc Bolan, Twiggy and other famous fashionistas of the era. It's doubtful many of these people knew the truth about how Iris and Romola spent their days, battling aliens, monsters and mad scientists to ensure the preservation of the Earth.

Here, in a portrait by Romola, they are captured in the aftermath of their defeat of a resurrected monkey spirit from Ancient Egypt. Note the bloodstain on the front of Iris' blouse.

(How I long for those parties! For short skirts and moon boots and free love. For cocktails and eyeliner and feather boas. Oh, Iris, can't we pay a little visit to Romola? Can't we? Your leopard print handbag would fit right in, and I'm sure your old self would love to see us.)

Celebrating the end of a successful case with Professor Archibald Angelchrist
(circa 1911, Arven Smith, charcoal and pencil)

A sketch of Iris on the Thames embankment, wearing an extravagant, wide-brimmed hat and a leopard-skin dress by St Michael. She's holding Professor Angelchrist around the waist in a rather familiar manner, although by 1911 they'd know each other on and off for almost a decade, regularly corresponding and meeting in London to share adventures.

A newspaper report of the time is most enlightening: 'Professor Archibald Angelchrist of the British Secret Service, along with a woman of undisclosed age and nationality, today caused a storm in the capital when they engaged a school of invading mermen in hand-to-hand combat.

Eyewitnesses report the woman used her carpet bag to drive the creatures away, once again saving the Prime Minister from an embarrassing situation.'

(He was all over her, the filthy beast. Wouldn't let up. I was forced to have a word. I have to hand it to him, though – Professor Angelchrist was always handy in a fistfight. He gave that Piscotorian a right punch up the hooter, just a few minutes before this sketch was made. Sent it scuttling back into the Thames with its proboscis between its legs. And he makes wonderfully exuberant jumbleberry jam. I always enjoy a good picnic with Angelchrist, even if he does have a penchant for 'borrowing' Iris' diaries for purposes undisclosed.)

Time considered as a bowl of juniper berries
(circa unknown, artist unknown, pastels)

Abstract.

An unknown graffiti artist added the Melton Mowbray pork pie at a later date.

(Tosh. Complete and utter tosh. I mean, what were they thinking? The pie looks reasonably appetising, though.)

On the battlements of space fortress Calixes
(circa 5614 Earth standard, Saul Ha'd'matek, Caprillian blood on dried Scorl hide)

This is Iris at her most regal, surveying the field of battle on the eve of the last night of the Caprillan-Scarlofen war. She appears quite incongruous against such a militaristic backdrop: an old lady standing amongst the castellation, her face drawn in a frown of disapproval.

It is said that she did not take part in the battle herself, showing a grave distaste for fighting, but aided in the settlement negotiations that brought an end to the conflict and helped to usher in a thousand years of peace between the two alien nations.

The etching is all the more impressive due to the primitive and grisly nature of the materials employed in its creation – the artist was an enemy soldier encamped around the base of the fortress, and used the hide of his dead steed and the blood of his dying comrade to scratch out an image of the women who had come to the aid of the Scarlofen in their hour of need.

(Oh, this is rich. Not to mention, utter bobbins. 'At her most regal', indeed! She told me about this one, once, in a rare unguarded moment. The truth of the matter is this – she got the two leaders together in a room and knocked their heads together. Quite literally. Then she gave them a right ticking off. They were so shamed by her performance, and so keen to get shot of her, that they hastily drew up a truce and called off their armies.)

Trouble on deck
(circa 1983, Mrs. Julie DeWinter, pencil sketch)

This slightly unflattering portrait shows Iris a little green around the gills during a voyage on a cruise liner around the Mediterranean. It is unknown whether she had been drinking.

(You can see by the frown on Iris' face that she wasn't enjoying the voyage. Indeed, she was quite green for most of the journey, and barely touched the bottle of Bombay Sapphire we'd sneaked aboard.

Additionally, she was properly fed up with that dreadful old woman in a bottle green coat, seen there in the background. She was a right troublemaker, I can tell you, sneaking around sucking up people's souls when they were least expecting it. Iris sorted her out, though, slipping a load of laxatives into the harridan's Bloody Mary and tipping her overboard while she was bent double with stomach cramps. Classy lady, that Iris.)

At rest on Hyspero
 (circa 1999 Earth standard, Art Critic Panda, biro)

The composition of this piece is highly irregular, and most difficult to decipher. The setting appears to be some sort of beach, suggested only by the bucket and spade to the far left of the picture. Iris is rendered in an almost cubist, impressionistic style, and the other characters have not yet been identified.

(The highlight of the collection, if I do say so myself. I wish I'd been able to find some proper paper, however – the lines from the exercise book are rather distracting. Nevertheless, despite being nought but a sketch, this is clearly a triumph of draughtsmanship and style. No wonder the curator cannot fathom its depth and meaning – it's years beyond him. A fitting tribute to a great woman, methinks.)

The Golden Hendecahedron

Cody Quijano-Schell

Heads turned towards Panda as his voice rang out through the auditorium. 'It's a *hendecahedron*, you hag!'

'Of course it is! I called it *'a shape with eleven faces'* for Tom's benefit.' More heads and other alien ocular appendages turned at the sound of Iris' voice. 'And what did you call me? What crawled up your…'

'Sshh!' Tom interrupted Iris and Panda's bickering. Even though the two had only recently met each other, sometimes Tom was amazed at how well Panda and Iris were getting on. They were already like old friends - or maybe even a married couple. 'I think they're about to start the demonstration.' He was amazed when both of them actually remained silent.

The silence only lasted a moment. One of the scientists in the row of seats behind Iris tapped her on the shoulder and very quietly and politely asked her if she might remove her hat (which was admittedly gigantic), or at least a few of the long frizzy feathers that rose several feet into the air. Iris turned around in her chair, testily admonishing the man for making such a racket while she was trying to pay attention to the presentation. The man, whose body resembled a transparent pineapple with a seahorse's head, turned blue in an expression of embarrassment. Once she thought she'd thoroughly shamed the man for having no respect for others, she turned around and sat expectantly, the feathers atop her hat settled in such a position that somehow ended up obscuring *even more* of the man's line of vision. Tom could only offer a sympathetic shrug to the pineapple man as Panda demanded to be lifted up onto his shoulder.

As the presenter, a stocky lizard-man-thing, walked out onto stage, Tom caught the eye of a light-green skinned individual already seated on stage. Sporting a black beard, it was fair to say that he was handsome. Very handsome, in fact, but with bizarre green and yellow upswept hair that came to a point. The hairdo looked almost like a giant bulb of garlic with small purple Brussels sprouts at the top. They locked eyes. Tom looked around the audience to see if the man could be staring at anyone else. With his hand held close to his own chest, Tom discreetly pointed at himself. The man's head nodded, just ever-so-slightly, as he maintained confident eye contact. Tom couldn't believe it, he was getting cruised on at a scientific conference on an alien jungle planet!

He smiled, and feeling awkward, looked down to read the brochure. The man's name was Zelopan, and was one of the Arboleans, a race of hybrid humanoid/plant people. The fat lizard-thing man was clicking and chirping away as his translator spoke into the microphone. Keeping one gecko-like eye on the audience, the other eye turned backwards, towards Zelopan. He raised a claw high in introduction: 'May I present the Person of the Time Span, Zelopan!'

The audience gave Zelopan moderate but not enthusiastic applause. Tom got the idea that his fellow scientists hadn't quite accepted the man's research as authentic, a deduction that was confirmed by Zelopan himself. 'I will make believers out of each of you. The Hendecahedron will be an amazing power source for entire planets.'

As Zelopan spoke, Tom quickly found himself unable to follow the complexities of the technical terminology. For a while he just watched the man's face and enjoyed the occasional electrifying moment of eye contact.

He thought back to when they'd first come into the auditorium. Panda had thought the strange geometric shape on stage was a sculpture and had started to analyze the composition, and the aesthetics of the texture of the chosen material. Iris quickly pointed out that it wasn't sculpture at all, but instead deceptively simple-looking technology that manipulated the forces of nature through geometric ratios. She had implied that the eleven-sided version of this technology was inherently flawed, and she wanted to find out how they made it work, especially in light of a total lack of documentation about the events leading up to the collapse of this civilization.

The shape was like a blockish football. It reminded him of the time he and Jenny Winterleaf had both been transformed into similar small purple styrofoam shapes by hostile aliens that wanted to hijack Iris' bus to the Andromeda galaxy. That was a long time ago, and Iris had changed a lot since then.

Iris was digging noisily about in her purse.

'Do you want some gum, Iris?' asked Tom in a whisper.

Iris responded in a loud stage whisper. 'No, I'm looking for my ciggies. There's no rules about not smoking in here because no one has done it for centuries! When we came in, I told them it's required for my species and they accepted it as the truth! We can smoke as much as we want here!'

Tom thought this was mean spirited of Iris, then found it funny as well. 'Give me one too then!' And it was true, some of the aliens in this room had the most unbelievable scents, and one even gave off tiny yellowish bubbles that floated about the room as part of their respiration. Other species did their best to tolerate each other's differences. As Tom lit up and exhaled smoke, he saw an alien in front of him tightly close some slits on her neck, but no one said anything. 'This is great! It's like the seventies!'

The two of them sat smoking as Zelopan prepared a demonstration of his energy source. Iris was chewing gum at the same time as smoking, and her bubbles would pop with a burst of smoke. She whispered 'The Hendecahedron is ultimately more powerful than the twelve-sided model they'll come up with later, but this version is horribly unstable under certain conditions.'

Panda was scandalised. 'Iris, are you saying we may not be safe here?'

'Oh we'll be fine, lovey, don't worry your fuzzy little head. As long as they don't use it to power any kind of time travel device, the Hendecahedron is safe as houses.'

Zelopan cleared his throat dramatically. 'The power is now building and we'll soon be ready to demonstrate our new discovery. Projecting objects through time!'

Iris sputtered and jumped to her feet. 'You can't do that, you don't know what you're playing with!'

Zelopan frowned. 'I've checked my research again and again. In fact, my colleagues, the famous Allis and Ballis also agree with me.'

Iris accidentally swallowed her gum and coughed hard, trying to catch her breath. She swayed in place, dramatically. 'Allis and Ballis!! Do you know what they…'

Zelopan raised his hands, motioning for her to sit. 'Please hold your questions until after the demonstration.'

Iris glared at the green haired man. She was desperate to take control of the situation. 'You're waiting for that power to build up anyway, why not take a few questions while we wait?'

Zelopan looked back at the Hendecahedron for a moment, then turned back to Iris and nodded.

'How do you compensate for microscopic matter distortions due to quantum-field instability at energy levels this high?'

'We use Micro-matter Field Suppressors.'

'Then how do you deal with the resulting *Macro*-matter Fields which are produced by that process? How do you integrate them?'

Zelopan looked around at the audience with a bemused expression and nearly everyone in the audience laughed along with him. 'That's a good question. There isn't an energy source that exists capable of producing a Macro-matter field. That would be like making a gold chain where each atom was a condensed star. Theoretically possible, but I assure you it's not going to happen.' Zelopan laughed.

Holding her cigarette between two fingers, Iris pointed at the Hendecahedron. 'That thing is unstable, buster!'

'It's perfectly safe. That is, unless there is a time travellers in the audience who are supercharged with temporal residue!' Zelopan turned to the audience and everyone laughed, except for Iris, Tom and Panda who looked at each other guiltily.

Iris turned around and grabbed her purse. 'Come on Tom, Panda, we've got to be going, thanks for the demonstration Mr. Zeloplitz, I hope everything…' she said, at the moment sparks flew from behind the Hendecahedron.

Zelopan ran to a monitor. 'Stay calm everyone! I'm sure it's nothing. We've done this a thousand times.' As he looked over the readings, the colour drained from the man's green face. Tom thought he looked almost Caucasian. Brandishing a hand-held device Zelopan scanned the room and eventually brought it to a stop, pointing directly at Iris. 'You! You *are* a time traveller! '

Panda put his paws on his hips. 'Time *travellers,* you mean! But our presence alone shouldn't be enough to cause this sort of disruption!'

More sparks flew and a high pitched whine began to rise. Zelopan moved his device across the audience. 'There's more of you! Are you historians that came from the future? To see this glorious demonstration?' He flicked the device off. 'Because I believe in my research, I believe in time travel. Any time traveller here is in grave danger and is also putting everyone else in danger. Power from the Hendecahedron will be attracted to you.'

A man in a simple grey jumpsuit on the other side of the auditorium stood up, pressed a control on his wrist and disappeared smoothly. A large alien in the back that looked like a blackened Christmas tree with yellow eyes disappeared in a swirl of orange. A blue lightning bolt flew out of the Hendecahedron and struck the spot the alien had just occupied moments before.

Tom grabbed Iris' sleeve. 'Iris, we have to go!'

'No Tom, it's too late. The damage has been done. Oh, I've been so stupid, I shouldn't have gotten curious. I have to fix this before all the space in this constellation is shrunk to fit the time it takes to encompass it.' She leapt out of her seat, then put a dramatic hand across her necklace. 'Unless this is the incident that causes the system to disappear? Oh my…'

Panda shook his head. 'That woman really does talk nonsense at times. Pick me up! Pick me up! I want to see what she's doing.'

Tom turned in time to see that Iris had run on stage and pushed Zelopan out of the way of a workstation. 'Shut it down, lovey!'

'I instantly initiated the shutdown, but it will take time. Now leave. We're all in danger while you're here. YOU are in the most danger! You're like a lightning rod.'

As if on cue, at that moment the high pitched whine rose again. Iris worked frantically at the controls, struggling to keep feathers out of her face. 'What an awful hat. I hate this bloody hat!' She took it off and threw it like a frisbee towards Tom and Panda. In midair it was struck by a bolt of energy and incinerated. Her face fell, but she continued working feverishly pushing buttons. 'My wonderful hat! I loved that hat!'

She pointed for Zelopan to work on another work station and he instantly saw what Iris was doing. 'You're a genius!'

Iris smiled. 'Did you ever doubt it, chuck?' The sparks stopped and the ambient noise slowed. 'You can always rely on Iris Wildthyme to take things in hand.'

Tom and Panda looked at each other worriedly as the noise started again, this time in a pitch deeper than before, and rising steadily. Iris bit her lip. 'Uh oh.' The Hendecahedron started to glow blue on one side, red on the other. Iris pressed buttons frantically. 'Temporal doppler, not good, not good, NOT FLIPPING GOOD!'

Zelopan grabbed Iris by the shoulders. 'It's too late, it's cascading. We have to go. Can your time device transport us to safety?'

Iris jerked herself away from the Arbolean scientist. 'Let go of my shoulder pads, greenie! I'm gonna yank the cord!' Iris ran to the base of the Hendecahedron to where there were eleven tiny pentagons soaking up energy from the shape. When she grabbed the cable and yanked it out, the blue glow and red glow of the shape suddenly reversed positions. From between the colours, a bolt of white energy streamed out of the geometric shape and directly into Iris' chest. The Hendecahedron went dark and Iris fell limply into the cloud of smoke that had covered the floor of the room.

Tom, carrying Panda, jumped up and searched where Iris had fallen. Zelopan checked the readings and confirmed they were out of immediate danger at least, but also that he was getting disturbing readings from another experimental version of the Hendecahedron at the far end of the diamond-shaped complex. He pointed at the map. 'We have to get here.' The two wings of the building spread out at angles then bent back inwards, creating a non-man-eating-jungle green-space in the middle of the complex.

Panda barked orders. 'Someone clear this blasted smoke! I mean, Iris has cast iron lungs, but the rest of us are more delicate.'

At that moment, Iris sat up and straightened her neck-scarf, as strangely deep and thick smoke swirled around her in slow motion. Tom breathed a sigh of relief; she was fine. He thought she looked like a bust of herself, the way the smoke obscured everything from her shoulders down. He avoided saying so because he knew the minute he did, Iris would make some horrible 'bust' joke.

Iris looked out at the small crowd that had gathered around her. Why wasn't the auditorium evacuated? She shook her head, missing her hat. It was typical of scientists to want to stay and see what happened. She enjoyed the attention, though. Looking up at everyone, she thought to herself how seductive she'd look if she were nude, with only wisps of billowing vapour covering her, modestly. Too bad the room smelled like burnt plastic, it spoiled the mood a bit.

Suddenly, an identical Iris sat up next to her and straightened her neck scarf. The two Irises stared at each other, bug-eyed with frazzled gray-blonde hair standing on end, momentarily speechless. 'YOU!' the Irises yelled in unison.

Shocked, Tom nearly dropped Panda, just barely catching him by the leg before he hit the ground. Panda hardly seemed to notice he was dangling upside down as he looked from one Iris to the other. The eloquent dignity of an art critic momentarily abandoned the small stuffed bear. 'Oh shite! There's two of her now!'

The two Irises sat staring at each other for a long time. One of them slowly reached out and poked the shoulder pad of the other. One jumped to her feet, which was impressive for a woman her age in high heels, and offered a red gloved hand to her twin, helping her up.

Iris looked at her glove as they released their mutual handshake. 'No Blinothingee, that's good.' The other nodded.

As far as Panda could tell, the two were identical. 'What happened? Were you duplicated, Iris? Is one of you from a parallel timeline? Which of you is the original? Duplicate Irises! This is simply unheard of! In all our travels through time and space, what are the chances of encountering a doppelgänger of one of us?' Tom rolled his eyes.

'I don't...' the two Irises started to say, nearly in unison. The one who was a half second behind the other let the first one speak. 'I don't exist in parallel universes, ducky.'

Tom stepped closer. 'Iris, you sound worried. No, worse than worried, you sound... serious!'

The other Iris responded as both of them started to look at data on Zelopan's screens. 'It is serious. As I was saying, time travellers like me don't exist in parallel timelines, we exist outside of them.'

'Except when we don't. And if we're right, this isn't a parallel timeline situation.'

Panda gestured with his arm. 'Iris, this Iris, have you had your hair done? It's more blonde now.'

Tom looked at the other. 'And yours is more grayish purple.'

The two nearly identical women shared a knowing look. 'It's true then.'

The other sighed. 'Yes, it seems so.'

Tom moved between the two of them. 'What's going on Iris?'

'That bolt. It didn't create a duplicate of me. It pinched my timeline.'

Tom turned to the more gray-haired Iris. For some reason he trusted her more. She reminded him more of the older, completely different Iris he originally travelled with when he accidentally crawled onto her bus one drunken evening. 'What does she mean?'

Younger Iris dug in her purse. 'Imagine that bolt of temporal energy was a cannonball, shot against my timeline, represented by this pair of control-top tights!'

She grabbed one toe and threw the other end to the older Iris. They pulled the tights taut forming an x-axis. The two Irises walked on opposite sides of Tom, using him to stretch the garment out into a bell curve along the y-axis. Tom cringed. 'Oi, are these clean?'

'Oh hush, Tom! We're trying to illustrate something. Right. *You*, Tom, are the cannonball, stretching my timeline out in both directions, at an perpendicular angle.'

'We're *not* two different Irises. I'm the Iris from the present...' she pointed to the crotch of the pantyhose '...stretching towards the past.' She wiggled the foot she was holding.

The other Iris mimicked the action. 'And I'm the Iris from the present, stretching towards the future. I'm getting older…'

'And I'm getting younger.'

'We're the same Iris' they said, in unison.

Panda jumped up into the older Iris' arms. 'So what happens when your timeline reaches its limits? Will you get a run in them?'

'Exactly, lovely. It will either rip in half, or…' Both Irises let go of the pantyhose simultaneously, which snapped away from Tom and collapsed, limp onto the floor. '…possibly my entire timeline will get ripped from its mooring points at both ends and I'll never have existed.'

Tom sighed. 'Either way, that's not good.'

The low-tech scientific demonstrations were interrupted as a low rumble coursed through the complex. As the vibrations grew stronger, everyone stood as best they could, not knowing what to do. At exactly the same moment, both Irises yelled for everyone to move away from the Hendecahedron. Cracks formed in the floor, radiating out from the large shape. The structural flaws soon widened into crevices. Finally a sinkhole opened up and swallowed the Hendecahedron, and the entire audience. Panda dabbed imaginary sweat off his brow with his cravat. 'Oh my.'

On one side of the crevice clung Tom and the youthening Iris, on the other, Panda, Zelopan and the rapidly aging Iris.

Zelopan yelled across the expanse. 'We have to get to the workshop at the other end of the complex! We'll go this way, you go that way. If you get there first, shut down the other Hendecahedron!'

From Iris' purse, he looked down into the darkness and imagined he could hear a distant scream. 'Poor devils!'

It was slow going through the complex. Tom and Iris had to climb over and crawl under all sorts of obstacles that stood in their way. Fallen support beams, chunks of organicrete, and at one point, a shattered futuristic coffee pot that left an artificially piping-hot puddle full of broken glass. Tom noticed that Iris was full of energy and able to circumnavigate these dangers fairly easily.

'Iris... You're getting so young. I just realised... You look a bit like...' But at that moment, Iris faltered, as if the exertion was catching up with her. 'Iris, what's wrong? Do you need to rest!'

'No, it's not that... but let's sit.' He and Iris sat on some orange chairs that must have been a part of a reception area in one of the scientific departments housed in the complex.

'Do you suppose that any of the labs have dangerous stuff that we should be watching out for?'

Iris shook her head. Her face had significantly fewer wrinkles and looked quite young. Her smile was just as infectious as ever. 'Tom, I'm glad I found you again. I know my memory isn't what it should be at times, but one thing I never forget are the good times.'

Tom laughed. 'Oh Iris, sometimes you remember nothing but the bad times! All the trouble, the danger, the horrible monsters!'

'Tom, those ARE the fun parts!' Iris laughed as she regressed in age. He'd never seen her looking so young and alive. Then something went wrong.

'Tom! Tom, I...' Iris collapsed to the ground face first, glowing, with lights swirling around her.

Tom grabbed her shoulder and tried to roll her over. 'Iris! Iris, are you okay? What's happening? Is your time line snapping?' When Iris flopped over onto her back, the glow disappeared and a new woman was in her place.

Tom realised what had happened. He knew there were different Irises, and that she periodically went through some sort of metamorphosis but he'd never witnessed it. She called it 'The Change' like it was menopause and just something natural that all women went through.

With her timeline running backwards, she'd just reverted back to a previous Iris, but it was one that he'd never seen before. She was an older woman, which seemed natural to Tom, with wavy, greying red hair. Probably just a faded dye job, actually. He opened her eyelids to check for concussion or response. One of Iris' irises was blue, the other was brown. 'Iris? Is that you? Your hair... Your eyes...'

'Dispersal of pigment.' The voice was deeper, steadier. 'One eye turned blue after I witnessed an explosion. My fault, really, since I caused it!' Tom realised she was talking about events that occurred when she was in this body.

'Why just one eye and not both?'

'Well, I knew I shouldn't watch the explosion. But it was in the vacuum of space and I wouldn't have been able to hear it, and I had to make sure it happened, didn't I? Tell me not to do something and I'll probably end up doing it. I just had to peek with one eye - hence the mismatched eyes. It's very Bowie, don't you think?'

Tom just stared and helped this 'new' Iris to her feet. 'You're an old Iris, aren't you? I mean, Iris when she was younger? The one just before the current one.'

Iris nodded. 'Usually *the Change* feels marvellous. Like slipping out of an old skin into a new one. I didn't expect it to feel just as good the other way around. Antimetamorphosizing… it's like slipping into a favourite old pair of bell-bottom jeans!'

'How are you remembering things if you're travelling backwards through your time line?'

'It's an oddity that applies to time travellers like me - not you. You have travelled a lot, but you're a total amateur. No offense, kid. Once you're sufficiently outside of time, memory is a different animal.'

'Outside of time?'

'Remember when I… the other Iris… was talking about how I don't exist in parallel universes? It's a part of being a time traveller. We travel between possibilities instead of branching off down the paths of infinity.' She rubbed her fingers together slowly as if she was feeling her own fingers.

Tom noticed this Iris was aloof. Easy going. A little spacey. 'So you're saying most people, every choice they make creates a parallel timeline, one for each possibility?' He was surprised when she let out a loud, bold pleasant laugh.

'That's right! But being adrift in time and space isolates you from that mundane reality. And that's why travellers like me… change the way we do.'

'When you become a new Iris it's not just your body healing itself…'

'…it's the cosmic balance of possibilities being restored. Oh, you'll get people trying to tell you it's just a survival mechanism, but the change goes beyond biology or even technology. It's temporal. It's cosmic chance. It's… infinite possibilities brought to life. Even removed from normal time, and all those branching quantum possibilities…the cosmos demands periodic change and new possibilities.' Iris ran her fingers through her long red hair and held it away from her, smiling at it. 'It's magic.'

'I've never seen you change like that.'

Iris' fingernails ran across her cheek and her mismatched eyes locked onto Tom's. 'I just thought of something. If I'm regressing through previous lives… then the other Iris must be…'

'…progressing through possible future selves!! Ha HA HAAAAAAAA!' Iris twirled a parasol above her head.

Panda thought this new Iris must have the most obnoxious laugh he'd ever heard. She hadn't stopped talking since arriving and was currently blathering on about how she'd always wanted to look like Phyllis from the Pruitts of Southampton. '…in fact, I wouldn't be at all surprised if I was the inspiration for Patrick Dennis' book 'House Party'. HA HA HAAAAAAAA!'

Zelopan shared an uneasy glance with Panda. 'What is happening? Why did she become covered in spider webs and emerge looking and sounding so different?'

'Marzipan my dear fellow, it's really just too hard to explain. You just have to accept this is Iris now. At least until we can iron out the issues surrounding this temporal energy that's warping her tights. Er,um, I mean her timeline.'

'Panda always gets flustered when ladies underthings are mentioned, don't you honey!' Iris swanned around the rubble filled corridor holding her parasol in one hand and in the other, a long cigarette holder. Despite her age, she was wearing a short green mini-dress with white go-go boots that came to elfish points in the toes. Her hair was a white wig made of candyfloss. 'Don't deny it, Panda, I've known you for a very *very*, long time. HA HA HA!'

Her laughter was somehow forced and automatic, but undeniably infectious. Panda shook his little head. 'My god, that woman is amazing and yet… unbearable.'

'She's frightening.' Zelopan leant down near Panda as Iris climbed a pile of fallen debris like an ancient mountain goat. 'So it's true. She is a time traveller. What does her travel device look like? Is she wearing it now?'

Panda scoffed and grumbled. 'No no, it's a craft, but disguised. It's not what you'd expect! It's a rickety old crate!'

Zelopan nodded.

Iris called from high atop the rubble. 'We can make it through up here! Come on you two, stop trying to look up my skirt, you better hurry to catch up with me! HA HA HAAAAAAA!' Her laughter made pebbles and dust fall. Fearing an imminent avalanche, Zelopan and Panda hurried after her.

Iris had changed yet again. Not a new Iris, but her clothes, her style. Through whatever temporal quirk, Iris was showing off the different fashions she'd worn in this body as they worked their way through the dangerous complex.

First, her blue eye reverted back to brown, and then she wore what Tom thought was a KISS-esque brown and orange faux-flames face-makeup with a corresponding brown and orange tribal get-up. It was all very glam and 70s, like tacky macramé decorations.

Now this Iris was back in her 70's garments, looking how she did when Tom first saw her, except for being slightly younger and with both eyes brown. She saw him inspecting her. 'Fashions come and go and return, Tom.'

Tom was suspicious. Was he being too trusting? 'So why haven't I ever met this Iris until now?'

'Haven't you? Tom, all of us, we're all the same person, you know.'

'Yes, I know but I mean… I've met many of you, the one before you…' mentally, he pictured the extremely young and vivacious Iris with honey-blonde hair. '…was quite old, wasn't she?'

She raised her eyebrows and looked Tom up and down. 'You seem well informed. You'll find out soon, I'm reaching the beginning of this life, in reverse. Which means another change.'

Tom kicked himself internally because this woman had fallen for his trap and confirmed false information. 'She's faking it. This isn't Iris'. He decided to continue playing along until they reached the other end of the complex.

The glam Iris collapsed, ready to be unborn. Instead of a pyrotechnic display, she simply faded out and another figure faded in. Last time the change had sparks and glitter and rivulets of light! The transitions between Irises were so inconsistent. Tom figured this was another sign that this was a deception.

The new figure huddled on the floor, wrapped in black robes. With great difficulty, she stood, and a long white braid fell into view. It came down past her waist. Tom knew this wasn't Iris' fourth youthful and vivacious self, but said nothing.

A croaking voice came from within the black robes. 'Tom, the effect… is accelerating. We have to…. get to the other device. But I need to…. rest… first, ungrow a bit less feeble.'

Tom watched with amazement. Perhaps he'd been wrong. The long white braid fell loose and slowly became more voluminous, blonde locks of vibrant hair. She smiled and her voice gradually smoothed out. 'It's funny, I waited so long for this body to get older. I spent years on the beaches in

Brazil without sunscreen, chain smoking, just trying to get some wrinkles and get some character into my skin! Being young is nice, but it just doesn't have the perks of being mature. I was in this body for a very, very long time.'

She threw off her robe, revealing a shiny, art deco skyscraper-esque space age leotard and shiny thigh-high high-heeled boots underneath. She smiled big and pulled out a laser pistol and blasted a hole in the wall with a hot pink laser beam. 'Let's go!'

Panda fell to the ground yet again as Iris flickered in and out of existence and her arms became intangible. 'Oh dear. I was worried about this. Being made of possible futures, I'm very unstable. Maybe if I…' and in a blink she was gone. The mini-dress fell to the ground heavily, and something clattered inside it.

Zelopan knelt by the dress. Panda paced back and forth nervously. 'Don't tell me she's turned into a baby. I can't abide babies. As a rule, I never walk anywhere, I never listen to dance music, and I can't stress this enough: I never… NEVER work with babies, animals or Martians!'

Zelopan carefully shook the contents out of the dress. It was a marionette with a long, exaggerated nose and chin, and permanently open painted-on eyes. 'It's… a dummy.' He suddenly felt the marionette shift to envelop his hand, latching securely on his arm, the wires for controlling the figure's arms jumping to his fingers. His lips didn't move as the words 'Who are you calling a dummy?

You're the dummy!' escaped his mouth in a feminine voice.

'Iris? Is that you?'

Zelopan turned a dark shade of green and held the strange figure as far away from him as his arm would reach. 'Please! Let me go!' he protested in his own voice.

His own barely-moving lips answered him back. 'I'm afraid that's not possible, buddy! Thanks to the Gamemaster, that's not how this works! You shouldn't have picked me up! Now you're stuck with me.'

'Please, no!' Zelopan's throat alternated smoothly between Iris' confident clear voice and his own sobbing, panic-filled voice. It made him ill as Iris used her will to force his mouth to say: 'I lost a cosmic wager over a game of interplanetary *Kerplunk!* and have to spent this entire incarnation in this form!' She cackled breathily, as if this was somehow funny.

Panda shook his head sadly. 'That's... horrible!'

Iris tilted her head and pretended to brush her yarn hair into place. 'What do you mean? I'm still glamorous aren't I?' Zelopan had calmed down but still had a trace of panic in his eyes. Panda found himself ignoring Zelopan totally, as if he wasn't there. He had to make a conscious decision to remember there was a being operating Iris' new form at all.

'Being stuck as a parasite puppet, I mean.'

Iris' painted-on eyes seemed to burn inside of her wooden head. 'Did you say.... puppet? *PUPPET!?*'

Panda cowered, a little fearfully. This was weird, even by Iris' standards. 'Maybe we should move on?' he suggested nervously.

Iris' wooden head looked in every direction and her inarticulate hands made motions as if dusting herself off. 'You're right, let's go… THIS way!' Zelopan was unable to resist moving Iris in exactly the fashion that she desired. He couldn't help thinking it wasn't Iris that was the puppet in this situation.

Tom was waiting outside the ladies room. Iris had ducked in to 'freshen up'. It had been a few minutes since he'd checked on her. She'd yelled something about leotards making it difficult to take care of business. Finally he heard her heels clicking down the hall.

He turned.

It was her. Iris. His Iris. The way she looked when he first met her. That raggedy green cardigan. The gleam in her eye. The trail of smoke her cigarette left as she marched down the hall towards him. Unexpectedly, he burst into tears. He knew that despite appearances, it was the same woman he now saw every day, but it was quite a shock. He gave her a crushing bear hug.

'It's a good thing I used the ladies room after a squeeze like that! What on Earth's gotten into you Tom?'

'Nothing. I'm just being daft. It's good to see you, I mean… like this.' He hugged her again. 'I have to tell you, for a while back there… I doubted you were really Iris.' He laughed.

Iris' expression changed. 'Oh, really. Tell me more.' She reached into an inner pocket of her cardigan and pulled out a laser pistol, brandishing it.

'Iris! I.. I…' Tom panicked. He'd been right? 'I was just being silly!'

'No Tom, you're usually a very perceptive young man.' She pointed the ray gun directly at his face. 'It's a shame in this situation…'

Suddenly Iris flicked her wrist a fraction of an inch and blasted some kind of mechanical spider that had been lowering itself towards Tom head!

'It's a shame… that you didn't notice that haywire surgical arachnidroid that was about to harvest your brain!' She pulled him close and hugged him hard. 'It's so good to see you too, Tom. But I think I was wrong about the damaged labs not posing a threat. Look. There's more of the beasts! We better hurry!'

Mechanical spiders feebly but steadily advanced towards them. She linked her arm around Tom's elbow. 'Do you know that yellow brick road dance from the *Wizard of Oz*? We could do that!'

'Me and the other Iris already had a *Wizard of Oz* themed adventure recently.'

'Oh. Well, let's just run and scream while I shoot my laser gun nilly willy behind us.'

Tom laughed. 'Let's!'

And they did.

Zelopan was wiping his hand on his jacket and repeating 'Ew!' over and over.

A new Iris shook her head. 'Well, I told you to hurry up before I changed, didn't I? We should be getting a move on anyway, to the other Hendecahedron.' Now Iris was tall, dark skinned and had loads of honey-coloured hair. Well, a honey-coloured wig anyway.

Panda cleared his throat. 'Iris, you are breathtakingly beautiful. Your makeup is immaculate. Your gown is radiant. You are, as they say, serving up Wildthyme realness. You have cunning, ubiquity, nostalgia and temporality. But is it just me, or are you... I mean, am I noticing that... Er... Are you...'

'Yes Panda?'

Zelopan butted in. 'Are you a black man?'

Iris tutted. 'Who says I can't be black? Or a man?' She laughed. 'I think I've been both, just not together. But the point is, I'm *always* a lady.'

Unexpectedly, there was a large cracking noise and Zelopan's scream faded away as if moving distantly downwards.

Panda jumped up and sat on Iris' shoulder, next to a large, ornate rhinestone earring. 'Well, you certainly look better than Tom does in drag. Ugh, one Halloween he gussied himself up, telling everyone he was 'Eartha Wyndenfire'. I suggested 'Hanna Barbara' as a drag name, but...'

'Panda, I think Zelopan's dead. Where he was standing there's now a rapidly expanding hole... oh shut up, Panda! This is serious.'

'You're right Iris! We better sashay away! Away from falling to our certain death!'

***

Iris sighed, satisfied. 'Finally! We've made it! This is the lab. That's the other Hendecahedron!'

Tom walked around it. 'But it's tiny! It's the size of a lunchbox'

'It's not the size that important Tom. It's the geometric interrelationships of the mathematical ratios. In other words, it's how you use it.'

'Iris… is it just me, or…'

'Am I black? Yes, I am Tom. Are you?'

'Well, yes, I am black, Iris, but I was going to ask if you're Scottish.'

'Very perceptive of you, Tom. In this form I went by the name Brenda Soobie. I performed in Vegas, Vega (the star) and all over the circuit. Released a ton of 45's doing all the hits that no one had heard yet. Hits from the future! 'Brenda Soobie: First Lady of Infinity!' they called me! Did you see how I just did jazz hands and then transitioned into adjusting my pink feather boa back up into place? That's an old trick I learned.'

Tom looked worried. 'The changes are happening much, much faster now, aren't they…'

'Don't worry your pretty head, Tom…' At that moment something struck the back of Iris' head.

'Iris!' He knelt where she fell and checked her. She had already changed again. She was unconscious, but very old, very regal. 'Iris can you hear me? Are you all right? What hit you?'

A figure stepped out of the shadows. 'Oh Tom lovey! I finally found you, chuck!' It was Iris. The current Iris, looking exactly as she did before all this started.

'Iris? What's going on? I thought you were aging through future possible selves?'

'Is that what this faker told you? Look here.' She leant over the elderly, unmoving first Iris. 'At the base of the neck. That device is of alien origin, put there by Zelopan.'

'Zelopan? The handsome, rugged scientist guy with beautiful eyes?'

'That's right lovely. He's of a race of cactus people who use their technology to change shape. They are also the ones that built these, these… Jimmy Hendrixagons. The imposter Irises took my place after the explosion. They are trying to get information out of you, trying to find my time craft!'

'Oh. That's a lot to take in, Iris. I'm glad they didn't trick me and get a hold of your… time craft.'

Iris laughed. 'Yeah, the *old crate*! Be it ever so humble, there's no place like home!' She inspected a pile of wooden boxes next to the door to the loading bay. 'Have you seen it about? We need to get out of here before the place goes up in smoke!'

A strange voice echoed from the other side of the chamber. 'Not so fast!' The voice was quirky, nasally, with a strange speech defect that made all her s's sound like shushes. The figure walked into the light. She was very tall, wearing a slightly more feminine version of a man's suit, in a gaudy floral pattern. She held an unlit pipe clasped between her teeth. Frothy white hair sat perfectly atop her head.

Tom frowned. 'Carol Channing?'

'Don't be silly Tom! It's me!! IRIS!' She went to hug him but he held out his hand warning her away. 'Tom, surely you don't believe all this nonsense. It's ME! Well, at least a possible future me.' She tilted her head and smiled, baring her gigantic white teeth. 'And look who's with me!'

She held open her suit jacket and out popped Panda. 'Ta-Da! It's Panda, Iris and Tom, all back together!'

The other Iris tugged at Tom's shirt and pointed a gun at the new arrivals. 'Don't be fooled by them Tom. They're not who they appear to be. Remember the device I showed you.'

The Carol Channing Iris (as Tom now thought of her) walked over to the collapsed figure of the first Iris. 'Oh, you mean this neck-implant device that lets you take someone's form while they're unconscious?'

'Don't touch that, Missy!'

The Channing Iris leaned over and swiftly pulled the plug out of the neck of the dormant past Iris on the ground. 'You should be ashamed. She deserves our respect!' She smiled down at the elderly woman. 'She looks ancient, but… she's really just a kid.'

'No!' gurgled the imposter Iris near Tom. Her skin started to bubble and bulge, quills erupting from green mounds on her face and hands. 'Tom, look what they're doing to me! Stop them!'

Carol Channing Iris shook her head. 'I just broke the link to us and now he's reverting to his original form. She's Zelopan, posing as an Arbolean scientist. Us, over here, we're the real

Irises. And we're running out of time. We're at the end of our ropes!'

Zelopan's voice emerged as the cactus-Iris gurgled. He slowly started to melt. 'Fine. The jig is up. I wanted to escape in her time-craft. Her *bus*.' He/she slapped her prickly forehead and sighed. 'The delay of the implant processing information is its greatest flaw. But while I still have access to part of Iris' psyche... Don't you think it's strange how well Panda seems to know Iris, Tom? Do you even remember how you met Panda?'

Tom thought about it for a moment. 'I...'

Panda looked at Tom pleadingly. 'Tom, we can talk about this later. Get the gun from her/him/hirm. We don't have much time! Iris' timeline is about to rip out from both ends and this Rubik's cube is about to explode!'

Zelopan covered everyone with his gun. 'We're getting on your craft and we're leaving!'

Carol Channing Iris spoke loudly in her strange voice, motioning with her pipe. 'But the survivors still trapped in the complex... Everyone in the entire star system... they'll all die? Didn't you learn anything from Allis and Ballis?'

'I couldn't care less about them. I only want to save my own neck.'

'Look into my eye, Zelopan. I'm from the future. I know this star system gets destroyed. I want to leave just as badly as you.'

At that moment something struck the disguised Zelopan at the nape of his neck, knocking him out. Tom, Iris and Panda looked in amazement as Zelopan collapsed to the ground. Standing behind him was a young girl, holding a solid looking length of metal pipe. 'Thanks for distracting him.'

Panda's eyes lit up. 'Lillith?' The girl smiled and knelt down to Panda's level.

Carol Channing Iris had tears in her eyes. Tom just looked confused. The elderly Iris was gone. 'Is that you, Iris? You as a girl?' She didn't respond, she just clamped her teeth down on her pipe.

Lillith hugged Panda long and hard. Panda felt her tense up as if in pain. 'What's wrong? Did I hurt you with my hugs?' Panda turned to look at the other Iris and saw Tom helping her stand. She was also in pain.

The impossibly tall Iris staggered over and helped Lillith to her feet. 'We have to hurry, have I mentioned that? We're running out of rope on both ends.' The woman and the girl held hands. The mini-hendecahedron crackled with energy and a wind started to blow in the chamber.

Lillith whimpered. 'It's too late. I can feel it. Our beginning, it's come loose!'

Carol Channing Iris nodded. She could feel her end of their lifeline had been severed as well. 'If we don't do something, we'll be lost forever.'

Tom thought about Iris' pantyhose. 'Iris, your laundry!'

'I have plenty of dirty laundry, Tom. It's the end, but now is the time to neither do it nor air it. Soon everything I've done will have never happened anyway.'

'No Iris! When you wash your pantyhose, what do you do?'

Tom looked down at Lillith. 'I don't wear tights yet, but I have some stockings.'

A light came on above Iris' head. 'I tie them together so it doesn't get all tangled in the wash! Tom, you're amazing!' He grinned.

Panda and Lillith looked confused. 'What are we doing?'

'We're tying the ends together, lovey!'

Panda shook his head. 'That's ridiculous. If you tie the beginning of your timeline to the end, there will be no beginning and no end. You'll be trapped in a bonkers loop! '

Lillith smiled. 'That sounds nice.'

Carol Channing Iris grinned too and her voice cracked as she laughed. 'Panda, there's endless possibilities, I'm in no danger of looping around. It just means I'll have a looser connection to reality than most people.'

Panda harrumphed. 'Oh, well that's nothing new. Get on with it!'

Iris and Lillith held hands, but each placed their free hand on the Hendecahedron. Soon they were joined by other Irises, also holding hands. Tom recognized all the ones on Lilith's side and Panda recognized the first half dozen strange, possible Irises standing opposite them as the double line quickly snaked down the hallway.

Tom saw the current Iris in line and waved at her. She nearly let go of the chain to wave back, but stopped herself in the nick of time. Instead she winked and blew him a kiss. The other Irises were all exchanging knowing looks.

Carol Channing Iris smiled down at Lillith, and the infinite number of previous selves holding hands in a procession that snaked its way all over the planet. 'We've done it. The hendecahedron is stabilized. We're going to be okay. We're free.'

Lillith looked up at the tall Iris and smiled and looked at what was waiting for her. 'It's going to be amazing!' She turned and smiled at Panda as she, and all the other Irises, faded from view. Except for one.

Iris - the current Iris - held out two red-gloved hands and hooted at the top of her taken-for-granted lungs. 'My boys! Tom and Panda! Come give your Auntie Iris a hug!'

Tom and Panda looked at each other. Panda grumbled. 'What is this, a soft drink commercial? I think there's been quite enough hugging and hand holding for one day.'

'What's wrong Tom? You look confused.'

He smiled. 'I admit I am confused about something, alternate Irises aside…' He looked at Panda and Iris, wondering what their connection was.

'What is it, Tom?'

'You said this star system gets destroyed. Have we changed history?'

Iris shook her head, surprisingly sad. Maybe she was just tired. 'No Tom. This star system still gets destroyed at some point, thanks to Allis and Ballis. The cactus people's planet is also destroyed. Come to think of it, some of the time-displaced refugees end up landing at Texcoco.'

Tom shook his head. 'I'll never get used to those weird alien planet names'. Iris laughed at Tom's confusion.

Panda harrumphed. 'Well at least you didn't destroy the universe this time.'

Iris grinned. 'The night's still young!' She hooked one arm through Tom's arm and the other around Panda and they marched back towards the bus. 'It's the witching hour, boys! We're perched between yesterday and tomorrow. Why don't we go see what we can stir up!'

Samsara

James Manley-Buser

That night, we held a funeral for the old woman.

Iris had been an odd one, I admit. I remember, looking back, when she arrived in my youth. I was not quite a man but no longer a boy, roaming the streets for something to do, unsatisfied with whatever offerings the day had thus far held. She had stumped out of the hills and into town, ensconced in outlandishly garish garb, muttering incoherently under her breath. Seating herself on a weather-stained bench with exaggerated labour, making a great show of her bad back and tired knees, she had shouted me over in some foreign accent I never have been quite able to place even after all these years. Lighting a fag of something foul and pungent, she jet-streamed acrid plumes from her nostrils as I cheekily gave her bad directions to the local mandiram, shit that I was.

I of course had thought this hilarious, and had gathered my fellow too-old-to-be-urchins to say so, boasting at the ridiculousness of this foreign fop. Later, after she had somehow tracked me down and given my ear a tweaking, I lead her, chastened and embarrassed, to the mandiram as she had wanted. When next I saw her, several days hence, she had commanded me over with but a sideways glance and the snap of her fingers, exclaiming 'Here will do' and demanding a put up. Since that day I had been her constant companion. We'd had many a good and memorable time over the last few decades. Over the years she had become well and truly oors. I cried yesterday, when she breathed her last and I knew that would not see my friend again.

The pyre was large and on the beach, much the same way Iris had liked her days and her drinks. I watched it burn down over the hours, seated under an open bar cabana, nursing a pint of something Amerikyan, piss-poor in taste and strength, and half-heartedly munching on oorga as people from town paid their respects to first the effigy and then to me. The crowd slowly ebbed with the tide, and for a spell I was lost in reminiscence. When next I was aware, it was well into the night and I was alone with my empty bottles, the blaze long since gone low.

From the silent darkness I saw a brilliant flash of aurora light and I idly concluded that I had probably had enough, even as I poured myself another. Not long after, there appeared a woman I had never before seen, meandering up the shore to stop in front of me. She was wrapped in a beach towel and barefoot, her skin a strange coffee blend, and her mischievous eyes framing a small ouroboros bindi. I noticed none of this at first, because her black bedraggled hair was smoking, random tangles lit with flame. It took a moment to realise she had asked me something. Still stuck on the burning hair, which smelled horrible, I said nothing, my not-quite inebriated brain not-quite knowing how to process the information. She rolled her eyes and reached behind where I was leaning on the bar, grabbing for Iris' hand-bag.

I had forgotten it was there, meaning to toss it onto the pyre before it dwindled, a last farewell to my old friend. She opened it and drew forth a pack of those noxious hand-rolleds, tilting her head sideways to light one with a burning shock of hair, and inhaling of it like one would take to water after days in the desert. As I stared at her a moment more, she gave me a wry look while idly putting out her tangles in my drink. Neurons fired, clarity occurred, and, smiling, at last I spoke.

'Shubh sundhya, Iris.'

At that she let out a throaty laugh, so familiar to my ears and yet so different all at once. It invoked strange feelings in my mind and heart.

'How did you know me?' she asked, rummaging through her bag and pulling out more random items of clothing than should have fit within, intermittently puffing away at her smoke. Her accent was new, more locally Indian than not, though still tinged with the Iris of old. I almost took a half-sip of my beer, bringing it to my lips before I remembered what she'd been doing with the glass. Setting it aside and folding my hands on the bar, I stated simply 'You have an unmistakability, my friend. You could be no one else.'

'How true,' she replied, as she picked out a debatably gaudy yet matching sari, petticoat, and choli from the growing pile of clothes that should not have been able to fit in that bag. 'Now turn you round while I change. Can't have you eyeing me up.' she said teasingly. I dutifully looked away as she dropped the towel and began to dress, grumbling about sand in her knickers. When I turned back after she gave the all-clear she was clothed and putting up her hair in to one side, long curls draping, somehow no longer looking like they'd been alight not five minutes ago.

'So,' I remarked, 'You're back.' Not quite knowing what else to say.

'Moksha thus far eludes me,' she commented, absentmindedly taking a drag on her beedi. 'Or is it the other way round, I wonder?' she mused idly to herself. While I pondered on that, she went into the cabana, rummaging through coolers, tutting at the beers, until she found a bottle of champagne I had meant to open earlier.

'So you've done this before? Been born anew?' I asked after a bit, awed and curious at the implications.

'Oh yes' she said, a sly grin creeping onto her face as she popped the cork towards the surf and let the foam dribble into the sand. She grabbed a pair of wine glasses from under the bar. 'A fair few times.'

'How very desi of you,' I said, which made her laugh. She offered me one of the glasses, and for a while we leaned on the bar in silence, watching the moon slowly languish towards the horizon and sipping champagne to the sounds of the ocean.

'I had grown tired,' she said finally. By way of explanation, I realised. 'No, that's not quite right. Maybe bored is a better word. Disinterested. I have been and seen and done so much. None of it seemed exciting anymore. I needed to let the universe get on with itself for a bit. So that when next I set out across it things would be fresh and new and unknown again.'

'Sabar ka phal meetha hota hai,' I offered, and she nodded, repeating the same.

Again we stood in silence for a time as I digested this information.

'So,' I began, 'you shall be going tooring then?' I asked, somewhat dismayed that my friend would be leaving again so soon after her at once miraculous and blasé return.

'Perhaps,' she replied. 'I left my old bus at a crap mechanic's in Tollygunge some thirty odd years ago before setting out on the random journey that settled me here. Now that life's gone and done, and it'll be an adventure in and of itself tracking the blasted thing down.' She thought for a moment and then turned to face me. 'You could always come with, you know, on my long route 'round.'

I brought out two wooden chairs from the cabana and set them a bit down the beach facing the just dawning sun, its rays casting rivulets of honey through the waves. I thought on it long and hard, enjoying her company while I contemplated leaving behind my life to travel the world. It was some time before I replied, and the gulls had already begun to cry out along the beach.
'You know me, Iris. I love it here. This is my home. I have never been satisfied travelling.'
'But there are such wonders to be seen!' she exclaimed with wistful jubilation. 'Many more than you could know or imagine' she added coyly. Settling down into her rickety chair, champagne at hand and ever-burning cigarette in the other, she took a long drag and let it out, choosing her words carefully before continuing, 'If you could feel the alien sands beneath your toes and listen to the sounds of ethereal shores lapping at the stars, if you could speak to the lights and touch the colours and dance with the elements, would that satisfy you?' Shooting another sly and amused look my way, giving a half cackle at my expression, me scarcely able to process the possibilities, she added 'or would you need a drink in your hand as well?'

Iris and the Caliphate

Eric Brown

It was sweltering in the Jurassic. The jungle throbbed with life. Insects and animals set up a continuous *a cappella* chorus. High above, through the canopy, the sun burned like a molten doubloon. It had to be, in Iris' opinion, one of the most hellish holes in which she'd ever found herself.

Panda whined, 'How much further?'

'How the blinking hell should I know? The co-ordinates were vague. I reckon we're within a mile of the camp.'

'But we've been walking that far already!'

'Illusion, chuck; it just seems so. We can't be far away...' This said more in desperation than certainty.

'What's that!' Panda cried.

Iris grasped Panda and dragged him behind a spray of fern. They crouched, peering out, as the source of the sound hove into view.

'That,' Iris said, 'is a brachiosaurus.'

Striped like a tiger, as big as a whale, it stank like a methane factory – and little wonder. A vegetarian, it consumed a quarter of a ton of vegetable matter every day. As it trundled past Iris and Panda, shaking the ground, its puckered anus the diameter of a manhole cover dilated and gave vent to a noxious gale.

Iris gasped, grabbed Panda, and ran. 'Duck!'

They sprinted under the vast hammock of the creature's belly, emerged on the other side, and fled into the shrubbery. The Brachiosaur's thunderous footfalls receded into the distance.

Iris paused and consulted her compass. 'This way.'

They were about to set off again when another sound assailed them, this the more ineffectual flailings of a human being accompanied by a torrent of cries, in French.

Seconds later a thin, bearded creature garbed in rags burst through the undergrowth and stopped dead.

'*Mon dieu!*' he cried. 'Am I hallucinating? Another human being, and... and a...?'

'Iris Wildthyme, at your service, sir, and this scabrous example of ursine fauna is my faithful sidekick, Panda.'

The man drew himself up, attempted to puff out his emaciated chest, and began, 'And I...'

'If I am not mistaken,' Iris interrupted, 'you're none other than Jules Verne. I recognise the beard.'

Verne squinted at her, suspicious. 'And are you allied with the scoundrels who imprisoned me?'

Iris clapped the writer's scrawny shoulder. 'I'm here to rescue you, Verne. You and all the others the Caliph is holding... somewhere.'

'I escaped from the camp last night,' Verne said. 'I thought, anywhere away from the prison camp! But...' He gazed about himself in fearful awe. 'Where in God's name are we?'

'You wouldn't believe me if I told you,' Iris muttered. Then: 'Where's the camp, Verne? Can you lead us to it?'

He gestured vaguely over his shoulder. 'Half a mile in that direction, but...'

Iris set off, dragging both Panda and Verne after her.

They wove through weird and wondrous plant life, dodged another grazing dinosaur, and came at last to a wire fence enclosing a compound. They hid in the herbage of a bountiful shrub and peered out.

Verne indicated a gap in the wire. 'Where I effected my escape.'

Beyond the wire stood a collection of timber huts, and slumped outside the huts, in varying degrees of despondency, was a sorry collection of human beings.

'And are you guarded?'

'They merely dumped us in this Godforsaken jungle and departed,' Verne replied. 'Guards are not necessary when monsters roam the jungle.'

Iris squinted past the barbed wire and made out several figures she recognised. The tall, portly gentleman with an impressive moustache and monocle was G.K. Chesterton, and he was in conversation with a small, thin fellow with a bushy beard – none other than Charles Dickens. She recognised Wells, Conrad, Conan Doyle, as well as Henry James, Lawrence (D.H.) – and Virginia Wolf in heated debate with Mary Anne Evans.

On the far side of the compound was a gaggle of scribes from more recent (if that had any meaning deep in the Jurassic) era: Martin Amis was buttonholing Norman Mailer, and Doris Lessing listened intently to whatever subject Germaine Greer was expatiating upon.

And closer at hand were still more of the great and good from the literary world: Achebe, Bellow, Carter, Dostoevsky... the list went on.

'One second I was enjoying a brandy in the Lyrique,' Verne said, 'and the next I was half-unconscious and being dragged through the alleys! When I came to my senses I found myself here, surrounded by a gallery of misfits and miscreants all claiming, to varying degrees, literary fame.' He stopped and said, 'But did I hear you correctly, madam, when you said that you intended to rescue me?'

'You and the rest of your pen-pushing fraternity,' Iris said.

'But how...?'

'I want you to get back in there and tell them that salvation is at hand.'

'You will transport us from this benighted land?'

'Away from this benighted land – and age,' Iris affirmed.

Verne cast her a long glance, and said at last, 'If you do not mind my asking, Mm. Wildthyme, just who are you, and how did you arrive here?'

'That,' said Iris, 'is a long story... but I'll cut it short.'

Riding the tides of time and space in her Routemaster, Iris and Panda had the misfortune to fetch up somewhere in the twenty-fifth century, along a time-line that had taken a very sad and sorry turn from the one she usually plied. These things sometimes happened; chronoclasmic pitfalls lay in wait of her trusty bus, and sometimes it tested her skill to land the vehicle without major mechanical breakdowns.

She had come to rest in the desert outside the walls of a great city, and concealed the bus in a tumble of ruins. The engine was out of water – the spare container had split in the rough and tumble of landing – and a trip into the city in search of a refill was required. Also, the bus had sustained engine failure, which after a couple of hours under the bonnet Iris had managed to fix. Her face was now smeared in grease – and she had covered her head in a knotted kerchief – and later she was to thank her lucky stars that she looked more like a frazzled mechanic than a female temponaut.

Stowing a complaining Panda in her knapsack, she set off for the impressive arched gate in the city wall, wondering where she had fetched up this time.

Her arrival at the great timber gate coincided with that of a camel train, some fifty strong, preceded by a team of sweating slaves bearing an ornate sedan chair.

The taller of the two guards addressed Iris in an unfamiliar tongue, his tone becoming aggressive when she failed to respond.

'Sorry, and all that. New to the area. Don't quite follow the lingo...' She held up her plastic container. 'I'm looking for water.'

The guard raged at her, and this had the effect of drawing a response from the personage in the sedan chair. A red velvet curtain twitched aside, and a hawkish face, possessed of a spectacularly ornate moustache, peered out.

He called something in his own flowing language and the guard snapped to attention and retreated to the gate.

The potentate's attention turned to Iris.

'Forgive the guard's ignorance, sir. He does not recognise a traveller from far lands when they arrive at our door. I am fortunate indeed that I have studied your language, though I speak it poorly.'

Iris considered correcting the man of his mistake viz her gender, then had second thoughts. A little voice told her that her accidental disguise might bear unforeseen dividends.

'You speak it well, sir,' said Iris. 'I certainly have come from afar, and I'm after a litre or two of water.'

'Water!' The potentate laughed. 'My generosity would be meagre indeed were I to furnish you only with water. Come! You are my guest. You will stay in my palace, and I will make it my duty to show you the wonders of my city.'

He pulled aside the curtain, revealing a divan, and Iris climbed into the sedan and sat down beside him. 'I am Yusuf el-Suliman,' he said, and snapped an order to his bearers, 'scientific adviser to Caliph Ali Halmani himself.'

The sedan rose with a precarious wobble and Iris and her host were born through the archway and into the city.

She was shown to a room looking out over the desert, with a bath of hot scented water awaiting her and the promise of a guided tour of the city before sunset.

She unpacked Panda, who stretched and looked around at the spartanly furnished room. A great bed stood on a bare marble floor.

'Odd that not a single item decorates the place,' Iris said. 'But then the entire city's about as functional as a Scunthorpe urinal, and worse.'

'Worse?' Panda lay on the bed, crossing his stubby legs.

'While we were carried through the streets I saw crowds in a market place.'

'And?'

'And there wasn't a woman among them.'

Panda cocked an eye at her. 'Kept under lock and key, no doubt.'

Iris nodded. 'And a good job it was that el-Suliman took me for a man.' She eyed the tub and the suit of clothes laid out beside it. The clothing would help maintain her disguise, so long as she covered her hair. There was no knowing the potentate's reaction should he discover the truth.

Thirty minutes later a servant boy rapped on the door and announced that Yusuf el-Suliman respectfully requested Mr Wildthyme's presence at a banquet laid on in his honour.

When the boy retreated, Iris said, 'You'd better stay here. I'll bring you something in a doggy bag.'

Panda's sarcastic reply was curtailed as Iris closed the door behind her and followed the servant through a maze of corridors.

Iris spared Verne the details of the feast that followed (she could see that the scribe had not eaten a square meal in days), but recounted in detail the subsequent events.

As flavoured water and fig juice flowed – what Iris would have given for an ice cold G&T – Yusuf el-Suliman quizzed her about her homeland.

'I have not travelled for many a year, and when I last visited Europe I was surprised at its... its barbarity.'

Iris was diplomatic. 'Why do you think I travel, sir? To marvel at cities like this, to understand enlightened and educated peoples.'

'And tell me,' said Yusuf el-Suliman, 'do your people still worship infidel images, and revere false prophets, and take instructions from evil books?'

Iris cleared her throat, buying time to frame an adequate response. 'All these and more, sir, but then what does an unenlightened race know of the truth?'

El-Suliman clapped his hands. 'I work closely with the Caliph to maintain my people's pre-eminence in the world. Through the application of science, we prosper. But my city awaits your inspection...'

As the sun went down over the desert, they toured the marble streets of the city, ventured into the Great Mosque, and then sat beside the soothing pool which stretched like a ribbon towards the sunset.

And nowhere did Iris clap eyes on another woman; nor did she see a single painting or work of art, no statues or sculptures or even so much as an ornamental garden.

As the last filament of the sun disappeared over the turreted horizon, Yusuf el-Suliman turned to Iris with a calculating expression and said, 'And now, sir, I suggest that a sojourn to the copulatorium might be in order?'

Iris echoed the word. El-Suliman laid a long finger beside his nose and grinned.

She was led across a courtyard to a great chamber. Men were coming and going through the arched doorway, and Iris quailed at the thought of what might be expected of her within.

Yusuf el-Suliman escorted her across a cool, bare marble floor to a line of archways, and paused before the closest.

He said, 'One moment, sir; a question, if I might, before we take our pleasure. I have heard tell, from recent travellers to your land, that woman are allowed to go abroad, and, moreover, share the same rights and status as their men folk.'

Iris inclined her head and stated that this was so.

'Barbaric!' el-Suliman cried. 'Monstrous!' He winked at Iris, a particularly vile and insinuating gesture, and indicated the arch. 'We, on the other hand, have formulated a solution to the Women Problem. Please, choose your pleasure...'

Heart thudding, Iris passed though the arch. She was confronted by a series of timber doors. Yusuf el-Suliman coaxed her forward. 'Go on, do not be shy. A great pleasure awaits.'

He took Iris by the elbow and eased her towards the nearest door, opened it and thrust her inside.

Iris stared in horror at what lay upon the bed before her, and it was all she could do not to release the contents of her recent meal.

'What?' Verne murmured as they squatted in the growing jungle twilight.

She shook her head at the recollection. 'A horror beyond horrors,' she whispered.

When she judged that an adequate duration had elapsed, she took her leave of the cubicle and awaited Yusuf el-Suliman. He emerged from a cubicle five minutes later, arranging his djellaba and grinning at Iris.

They stepped out into the cooling night, and Iris took a long, head-clearing draft of air.

'But this is not the limit of my Caliph's greatness!' Yusuf el-Suliman went on.

'It isn't?'

'By no means. How do you think that the Caliph ensures that my people, that our society, maintain our current pre-eminence.'

'I'm sure I'm at a loss to know.'

Yusuf el-Suliman leaned close and whispered, 'We eradicate all subversive influences! The people you know as… artists – we banish them! Writers and painters, singers and song-writers, every one of their dangerous, perfidious tribe! Through a God-given stroke of fortune, just one month ago the Caliph came into possession of a miraculous machine, and it is with this that he maintains the rule of law!'

'A machine?' Iris said.

El-Suliman stared at her, calculating. It seemed to her that he was drunk on the wine of hospitality, or on the ego-trip of showing her the wonders of his city.

'Come! I will take you!'

He led Iris into a great marble palace, and through a warren of corridors to a high, arched door. She wondered what terrible apparatus awaited within.

They passed into the room; el-Suliman pointed with great pride.

She thought at first that it was Aladdin's lamp, but a greater version of that magical object; it stood as big as an automobile, gold and glowing.

As el-Suliman led her across the chamber, Iris saw that it was not a giant lamp at all, but some form of carriage, with a padded divan inside a small cabin.

He gestured her inside, and she climbed aboard and sat before an array of familiar controls.

'I have it from the Caliph's very lips,' Yusuf el-Suliman went on, 'that this machine appeared as if by magic one evening thirty days ago, on the eve of the Caliph's twenty-first birthday – a propitious gift from God! It was controlled by operatives who, under torture, disclosed the true nature of the machine, and its workings.' Yusuf el-Suliman laughed. 'The Caliph had the infidels put to death, and had his craftsmen scrap the old frame of the machine and fashion a new, more pleasing one in its stead.'

Iris stared at the control of the time-machine – an old, but serviceable, Mark II that had belonged, once upon a time, to operatives from The Clockworks. As to what they had been doing here, that was a mystery which she might never fathom.

Yusuf el-Suliman went on, 'This machine, though you will find it hard to believe, is capable of travelling in *time*.'

Iris made an appropriate expression of wonder as El-Suliman went on, 'We used it to rid the land of infidels and undesirables, and then the Caliph had an inspiration. Why limit this *cleansing* to the present? Why not cleanse the past, too, of all those that God deems undesirable? To this end we send out agents through time, apprehending God's enemies and... and transporting them to Hell!'

Iris murmured, 'Writers and painters, singers and song-writers...?'

'Exactly so!' he said. 'Starting with the writers. It is an onerous task, and ongoing, but with God's grace and patience...'

'And this Hell?' she ventured.

'A sultry land inhabited by all manner of evil serpents and monsters!'

She eyed the controls. If only she could distract el-Suliman's attention long enough to...

'This is truly a miracle. Would you mind if I sat awhile and contemplated its wonder?'

Yusuf el-Suliman smiled. 'By all means. Be my guest.' He climbed from the cab and stretched.

He gazed lovingly at the coachwork of the craft, and ran a hand along its lines. Iris watched him like a hawk, and as he moved around the front of the vehicle, trailing a hand across its golden fender, she fell to work.

It was done in ten seconds, and, when Yusuf el-Suliman came around to her side of the cab, he was none the wiser.

She sat back, and el-Suliman took her relieved breath as a sign that she was overcome by the wonder of the vehicle and the bounteousness of his God. 'Truly, we are blessed,' he said.

She slipped from the cab and Yusuf el-Suliman led her from the chamber. As he was returning Iris to her room, he paused on the ramparts and gestured across the desert.

A familiar structure scintillated in the starlight.

'All that remains from before the time of the Last War,' el-Suliman said. 'And built beneath that structure, a holy temple which houses the only book which God, in his greatness, allowed to survive the cataclysm...'

Open-mouthed, Iris stared at the distant shape of the Golden Gate Bridge.

'Okay,' Panda said, sitting up on the bed, 'where's the doggy bag?'

'Move yourself. We're getting out of here.'

'What?'

She ran to the window and peered out: a sheer thirty foot drop to the desert below. She calculated that the runs which concealed her bus were half a mile away to the west.

'Ever made ropes from silk bed-sheets?'

'Would you mind explaining what's going on, Iris!' Panda wailed.

As they tore and knotted sheets, Iris did just that – describing everything from the banquet to the guided tour (not forgetting the copulatorium), and the revelation of the Caliph's time machine.

She pushed the bed to the open window, tied one end of the makeshift rope to the headboard, and flung the rest through the window. She peered down. The rope terminated six feet above the sand, which was close enough.

Panda said, 'But... the copulatorium?'

She grabbed her knapsack and, before stuffing Panda unceremoniously inside, said, 'They remove their women's brains at birth, Panda, and grow the bodies in vats... and then when they reach maturity employ them...' she closed her eyes and sniffed back tears, 'they *use* them in their hellish brothels.'

She closed the knapsack on Panda's questions. She filled her canister with water – the reason for her presence in the city in the first place – and fastened it to her knapsack. Then she slung the lot over her shoulder and climbed over the window sill.

She slipped down the rope, none too elegantly, and dropped to the ground with a thud. Cursing, she picked herself up and ran through the thick, impeding sand towards the ruins.

Panda squirmed from the knapsack and peered over her shoulder. 'But their time machine?' he began.

'I fixed it!' she panted. 'But not before I'd accessed it's history and found out where it took the writers.'

'Fixed it?'

'Activated it's motile drive and sent it on a one-way trip into the future, but on a time-delay. I reckon the machine should be leaving the city, for ever, just about now.'

She laughed.

'What?' Panda asked.

'I'd like to see the look on his face when el-Suliman finds the time machine missing!'

They came to the ruins and Iris jumped aboard the bus. She filled the tank with water and slipped into the driving seat with a shudder. She had no desire to spend one further second in this corrupted age.

She started the engine.

'Where are we going, Iris!'

'Hold on tight!' she cried. 'First stop, the Jurassic!'

Iris glanced at her watch. They had been waiting fifteen minutes since Verne had squirmed back through the wire.

'What on Earth is he doing in there?' she hissed.

Minutes later she heard a sound, and saw a shadowy figure emerge through the gap in the fence. He was followed by Joseph Conrad, Emily Bronte, and a thin man in doublet and hose who could only be William Shakespeare. Others awaited beyond the fence for their turn to crawl through. Among them she spotted Greer in animated debate with Virginia Wolf.

'You took your time!' Iris whispered to Verne.

'Some individuals were harder to convince than others. They thought it might be a trick.'

'But they're all here?'

'All except the cynical Mr Bierce, who effected his own escape earlier.'

'We can't hang around waiting for him,' Iris said.

When the camp had emptied, and more than a hundred scribes milled in the margin of jungle beside the perimeter fence, Iris told Verne, 'Spread the word. Single file through the jungle. Follow me.'

She led the way, from time to time consulting her compass with the aid of a flashlight.

With luck, the dinosaurs would be sleeping after their daylight exertions; the jungle would be populated now only by snakes and poisonous insects. She tried not to dwell on that possibility.

Ten minutes later she found her bus, glowing in the light of the moon, and stood beside the passenger door as the bemused writers filed in one by one.

A thin, plain women in crinolines asked, 'But how do you hope to drive your vehicle – whatever it is! – through a jungle as dense–?'

'Just watch, Ms Dickinson,' Iris said, hoisting herself into the driving seat and starting the engine. Beyond the windows the jungle vanished, replaced by the kaleidoscopic, multi-coloured swirl of space-time.

She turned from the controls and addressed the alarmed crowd. 'Silence! Silence, please, ladies and gentlemen! Now, Panda will go among you and if you'd be so kind as to give the precise date you were kidnapped, I will do my best to return you to that time within minutes.'

She raised a hand to quell the babble of questions. 'But – and please forgive the pun – that might take some time.'

For the next few hours, as the number 22 Routemaster raced through the ages with its cargo of scribes, Iris Wildthyme did her best to explain what singular fate had befallen the august gathering.

Iris dropped Jules Verne off in a narrow alley beside the stage door of the Lyrique theatre on the fine Spring evening of July, 1855.

'A pity about Monsieur Bierce,' Verne said.

'I'll go back, one day, and do my best to find him,' Iris promised.

'My gratitude knows no bounds, Mm. Wildthyme. And your tales have stocked the larder of my mind with much food for thought.'

'Glad to be of service, chuck. I'll make sure to read your books.'

'Alas, I have yet to write books – just plays that fail to find much favour.'

Iris clapped him on the shoulder. 'You'll write volumes which will become best-selling classics,' she reassured the doleful Frenchman.

'I will?' Verne waved her off. '*Au revoir*, Mm. Wildthyme! *Bon voyage!*'

Soon only Greer and half a dozen others remained, as the bus rattled trough time. Iris left the controls and joined her on the back seat, the germ of a miraculous idea forming in her mind.

'The things you must've seen, Iris!'

'The wonders, and the horrors,' Iris said, and described what she had experienced in the Caliphate of the twenty-fifth century.

They parted with hugs and the promise, on Iris' part, to look her up when she was next in Cambridge.

All that remained was to stop off at Foyle's to make the requisite purchase, and then continue on through the time-line that would see the Last War and the inauguration of the Caliphate of the Golden Gate Bridge.

But not before Iris had paused to deposit a book in the ruins beneath that rearing structure.

She concealed the bus in the tumble of stone outside the city walls and, with mounting apprehension, approached the timber gates.

They were open wide, with no guards monitoring who passed in and out this time. Iris stepped through, with Panda in her knapsack.

Brightly-dressed crowds promenaded as the sun went down. Citizens walked arm in arm along wide boulevards. Street-markets sold food and wine, and strolling musicians entertained crowds with songs of adventure and romance.

'I don't know about you,' she said to Panda. 'But I'm famished. And I could kill a G&T. Let's eat, and then maybe we could stay awhile and party.'

Yes, she thought as she strolled through the crowds towards a likely looking café-bar; I could do with letting my hair down.

'I'm curious,' Panda said later as they sat down. 'What was the book?'

'I'll give you three guesses,' Iris said, as a café worker approached their table.

'And what can I get you today?' asked the waitress.

Mix Her Own Adventure

Patrick Magee

1

There's a woman at the bar. She looks middle-aged, although she could be older or younger in a different light. Her clothes are vaguely bohemian, probably – you're a bartender, not a fashion critic. As you approach, she looks up at you.

Or tries to, at least; she moves like an ancient housecat who refuses to die. There's a half-finished gin and tonic in front of her, and it's clearly not her first.

Tony, the other bartender, is finishing his shift. You gesture to the woman, asking who she is.

'No idea, mate,' says Tony. 'Showed up after lunch and hasn't moved since. Just keeps ordering G&Ts and going on about how they all leave her in the end.'

'Oh right,' you answer. 'Makes sense.'

'Yeah. Listen, I'm off. Have a good one.'

He leaves. You take up position behind the bar and start polishing a pint-glass, for want of anything better to do. There are a couple of younger lads playing snooker in the corner; could be trouble later, you think.

Tony sticks his head back in the door. 'Heads up mate, there's a bus parked out the front. Means there'll probably be a coachload of tourists wandering round. Might end up being a big night after all.'

'Here's hoping,' you reply. Tony grins without enthusiasm, and pops back out.

The pint-glass is sparkling by now, and you put it back on the shelf.

''Nother G&T,' you hear, and it's only after a moment that you realise it's the woman at the bar.

Her voice is oddly sexy, with just a jigger of maternal weariness, and it's difficult to resist her request. Even so, she's clearly had enough already.

Do you serve her another drink?
If yes, turn to page 3
If no, turn to page 2

2

'Sorry love' you say, 'but I think it'd be better if you had a glass of water.'

The woman stops mumbling, and looks up at you. The hatred in her eyes is like a shot of ethanol straight to the chest, and you involuntarily stumble backwards.

'Water?' she splutters, knocking over the tumbler in front of her and spilling ice cubes and lemon wedges across the bar. 'Who the hell do you think I am?'

'I've got no idea,' you reply, artificially calm.

The woman smiles, triumphantly, *predatorily*. 'No, and now you'll never find out!'

She stands up, or rather falls into a vaguely vertical position, and starts to head for the door.

'Do you want me to call a cab?' you ask.

She shakes her head. 'I don't need a cab, I'll catch the bus.'

You snort. 'There's not a bus-stop for miles...'

It's too late, she's already out the door.

Shrugging, you get back to your bartending duties. There's a match on the telly, and you turn it up extra loud to drown out the noise of teenagers and billiard balls.

But that night, as you lock up and start to walk home, past the disabled parking space where a double-decker used to be, you're gripped by a gnawing sense of regret.

While tugging your duvet tight around you, you realise it feels exactly like the time you didn't ask Anne Rutimeyer to the school dance and she ended up going with that rugby player who became a fairly successful investment banker in the City.

THE END

3

'Yeah, alright. Why not?' you mutter, and turn to the spirits shelf.

Do you choose Hendrick's? Turn to page 7
Grey Goose? Turn to page 6
Or Gordon's? Turn to page 5

4

She lifts the Hendrick's & tonic to her nose, inhaling the aroma of juniper berries, citrus and the slight infusion of cucumber and Bulgarian rose, before knocking back the drink in one lascivious gulp and slumping back on the bar.

'Lime,' she murmurs. 'Good choice.'

You're slightly taken aback, and more than a little offended. Doesn't she know how much concentration went into mixing that drink?

'Right,' you say, ringing it up. 'That'll be…'

The woman raises her head, and her eyes meet yours. Suddenly, they're no longer the rheumy eyes of a middle-aged drunk: they're eyes that watched suns eat worlds for breakfast; eyes that blinked in the first, broiling light of the universe; eyes who know that there are some corners of the universe which have brewed the most terrible drinks. And now those eyes are turned on you.

'What did you say your name was?'

You tell her. She shakes her head. 'No, that won't do at all. I'm in the mood for a spacey-sounding one this time.'

She starts trying out names, rolling them around in her mouth like a fine wine or gobstopper. 'Something with a Z in it. Zargon. Zorbum. Azrok.' She waves her hands. 'We'll work out the details later. I'm Iris, by the way,' and before you know it she's bounded out the door.

Do you follow her? If you do, turn to page 8
If not, turn to page 9

5

You reach for the Gordon's.

'Oi!' slurs the woman, wetly slapping her hand on the bar. 'I don't drink Gordon's after 1953, it's 'orrible. Give us the Hendrick's.'

You turn back to her. Maybe she has had enough after all.

Is it time to cut her off? Turn to page 2
Or will you throw caution and the responsible service of alcohol to the wind, and give her the Hendrick's? Turn to page 7

6

Grey Goose? *Grey Goose?*

Grey Goose is a premium brand of vodka, invented by Sidney Frank and produced in France.

It's suitable for a Harvey Wallbanger, and goes very well in a Cosmopolitan, but lacks the essential quality of 'being gin', thus rendering it completely inappropriate for use in a *gin and tonic*.

Go back to page 3 and think very carefully about your choices as a bartender.

7

The secret to a good G&T is to balance the bitterness of the tonic against the sweetness of the gin, usually with a fifty/fifty blend of spirit and mixer. You drop four or five ice cubes into the tumbler, enjoying the cold, glassy clink of the impact, and half-fill the glass with the Hendrick's. Then you take a bottle of tonic water from the fridge and top up the drink.

(The woman is watching you the whole time, her eyes sharp and hungry. For a brief, hallucinatory second, it almost feels as though she's in your mind, guiding your decisions…)

Some people think you should have lemon in a gin and tonic, and your co-worker Tony is one of them. This, of course, makes him an idiot; most gins are already infused with lemon, so to add more is over-egging the pudding. Fresh lime should always be used, and drizzled slightly before garnishing. This complements the flavours and keeps the drink crisp.

(Time seems to have slowed down, as though this had suddenly become the most important drink in the world.)

You slide the finished product across the bar to the woman, leaving a snailish trail of condensation behind it.

(The universe holds its breath.)

Go to page 4

8

By the time you're outside, Iris is standing on the steps of the double-decker.

'Should I call last order-' you start to ask, but she clamps a hand over your mouth.

'Don't ever, *ever* say those words. If you're going to travel with me, you should know there's one rule,' she says, dragging you aboard. It's cosy inside, with a vague sense of summer holidays and grandmother's house; there are various items of furniture and clothing strewn about, and propped up on the dashboard is a framed photograph of a slightly attractive young person.

Iris catches you staring, and turns the photo around. 'Never mind that,' she says.

'Well?' you ask.

She looks confused, and brushes a rum-coloured lock of hair away from her face: 'Well what?'

'You can't just say 'there's one rule', and then not say what it is,' you point out.

Iris pouts. 'They'd usually cut straight to me telling you what it is.'

She starts the engine, and settles into her chair.

'So what's the rule?' you ask, taking a seat behind her.

'There's always time for another drink!' she roars, as the bus flies away on another adventure.

THE BEGINNING

9

You are left there, vaguely aware that you might have missed something important. And that the till isn't going to balance at the end of the night. You wonder if it's worth chasing her out the door.

But then one of the locals comes up to the bar, and you find yourself pulling a pint and starting another pointless conversation about the horses. The woman – wild thing? – fades away into the underused neurons of your memory.

For the rest of your uneventful life, you're followed by a constant niggle that somewhere, sometime, you left a metaphorical pot on the figurative boil, and never bothered to check it.

THE END

Time to Exist

Andy Smillie

Time is the oldest thing in Existence. There are however varying opinions on this. In the light that time is the oldest thing in Existence, people have raised the point that for time to be in Existence, Existence must first have existed. However it has generally been accepted, due to people not liking to ask questions and the usual lack of answers to said questions, that Time is the oldest.

Time passed by. He had been doing that a lot of late. Too much perhaps. It wasn't that he particularly minded doing it, it was after all what he was there for, but it was rather repetitive, and he felt, on balance, he was overdue a holiday. Existence could do without him for a little while.

He doubted it would really miss him anyway. If he were gone, there'd be no time, and without time to pass, would he ever really have been gone? Deciding to stop that particular train of thought before he developed a headache, Time stopped thinking and headed for the one place he'd never been.

The Gap, or Great Abyss of Perpetual Nothing, is a chasm between Existence and Non-Existence, a giant hole in the middle of everything. Like most holes, nooks and forgotten crannies, it has over time filled up with a whole lot of junk. The young philosopher, Edwin I. Clank, once remarked, 'For A Great Abyss of Perpetual Nothing, the Gap appears to contain an awful lot of something.'

Edwin was right - the Gap contains a vast assortment of things. Everything ever permanently lost by anyone is down there somewhere. All manner and sizes of keys, socks, remote controls: literal mountains of stuff. It even contains a rather fetching assortment of scarves.

But, up until that particular moment, the Gap had never contained a No.22 double decker bus, never mind one which should really have been headed for Putney Common.

'Why are we here?' Panda huffed. He was sitting on the dashboard, his head pressed up against the front windscreen. 'It's pitch black and full of rubbish.' He indicated the mounds of debris illuminated by the bus's head lights. He sighed, raising his shoulders and dropping them again for effect.

'I don't suppose you'll have any problem fitting in then,' said Iris with a smile as she pulled on the lever and opened the door. He ignored the jibe, too hungover for their usual bout of sparring. He made a mental note to make fun of her later, and closed his eyes. The windscreen was soothing - cool, and the droplets of moisture running down onto his lips were the only clean liquid he'd had to drink in quite a while. He half expected them to taste like gin.

'You know why we're here. We travel through Time and Space, Panda love,' she said, gesticulating like an epileptic conductor as she descended the stairs. 'If one of them ups and decides to go on leave, well... it's a problem. And not a small one, you understand. Existence needs Time, without it nothing will happen, everything will just... stop.'

'Might be nice to have some peace and quiet for a change,' said Panda without lifting his head.

'Don't be dense, love. When you run out of time, you die. Don't much matter how that comes about. We were bloody lucky we were on the bus when ol' Timey decided to go for a walk.'

'Lucky?' asked Panda. 'There's no drink on the bus.'

'Exactly! And who's going to distil us more if every bugger's dead? An eternity without gin? Not for me pet.'

Panda sighed. Iris was like a child on a sugar-high at times like these. Still, at least his headache was starting to ease. 'What exactly do you propose to do about it?'

'I'm not sure yet but that's the fun of it, isn't it?' She smiled and stepped off the bus.

'If you say so.' He shot a glance over his shoulder, catching the edge of her coat as it disappeared through the doorway. She could go on her own. He'd take the bus and fetch some pain killers, and maybe some more gin. No, definitely more gin.

'I'll see you in a while,' he called after Iris, and was about to shift to the driver's seat when she reappeared at the door, a set of keys bobbing up and down in her palm.

'Oh, marvellous,' he said. She'd taken the bloody keys. Knowing his luck, the mad bint would lose them and he'd be stuck here with nothing to do and more importantly, nothing to drink. 'Fine, I'll come,' he grumbled and got off the bus.

Dropping off the last step, he collided with Iris's back. 'A fine place to stop. Why don't you just lie in the doorway next time.'

'Shush,' said Iris, pressing a finger to her lips and gesturing ahead of them with her head.

'What is it, woman?' Panda strained his eyes but they hadn't yet adjusted to the gloom. Iris continued to gesticulate with her head. 'I knew that hat was too tight when you bought it,' he said.

Iris frowned, reaching up with both hands to fondle her hat as though she had forgotten it was there. 'This? No. Look,' she gestured again, this time with her hand.

Panda drew level with her and squinted. 'Right. Why not?' he sighed, catching sight of the Emperor Penguin standing in front of him.

The naturally well-dressed Penguin had gone a step above, and was sporting a fetching waist coat of tan tweed, a monocle, and a smart looking leather briefcase.

'Hello, Mrs...?' the animal said as it took a step forward.

'It's Miss,' answered Iris without missing a beat, a smile completing the mischief look spreading across her face.

Panda felt his headache returning. He was in no condition for that smile.

'Of course, Miss…?'

'Wildthyme. Iris Wildthyme.'

'A pleasure, Miss Wildthyme.'

Iris preened, delightedly. 'Oh I do like his manners. Don't you, Panda?'

'He's a bloody penguin, Iris.' Panda threw an arm out in exasperation. 'His manners were not my first concern.'

'How astute. One would never have thought a teddy bear capable of such quick deduction,' said the penguin.

'I'm a panda, you ridiculous avian! Don't make me beat you black and white to prove it!'

'I'm sure.' The penguin looked down at his black and white feathers and shrugged. 'Well, whatever you call yourself, there are several other pandas over in the Valley of Forgotten Toys if you want to go play? Most of them are missing limbs so you'd be at quite the advantage, even if you are a little slow.'

'I like him,' Iris barely stifled a chuckle. 'And you are?' she asked, addressing the penguin.

'I am Cornelius Smith the nine-hundred and seventy-third,' he said, dipping his head in greeting. 'I am one of the Welcomers here'.

'And where exactly is here?' snarked Panda.

'A good question,' Cornelius nodded and smiled, as though rewarding an infant for naming an object correctly. Placing his briefcase on the ground, he pulled out a large, leather bound volume.

'Jesus, not the Bible.' Panda sighed. 'I meant, where are we geographically. I'm not after some metaphysical hand-waving bollocks.'

'Oh, on the contrary,' said Cornelius, unperturbed. 'This is the Book of Pages.'

He held the book up so they could see its stained leather cover. It didn't look to have been made from a single piece of hide, but was rather a rough collection of stitched together scraps. Cornelius moved to a waiting lectern, placed the book on it, and took a step back.

The pages, oddly numbered and all of differing sizes and paper stock, began to turn themselves. They jostled to-and-fro for a bit, before settling, dropping open around a third of the way into the volume.

'I'd read the Bible if it could do that,' said Panda.

'Shh,' Iris punched him in the shoulder.

Then, in a voice that wouldn't have sounded out of place on a Barry White album, the Book of Pages began to read itself aloud.

'Before the dawn of Time there was nothing. After that, there wasn't much either. But a while after, a good long while, something took the place of nothing.' The book paused, coughing as though to clear its throat. When it continued its voice had changed to that of a young girl. 'Over the course of many millennia this rather large something became known as Existence. A huge, sprawling character, Existence took up almost all known room. However there was a place where even Existence didn't dare venture.' The book coughed again, and once more its voice changed, this time to a man who sounded like he was suffering from a bad head cold. 'Due to the lack of Existence in this forbidden place it became known as Non-existence – and Existence hated Non-existence, who was always pressing the point that without her, Existence would have no purpose. Existence was quick to dismiss her claims, insisting that she was merely there to fill the space he couldn't be bothered occupying.' Another coughing fit and another new voice. 'Tired of the arguments, Existence and Non-existence went their separate ways. Where their borders once met, now only a gap remains, a great abyss of perpetual nothing.'

'Why does its voice change?' asked Panda.

The pages flickered, turning towards the back. 'When someone loses their voice for a period, the missing segment turns up here and joins with the Great Narrator,' the book said in a perfect baritone.

'And why is it so dark down here?' asked Panda, louder this time.

'Light has never appeared in the Gap, they need it too much in Existence. Still it may need a vacation. Darkness on the other hand has always been here. The young philosopher, Edwin I. Clank, once theorised that darkness was there before Time and that darkness was bigger than Existence, Non-existence and the Gap put together. How else, he reasoned, could it be everywhere at once. However, Edwin's life was tragically curtailed, as he began to age at ten times the normal rate. This was put down to a severe case of R.B.A.R.I.L.B.A.B.T.O.T, otherwise known as "Really Bad And Rather Inconvenient Luck Brought About By Ticking Off Time. Still, it's not a bad place to live,' said the book, in the voice of a young man, 'as long as you don't mind the darkness.'

'But it's raining,' Panda held out a paw to illustrate his point. 'It rains in Existence too. So how come it's raining?'

'It rains everywhere,' the Book of Pages said flatly.

'But-'

Iris put her hand over Panda's mouth, 'No more questions.' She looked to Cornelius. 'We've come to find Time.'

'Ah, yes,' Cornelius adjusted his monocle, 'Time.' A troublesome fellow. He showed up-' he paused, a line of concentration creasing his brow. 'Some time ago, I suppose.'

'Do you know where we can find him.'

'No, I'm afraid we're not exactly sure what he looks like or where he's gotten to.'

Panda shot him a quizzical look.

'The Welcomer who met him got very old, very fast, and the poor fellow has quite forgotten every detail about their encounter.'

'We'll just have to go look for him then,' said Iris.

Panda felt tired just catching the glint in her eye. 'And where exactly do you propose we start? I'm not driving around all night, you know.. I mean, how big is this place anyway?'

'I'm afraid no one knows. But perhaps this will help.' Cornelius produced a map from his briefcase.

'Thank you,' said Iris, blowing a raspberry at Panda. She took the map and unfolded it by the light of one of the headlamps. The map was made of a cheap wax paper of the sort given away at family attractions and cheap hotels. On this particular one, someone had coloured over the entire thing in black marker, and then used red crayon to write, you are here on it. Presumably to avoid any confusion, they'd also circled the words a few times in yellow.

'Well this is... nice,' Iris tilted the map so that Panda could see. 'I don't suppose you have one with a little more information on it?'

'Oh that's all any of our maps contain. You see, things turn up here all the time. Take yourselves, for example,' Cornelius said, pointing to the bus with a shrug. 'The landscape changes so much, we found it's only really practical to know where one is at any given moment. Best to let everything else worry about itself.'

'Maps don't work without-' Panda clasped his head in frustration. 'This is useless.' He snatched the map from Iris and threw it away.

'It depends on what you're using it for I guess.' Cornelius shrugged.

'No it...' Panda stamped a foot. 'Look, can't we ask the sodding book where Time is?'

'My dear bear, the Book of Pages is not a toy.'

'I warn you, I'm going to hit you.'

'Now, now,' Iris held up her hands. 'Cornelius, you must have some way of finding things down here.'

'To be honest, no one here has ever really bothered looking for anything. Except...' Cornelius stroked his beak. 'Except for the Navigator.'

'Who?'

'The Navigator. John, I think his name is. He has travelled the Gap a fair bit, he collects keys when they turn up.'

'He can find Time?'

'I should think so. He once found the edge of the world, which I imagine is harder than one might think, being that the Earth is a globe.'

'How did he end up here?'

'Sailed off the edge, I believe.'

'Right. Of course he did. So we're trusting to the tracking skills of a man who wasn't able to keep his boat on the planet?' Panda shook his head.

'It was a ship, rather than a boat, but yes, that's essentially correct.' said Cornelius, nodding.

'Splendid!' declared Iris. 'I'll drive, Panda, you can help Cornelius navigate. And before you argue, you know your eyesight is better than mine.'

'So's my driving,' he mumbled.

'What?'

'Nothing.'

'Right, come on then.' Iris ushered a reluctant Panda onto the bus, and turned to Cornelius. 'Are you coming?'

'Me?' Cornelius gestured to himself.

'Yes, you. Who else is going to show us round?'

'Well, I suppose I could.'

'Then it's settled,' Iris grabbed him by the wing and dragged him on board after her. 'Oh I do love a group adventure,' she grinned and bounced down into the driver's seat.

'I hate you,' Panda glared at Iris.

She had one of her stupid grins plastered across her face, and was enjoying herself far too much. He on the other hand, was trying his best not to fall off the dashboard as the bus rattled and shook around them. Cornelius had led them to a road alright. A great big line of golf balls smashed together like an idiot's version of silly-paving. 'This entire thing is ridiculous.'

'Do cheer up, Panda. This mood of yours is rather tiresome,' said Iris, gripping the steering wheel as she bumped up and down on the seat.

'Rather tiresome? You've been listening to this pompous idiot too much,' Panda gestured towards Cornelius.

The penguin was sitting behind them in the front row of seats, gawping out the window like a newly-landed tourist. 'I have never come this way before,' he said. 'It's much quieter and certainly far less resentful than the Avenue of Abandoned Kittens,' he held up a flipper to demonstrate, indicating several raw scratch marks.

'There! Finally!' In his despair-fuelled excitement, Panda almost punched out the window, as he pointed to their eleven o'clock, indicating a lumpen shape which the bus's headlamps were doing their best to illuminate.

'Where?' asked Iris, shaking her head without really looking.

'There!' Panda pointed again. 'Look woman, Sock Mountain.'

'Ah, gotcha!' said Iris, clamping eyes on the looming pile of socks that rose up like the universe's largest laundry basket. Except, owing to the large assortment of colours, shapes and sizes it would have been a terrible mistake to wash them all at once. Hoisting the wheel with her arms outstretched, Iris altered course as though she were steering a tanker. The bus juddered and lurched onto two wheels as she took them around the mountain's right side.

'Is the vehicle supposed to do this?' asked Cornelius as his genial view of the road became a severe close up.

'Only when she drives,' answered Panda.

'Well that is a lot of socks,' said Iris, rolling down the window for a better look.

'Several million I should imagine,' said Cornelius.

'And they just keep coming?'

'Yes.'

'What happens when they reach...' Iris hesitated a moment, staring up at the unending pile of cotton, 'the top?'

'I'm not altogether sure there is a top.'

'Has anyone ever been up to take a look?' asked Iris, craning her head out the window.

'Eyes on the road you-' Panda snapped, as the bus went over a bowling ball and the resultant shock sent him into the window. 'Jesus woman. Give me that,' Panda hopped into her lap and took the wheel.

'A few, that I know of,' continued Cornelius.

'What happened to them?'

'I suppose the smell was too much for some. Others I think, found it marvellously comfy. They simply lay down and didn't bother to get back up.' Cornelius swapped seats, moving to the other side of the bus and away from the mountain. 'In any case, it is a fool's errand. Socks come here so often we don't even bother welcoming them, and they pile up far faster than anyone could possibly hope to climb over.'

'I wish you hadn't said that,' groaned Panda. 'She does love a challenge.'

'Perhaps another time, eh Panda? Eh?' Iris joked, nudging his side with her elbow.

He was about to reply, and threaten her with violence, when she leapt from the seat, forcing him to cling onto the steering wheel.

'Oh look at the lake!' Iris stepped to the door. 'Stop the bus, Panda.'

'Why?'

'We're almost there, aren't we?' she looked to Cornelius.

'I believe so, yes.'

'Grand, then we can walk the rest of the way. I don't want to miss the lake.'

'Fine,' Panda sighed and slammed his feet hard on the brakes. He turned , expecting to find Iris planted into the dashboard. Instead, he found her smiling at him, her hands braced on the safety rail.

'Door please,' she winked at him, leaping off the bus as he pulled the lever and the doors swung open.

'She has rather a lot of energy that one,' said Cornelius as he filed off the bus.

'Yes, and you haven't even seen her pissed.'

'Oh it's marvellous!' Panda could hear Iris before he'd even left the bus.

'I wish I were pissed,' he said to himself, slumping off the chair, and joining her by the lakeside.

'Isn't it marvellous Panda? Isn't it?'

Panda followed the glow of the headlights as they cut through the darkness to skim the lake. Except it wasn't really a lake at all. Most dictionaries he'd cared to read over the years defined a lake as a large body of water surrounded by land. He looked again at the multi-coloured, fizzing, popping liquid that splurged out in front of him. It was more sugar than water, and judging by the sharp tang wafting from it, contained more additives than his last meal. He even saw some milk glomming towards the centre. 'It's fantastic. Where now?'

'Just up here, around the lake.' Cornelius led them to the end of the road, and down a shallow embankment where clusters of yellow batteries stood in the ground like bunches of lilies.

'This way, comecomecome,' said Cornelius from up ahead.

Iris nudged Panda. 'The stiff bugger seems to be really loosening up. I think he might even be starting to enjoy himself.'

'I'm absolutely delighted for him.' Panda glared at the penguin's back. 'He walks like a fat baby you know.' He sighed, and looked back towards the lake, briefly wondering if there might have been some gin in it. He sighed, again, and started after Cornelius, following him through a maze of upturned boats and wrecked rigging. It was a graveyard for seafaring vessels of yesteryear. Anchors were dotted around like tombstones, and felled masts were stacked upon one another, like pyres ready to be lit.

'He should be around here somewhere,' said Cornelius.

'Are you sure he's still alive?' asked Iris.

'Oh yes, quite sure. It is rare indeed that Death visits us here, and to my knowledge, he hasn't been since John arrived.'

'What the arse-biscuit is that?' Panda gestured to a the only ship that seemed to be in one piece. It was huge and it was shining; a glittering galleon of silver and bronze with masts that seemed so opulent he doubted his Christmas sheets were pure enough to string between them.

'Ah, you found him,' said Cornelius.

'Found him? He's hardly hiding, living in that. And while we're on the subject, I have a question.'

Cornelius raised an eyebrow.

'If there's no source of buggering light here, how come the ship's twinkling?'

'It is beautiful,' replied Cornelius. 'All beauty shines.'

'Oh, do sod off.' Panda put his head in his paws. If his headache and that god-forsaken drive over the golfballs weren't enough to make him throw up, such a nonsensical sentiment would just about do it. 'I hate this place,' he said but no one was listening.

Iris had already skipped down to the galleon and even the penguin was waddling off ahead of him. He sighed, again and trudged down the hill after them.

Up close, it became apparent that the ship had been fashioned from thousands upon thousands of keys, and seemingly without any adhesive or welding. They'd just been balanced together, arranged like a masterful dyke wall. Around the vessel were strewn piles and piles of the keys, like the incidental and leftover materials scattered around a building site.

'No, no, no...' a man appeared from behind one of the mounds. He was sifting through a selection of keys in his palm, tossing them away one at a time as they failed to meet whatever requirements he was judging them by. 'No, no, no-' He stopped when he realised he wasn't alone.

'Hello Navigator,' said Cornelius. 'I've brought some people to see you.'

The Navigator regarded Iris and Panda, standing stock-still for a moment before a wide grin split his face. 'Do you like her? Made her meself,' he said, indicating the galleon with a thumb, and pushing his chest out.

'Oh she's wonderful,' said Iris sweeping her arms out to encompass the ship. 'What's her name?'

'I call her Yale,' the Navigator placed one hand over his heart and gave a salute with the other.

'That's a terrible name,' said Panda, prodding the hull in the hope it would collapse.

The Navigator lowered his hand, deflated by the comment.

'Quiet,' snapped Iris.

'But it is. He's just read it on one of these keys.'

The Navigator, crestfallen, looked to Cornelius for support. The penguin shrugged.

'Panda, love, shut up.' Iris stepped between Panda and the Navigator. 'I think it's a fantastic vessel.' The Navigator visibly perked up at her words, craning his neck to nod at Panda as though Iris's vindication was absolute. 'We were wondering if you could help us,' she said.

'Al do me best, luv.'

'We're looking for Time.' said Iris.

'Oh is that right? Well, findin' 'im should be easy enough. Just follow the ol' stuff. The closer you get to 'im the more it'll have aged.' The

Navigator turned away and set about rummaging through a pile of keys.

'All the same, I'd just as soon have you come with us,' Iris pulled a crumpled polaroid of the bus from her jacket. 'You could be our navigator.'

The Navigator examined the picture, 'Ain't never sailed in one of those before.'

'You'll come then?'

'That depends,' he scratched his chin. 'What's in it for me? I means, the closer I get to ol' Time, the quicker the years will fall off me. I ain't ever been ready for the grave-locker.'

Iris thought for a moment. 'Well, all the more reason to find him quick. Then once he's gone you'll stop ageing.'

The Navigator seemed to weigh up the sense of her argument before answering. 'Nope, can't do nothing for nothing,' he shook his head and folded his arms, revealing the tattoo on his forearm. 'I'm gonna need something.'

'How about this,' asked Iris holding up a bronze key.

The Navigator's eyes flashed to the key and then to a small gap on the side of Yale's hull. 'By Davey, you're on,' he said, his wide, toothless grin making him seem madder even than their bizarre surroundings.

After countless wrong turns, false-starts and winding detours, it soon became apparent that the only way the Navigator could have found the edge of the Earth was by pure chance, luck or some other random happening that he himself had very little to do with.

'Arse duck,' Panda spat as the Navigator indicated they should turn around, again. It wasn't his finest insult or even one he'd rank among his top ten. It was simply all he had left. He'd spent the last God knew how long slinging around an unceasing barrage of colourful curses, some of which would have made Iris blush on her worst day. 'I'll be up the back. Come get me if we find Time or someone dies. Either way I'll come to celebrate,' Panda shot Cornelius a glance that he hoped said quite clearly, I could eat penguin, and retired to the back of the bus.

Away from his companions, the view was slightly less stupid.

The bus carried on through the endless dark. Indistinguishable shape after indistinguishable shape rolled past the window. Once in a while, Panda thought he saw the shadow of something interesting, though each time it turned out to be just his reflection, distorted by the weird demi-light that had settled in the bus. I look rough, he thought as he caught another glimpse of the dark rings under his eyes. I need a drink. He sighed, and took to counting as a way to take his mind off the dryness in his throat. Somewhere around seven-hundred and forty-five, he fell asleep.

He woke up when his head hit the window, a sensation he was growing rather tired of. He pushed his fist into his eye. If they still hadn't found Time he was going to be displeased with someone; probably John the Navigator but probably Cornelius too. 'Have we found him yet?' Panda dropped off the chair into the aisle and—

'Stop!'

Panda had just enough time to grimace before being hurled like a bowling ball down the aisle into the console at the front.

'Hi Panda.'

He looked up at Iris. 'Don't,' he said.

She grinned anyway.

'Ahoy! Look ye well. We've found him,' the Navigator was a carnival of motion, waving his arms like the first sailor to see land, and pointing out the driver's side window.

Sitting by the roadside, with his back to them, was a forlorn looking reindeer in a pinstripe suit.

'That's...' began Iris.

'Time, yes. True as true,' the Navigator assured her.

Iris looked to Cornelius.

The penguin shrugged. 'I suppose it could well be.'

'Good enough,' said Iris, tossing the Navigator the key she had promised him.

He snatched it from the air, and kissed it, holding it up in front of his eye like he was examining a diamond. 'A fine bounty,' he said and swallowed it.

'Odd fellow,' said Iris as the Navigator threw them a quick salute and sped off the bus.

'Quite,' agreed Cornelius.

The pair stared in silence for a moment at the void left by the Navigator.

'I hope that wasn't the key to the bus,' said Panda.

'Of course not.'

'Then what key did you give him?'

'If I remember right, I think it opens the door to the Special Reserve Vault at the Gordon's Gin distillery,' said Iris.

'What? How could you?' Panda's face fell. Iris hadn't seen him look so dejected since that time she'd bought him a single rather than the customary triple.

'Ahem,' Cornelius cleared his throat. 'Time?'

'Ah yes!' said Iris. 'Come on everyone, let's go and save Existence,' she beamed, skipping from the bus.

'Please, after you,' Panda shook his head and ushered Cornelius towards the door.

Outside, for what he truly hoped was the last time, Panda watched Iris reach into her coat and pull out a bottle of gin, a can of tonic and a set of two glasses. He glared at her, hoping his eyes might somehow burn into her soul or at the very least singe her jacket. 'You told me we'd drunk it all.'

'No, no that's not true,' said Iris, 'I told you there was nothing more for you to drink.'

'I hate you.'

'No you don't,' she smiled and turned to face Time. 'Gin and T?'

Time looked up from his feet. 'I'm sorry, I was miles away.'

Iris laughed.

'What's funny?' asked Time.

'Well, the idea of you being miles away, it's funny. I mean, you're just always there. Around I mean. It's annoying too,' she said pulling on the loose skin of her face to demonstrate. 'I for one could live with you being quite far away. Still that's not really how it works is it?'

'No,' Time shook his head. 'I came here to get away... but I can't switch off. I still feel myself being me,' he plucked a battery from the ground and stared at it as it began to rust and dissolve.

'Ah cheer up. This'll sort you out,' said Iris, settling herself down beside him.

'What will?'

'Gin and tonic, cures what ails you,' she held out a glass. Time looked at it and shook his head. 'Don't worry,' said Iris, 'these were me Aunts'. They're well aged. I doubt there's much more harm you'll do to them.'

Time attempted a smile, and took the glass. Iris loosened the cap on the gin and filled his glass almost to the top, 'We're light on tonic,' she said, opening the small can of tonic water and adding a splash to his drink.

Time sniffed the glass. 'It smells awful.'

'Tastes awful too, at least for the first couple,' she grinned, pouring herself one, 'but give it a chance.'

Time paused, staring at his drink as though it might bite him.

'Go on, you're on holiday aren't you,' said Iris.

'I am, aren't I?' Time seemed to brighten up at that, and knocked back the drink in one.

Iris chuckled as his face contorted.

'Are you sure this gets better?' he asked.

'Trust me,' Iris slapped him on the back and refilled their glasses.

Time downed the second one, and a third, and a fourth. Knocking them back one after another as though speed improved taste. After the sixth he stopped for a moment to tell Iris about when he'd decided to go as fast he could to see what would happen. Turned out it caused some sort of big bang. The noise left him with the worst headache, and so he'd decided it was best he never do it again.

'You were right, this is helping,' Time held his glass out.

'None left, me pal.'

'None?'

'Nope,' Iris tipped the bottle up as proof.

'Really?'

Iris shook the bottle. 'Nope.'

Time's eyes dropped to his empty glass, which he retracted and cradled in his lap.

'We've drunk it all,' said Iris.

'Can we get more?' asked Time, his face alive with hope.

'Not here.'

'Where?'

'Back in Existence, there's plenty,' said Iris, 'We just-' she turned around to find Panda tugging on her sleeve. 'There's no gin left, Panda. None.' She tipped the bottle up again to show him.

'Yes, so I see,' Panda sighed. 'Look, you've managed to get Time blotto. Great. Fantastic. That's certainly one for the books. But are you sure helping Time get drunk on a more regular basis is a good idea? We all sort of rely on him to behave.'

'You don't think he should drink?'

'No. No I don't think Time should be drinking, in the same way I don't think politicians should have an expense account.'

'Nonsense.' Iris said firmly. 'At least to the first bit,' she clarified. 'So ol' Timey will run a little slow sometimes and a little incoherently at others. At least he'll be there. Won't you?' she asked, turning to address her drinking partner. But Time had vanished.

'Hey!' cried Iris, 'he took my glass.'

Panda shook his head, 'Fine, but don't say I didn't warn you. If he starts repeating himself and something breaks somewhere then don't go dragging me on some quest to mend it.' He turned and walked away.

'Where are you going?' asked Cornelius.

'Back to the bus,' said Panda. 'We're done here.'

'Perhaps,' Cornelius coughed, clearing his throat. 'Perhaps...well I have rather enjoyed myself,' he coughed again. 'Perhaps I might impose...'

'You want to come with us?' Iris stumbled to her feet.

'No,' said Panda.

'Yes,' said Iris. 'Panda you can drive us,' she said, tossing him the keys.

Panda sighed as the keys landed just beyond Iris's feet. 'Where to now?'

'London,' she said.

'About time,' said Panda.

Scream in Blue
Dave Hoskin

Saskia feels the air change just before the bomb goes off.

It wasn't like the bombs Saskia has seen on TV. She doesn't see it directly, but feels a reverberation in the corner of her eye and just catches sight of one of the other passengers as they explode. Saskia is very sensitive to sound. Rather than a 'boom', this explosion is strange, sounding like shattering glass as the man's head flies apart like dandelion fluff. Even stranger is the lack of blood. Each fragment of the man's body simply cascades down the interior of the bus, tearing away the curtains, the paintwork and somehow... revealing something new underneath. Saskia stares as the damage seems to spread, as if the reality of the original wall is being rewritten somehow. Beneath the camp, chintzy surface, a new, gun-metal gray skin is peeking through. Just looking at the contiguous parts of wall makes Saskia uncomfortable. They feel like metaphors – gaps between something factual and something poetic - and she isn't good at those. Metaphors make her feel *wrong*.

A boy with a rapper on his T-shirt is yelling at her, his frantic words a cerulean blue. She reminds herself that when someone is yelling at her, it's because there's something important going on. Pay attention, follow the cues, figure out what's going on.

The boy is yelling about the explosion. He's telling her to get down, get to safety. Saskia can't see why she should. The bomb's already exploded - there can't be more, can there? Instead she turns her head, scanning around to see what's going on.

The driver is standing up, looking down the aisle at the aftermath of the bombing. The bus immediately careers into oncoming traffic. Swearing, the driver spins around and does something to the dashboard. The bus veers back into the correct lane and keeps driving, even when the driver takes her hands off the wheel again. Apparently the bus has an automatic pilot. Saskia didn't know that buses came fitted with those, but then she's no expert on the subject.

The driver's face is strange. Saskia hasn't paid attention before now, but it's like getting slapped with a hurricane made of crayons.

This face is *alive*.

Saskia can't normally read emotions very well. She can recognise expressions and match them to what she's been taught are the appropriate cues, but for the most part she's got used to perceiving other people like an astronaut behind a faceplate.

But this old woman's face *radiates* emotion. Her hair is a purple bird's nest, and Saskia can feel her eyes burning with energy, barely contained behind her chunky white glasses. She's not a big woman, but now that she's visible it's like she fills up the world; a flapping pink sheet in a line of lank, white tea-towels.

Saskia doesn't know how she understands that tea-towel metaphor, but she does.

'This! Is! Brilliant!' hoots the woman, her words fireworking off the walls. Saskia is surprised to see the words look different somehow, and now that she thinks about it, the boy's blue scream also had a strange quality. Like there's something in the air that's interfering with the colours, making them... she blinks slowly, resetting. Pay attention, follow the cues, figure out what's going on. The old woman is staring intently at the gun-metal grey patch left by the exploding man and smiles a completely irresponsible smile. 'Now,' she says. 'Who's responsible for that, eh?'

A panicked chorus of screams from the passengers. The old woman spins back to check the road. Up ahead: a red stoplight. Vehicles braking to a halt. Clearly the automatic pilot can't handle the bus entirely on its own. The old woman flicks a switch, leaps behind the wheel, but doesn't hit the brakes. Instead she cranks up some music that sounds suspiciously like a disco version of Ride of the Valkyries and swerves around the banked up traffic. Oncoming traffic is honked out of the way, and she leans on the horn all the way through the intersection.

Miraculously, nobody hits them.

Saskia thinks she hears sirens start to wail. Sirens have no colour, she thinks absently. Not even a boring colour like grey or khaki green. Saskia can name all the colours and all the shades. It's one of the things she's really good at.

There's a satisfied cackle. Saskia watches the old woman reset the automatic pilot. Then she beckons a male passenger forward, gives him a quick primer on the accelerator and the steering wheel, and dubs him the newly designated driver. Saskia thinks the new recruit might be reluctant – he sits down in the seat very slowly – but the old woman pats him on the shoulder and says, 'Now lovey, I need you to keep up the pace. Eighty kilometres an hour, think you can do that?'

'Why don't you just stop the bus?'

Another of the passengers is standing now.

The old lady turns to look at her. The passenger is a chubby-faced, floppy-haired girl. Saskia can see that the girl's lips are twisted upwards, and recognises that this is a smile. She saw that look on so many girls back when she was at school; saw it when they were saying things to her that have more than one meaning. Saskia's very bad at telling when things have more than one meaning, but she's learned to track back and parse the statements that qualify when she recognises this particular smile

The old lady's eyes narrow. 'I don't remember picking you up, love.' Saskia sees a thread of sharp orange inside the fluffy pink of her words.

'Don't you?' Chubby-face continues smirking. Her words are vanilla. 'Maybe I was in disguise?'

'I doubt it. You strike me as the type who always forgets their costume when they go to fancy dress parties.'

Saskia hears the driver grind the gears. The bus slows for a moment, and everybody lurches slightly as it struggles to regain momentum.

The lips twist upward again. 'I'd still like to know why we don't just stop?'

There's a murmur from the other passengers. They'd like this answered too.

The old lady glares. 'What's your name, pet?'

'Sanna.'

'Well, Sanna, it's traditional in situations like this to keep the bus going like the clappers. Bombs on speeding buses are a speciality of mine...'

Saskia's eye twitches.

The old man sitting across the aisle from her winces. Saskia notices that he's cut himself shaving that morning, and that's where the explosion begins. The cut widens, as if dragged apart by invisible hooks, and the man's head and neck peels open like a banana. For a moment his skull is visible, jaw working in pain, and then his whole body falls apart, bouncing up the walls of the bus as if it weighs nothing at all. Screams seem to propel the debris, wordless blue waves heaving it over the heads of the passengers, and everywhere it lands pieces of the floor and ceiling are eaten away.

As if from a very long way away, Saskia thinks she can hear a low mechanical groan.

She looks back at the old woman. Her face has gone very still, all its fierce vibrancy drained away. Then, like a garage door slamming down, she glares at Sanna.

'You knew that was going to happen, didn't you?' Another curve of the lips. 'Right then. Where is it?'

'Where's what?'

'Don't piss me about...' Like a kicking mule, the old woman suddenly swings her handbag at Sanna's head. Sanna doesn't even duck. It connects just below her ear, and there's a meaty thud. The handbag must be heavy, Saskia thinks. It should have hurt Sanna quite a bit. Should at the very least have caused her to recoil from the impact...

...but instead Sanna doesn't even blink. Saskia is confused. The cues are all wrong. Sanna should have winced, staggered, or perhaps started crying. Instead Saskia sees the lips begin to curve upward again.

'Excuse me, driver, what's your name?' Sanna calls.

'Um. Donald,' the driver replies.

'Are we still doing eighty, Donald?'

'Just like she told me.'

'Thank you.' The lips curve at the old woman in triumph. 'Care to have another go? Or would you rather slow down and take your chances on another bomb going off?'

The old woman swears at her in a colour Saskia can't name. Sanna tut-tuts and then begins to unbutton her overcoat. Everyone in the bus begins to edge as far away as possible.

A body crashes through the window.

Saskia's head whips around to see a police van roaring alongside the bus. Two muscle-bound men in flak jackets are watching the passengers through the hole in the window. Saskia looks down to see their compatriot picking himself off the floor. He doesn't seem as injured as he ought to be after a stunt like that, and Saskia wonders if it has something to do with the interior of the bus. Given the change in the colour of the words, not to mention Sanna's insinuations about the speed of the bus allowing her to shrug off a wallop from a handbag, Saskia was picking up the cues and forming a picture of the new status quo.

The next thing she notices is that the officer is beautiful. Angular, slightly Asiatic features, smooth skin and short hair. And so young; boyish really, not much older than Saskia herself.

The old lady makes a beeline for him. 'Can I help you officer?'

'Ma'am! Is there a reason! Why this bus! Is speeding through a built-up! Area?!' Saskia is confused. The police officer seems to place the emphases in his sentences in all the wrong places.

'There is a reason, yes. There's a bomb on this bus, and I'm sure that if we slow down the bomb will go off.' The old woman takes the officer's hand between hers, almost girlishly. 'I'm sure a man of your experience will have seen something like this before.'

'As a matter of fact! Ma'am, yes I have!' The officer turns to address the bus. 'OK, listen up! People I have been! Informed that it! Is impossible! To slow down! This bus! Therefore we! Are moving to Plan B! I and my fellow! Officers over there...' The officer points out the window. The police van screeches around the corner, shadowing the bus. '...are going! To evacuate! You! To our vehicle!'

'Excuse me,' Sanna pipes up. 'But what if we're perfectly happy here?'

'That's the bomber,' the old woman mutters. 'I think she's got something dangerous under her coat.'

The officer's eyes dart between the two women. Then he pulls a gun. 'Ma'am! Will you please! Remove! Your coat?!' His words are like brass arrows.

'Is now really the time for...'

'Ma'am! I'll give you! To the count of three!'

'One,' says Sanna helpfully.

'I'm absolutely! Serious, ma'am! Two!'

'Three.' Sanna's hand reaches for something inside her coat.

The officer pulls the trigger. Nothing happens.

'I should have told you,' the old woman whispers. 'We don't have time for the long version, so just believe me when I tell you this is a special kind of bus. If I rev her up to eighty kays an hour, a sort of... grace thingy happens.'

'Grace thingy! Ma'am?!'

'No violence inside the bus. Not if she feels like we're about to take off.' Another blank look as the bus screeches into another corner. 'We can't take off because the first bomb damaged the... Look, never mind. I'll explain later.'

Sanna starts unbuttoning her coat again. 'A special kind of bus, you say? I did wonder what happened to the regular service.' She untwists the final button. Saskia can't quite see what lies underneath, but she's heard about the terrorists and their suicide vests. 'So... would I be right in saying you're not employed by the bus company?'

'I would have thought that was obvious.'

'They don't seem to think so.' Sanna looks at the other passengers. 'I think they thought you were doing the usual route on the usual timetable. But you're not are you?' The old woman doesn't say anything. 'So. Why did you pick all these people up? Why fool them into getting onto your tatty little bus?'

The wheels screech. The old woman smiles in triumph. Saskia sees something magnificent inside her draw itself up to its full height. 'I was giving them an adventure!' she said. 'The trip of a lifetime with the notorious Iris Wildthyme!'

The police officer gives a tiny squint. Saskia can't tell what the look means. It might be that he recognised Iris' name. It might be that he was feeling the first twinges of a toothache. He opens his mouth. 'Whoa...' he says, very quietly.

Then he explodes all over the front of the bus.

Sanna calmly walks down the aisle, her open coat flapping in the wind from the broken window. When she reaches Iris at the front of the bus, she stops. Iris punches her in the face again, but

Donald's managed to get the bus back over eighty kilometres again, and Sanna simply shrugs away the blow. She delicately brushes something off the old lady's shoulder, and Saskia realises it's a stray shred of the police officer. Then Sanna eases past Iris and steps into the ruined grey stairwell, regarding the devastation wrought by the explosion. Almost half the bus is scorched a different colour now, and as she places her hands on the dashboard, Saskia hears that low mechanical groan again.

'That grace thingy doesn't seem to be doing much of a job,' says Sanna. She's found a crack in the dashboard, and Saskia watches as she forces her fingers inside.

'What are you doing to my bus?'

Sanna doesn't even look around. 'Whatever I like.' She shoves her fingers deeper into the crack in the dashboard and there's another groan from the bus. Saskia blinks. Just for a second she sees a thin mist of turquoise hanging in the air.

'Donald?' says Iris.

'What?'

'Brakes.'

Donald doesn't understand the command, but does as he's told. The bus lurches slightly, and just as the speedometer dips below eighty, Iris swings Sanna around by the shoulder and punches her in the nose. Sanna's mouth falls open, and then she collapses in the stairwell.

Iris hisses in pain and shakes her hand. Apparently the punch hurt more than she thought it would. Then the garage door slams down again, and the devil-may-care expression beams out so intensely that it almost hurts Saskia to look at her. 'Thank you, Donald. You were almost as brilliant as I was. Now. You blokes down the back there. Come and help drag Miss Clever Tits out of here.'

As two men in tracksuits gingerly start to haul Sanna's body out of the stairwell, she stumps over to the hole in the window to address the police van. 'Get out in front of us and clear a path!' she bellows. 'It's the best thing you can do at the moment!'

The police don't look happy about this, but after some waving of arms and shouting of arguments, they do as they're told. Iris goes to check how Donald's holding up – she mops his brow with a feather boa, and one of the pink feathers sticks to his forehead – and then returns to examine Sanna's body. The other passengers gingerly gather around and watch as she lifts Sanna's coat, spreading it out like a mounted butterfly's wings.

'Er. Where's the bomb... vest? Belt? Whatever?' says the first tracksuit guy.

'She's not wearing one. No bomb. And no trigger either,' says Iris, going through Sanna's pockets. 'Clever little cow was bluffing. Make no mistake, she's our bomber, but she's not actually setting them off.'

'Do you know her? She seems to know you.' says the second tracksuit guy.

'Never met her in my life, lovey.' Iris stands up. 'Right, here's the good news. She's not going to explode on us, so there's lovely. Bad news is we're not out of the woods. The combat veterans among us might have noticed these explosions are a bit weird. That's because I think they're psychic bombs.' Iris taps the side of her head. 'I think what our Mad Bomber has done is alter the atmosphere in here. Given a particular type of trigger, somebody explodes. It's not that you've had something implanted in you beforehand. She couldn't have known the delectable copper was coming aboard and he died like everybody else.' Iris elbows Saskia in the ribs. 'Good bit of deduction that, eh?'

Saskia nods. It seems the easiest way to get Iris out of her ribs.

'Well... what is the trigger then?' asks the boy with the rapper T-shirt.

'I wish I knew, lovey.'

'So we have to keep speeding around until we figure it out?'

'I know! It's going to be brilliant!'

Sanna springs off the floor and slaps Iris across the cheek.

For a moment, it's as if the sound of the engine, the sirens and every other noise just disappears and the only thing that's audible is the flat smack of palm on cheek. The two track-suited guys grab Sanna's arms and haul her back, but she doesn't make another move to strike. Nor is she smiling, as Saskia expected she might. Instead there's a hard look on her face, a kind of... Saskia can't quite make it out. Based on the sequence of events, she'd say hatred, or contempt, or loathing, but really she'd just be guessing. What makes things even more inexplicable is that Saskia's sure that the bus hadn't slowed down. Sanna's slap couldn't have actually hurt Iris, not with the grace thingy working.

'You. Fucking. Sicken me.' says Sanna. Her voice is very low, and purple like a bruise. 'Litres and litres of horseshit just pouring out of your mouth. Why don't you tell them why you fucking kidnapped them today? Go on, tell them you pathetic old bag of piss! Tell them why they're on your grand fucking adventure!'

Saskia watches the first beginnings of Iris' shocked response... and then, as if she knows on some fundamental level that something dangerous is about to happen, cuts in.

'I can see what you're saying,' she says. 'Like colours. Colours in the air.'

Iris freezes, her words stillborn on her lips. Her eyes narrow as she stares at Sanna, trying to understand exactly what's going on. Then she unclenches her fists – Saskia sees her wince a little – and turns away from her accuser. 'What do you mean colours, dearie?' she says.

Saskia sees the mad scatter of emotions on Iris' face beginning to focus on her exclusively, like a tornado's throat funnelling down to make landfall. 'I mean... when you speak, I can see the words come out of your mouth. And the words make colours. My doctor calls it synaesthesia.' Saskia can see the gears turning rapidly beneath Iris' face. She was a blustery old hen, but Saskia could tell she wasn't stupid. 'I can see the words moving through the air,' she went on. 'And when the words hit the man before... that's when he died.'

Iris nodded slowly, processing what she'd said. Then she spun to face the other passengers. 'What about the rest of you?' The tornado leaps from face to face. 'Can you see it too? Because let me tell you chickens, I bloody well can't, and I'm usually the first to see the weird shit.'

There's a slow, herd-like shaking of heads.

Iris spins back and Saskia sees the mouth of the tornado beginning to widen as her mind processes the new information. She sees Iris is about to speak, and Saskia knows it's very important that she interrupt her again before something terrible happens.

'The explosions happen when you lie.'

She knows her voice is often flat, the words a simple black and white, but she also knows she has to proceed very carefully. Normally it was hard to anticipate other people's feelings, but Iris was different. Her feelings were... *bigger*, easier to read. And Saskia knows that what she's saying will hurt Iris, and while that was necessary to stop another explosion, it still wasn't something she wanted to do. She takes a step back, anticipating an angry response, and lowers her eyes.

The response doesn't come. Saskia looks up again.

'When I lie, you say?' says Iris quietly. 'How can you tell?'

'The colours are different... when you...'

'When I'm talking a bit of fairly obvious shite, is that it dearie?' Saskia nods. Iris nods back, and smiles at her. 'Do you think it's just me causing the explosions?' she asks.

'I can't tell,' says Saskia. 'It's just that you're the only one I'm sure about.'

'She's right, you know.'

Sanna is smiling at them both, still held in check by the tracksuit twins. Iris shakes her head. 'When did I piss in your cornflakes, pet?' she says. 'Am I really worth all this?'

'Ha!' Sanna's face looks strange as she makes the laughing sound. It doesn't look happy at all. 'It's not all about you, Iris. It's your bus I'm interested in.'

'My bus...?'

'But since you asked,' Sanna snarls. 'I hate the fact that there's not a single part of you that's not made out of chipboard and papier mache. I hate the fact that you're all over the shop, so bloody unreliable. I hate the fact that you never listen, and that you don't make any sense, and that you never, *ever* tell the truth.'

Iris raises an eyebrow. 'You've been practising that chipboard and papier mache one, haven't you?'

'You're the one that killed all these people. And she saw it happen.' Sanna jerks her head toward Saskia. 'I know what you're like Iris. I knew that I could bury you with your own bullshit if I set the stage just right. And here you are. One bomb away from losing your bus altogether.' She balls her hands into fists, and the mechanical groan sounds again.

'Leave her alone!' snaps Iris. The gun-metal stain, the *ordinary* stain, flexes in concert with Sanna's fists, bleeding into the little remaining territory that hasn't been sterilised by the exploding passengers. Sanna simply closes her eyes and ignores the old woman. Her fists flex again.

And Saskia's eye twitches. She realises what's going on.

'I need to tell you something,' she says.

'Not now, love,' says Iris.

'I think I can feel the bomb inside me. I wasn't sure before. But I feel something different. Something's changed.' Saskia doesn't feel afraid when she says any of this. All of it was the truth. The bomb inside her won't go off if she tells the truth.

'Are you sure?'

'I feel like I'm... ticking.'

'Well that can't be good.' Iris mutters, sitting down on one of the seats. Saskia sees her wince again as she attempts to steady herself with her hand, and she wonders whether Iris broke something when she punched Sanna in the face. There's a glamour about the old woman that can keep ordinary, boring things at bay, but sometimes that glamour slipped. In that moment, Saskia realises that Iris is a thing meant to be in motion. It's only when she comes to rest that inertia drags at her and pulls her out of shape.

'Here's the good news, lovey,' says Iris, tiredly. 'I think I can get that bomb out of you. But it won't be easy.' She looks around at the rest of the bus. 'Right then. The lot of you get to the back of the bus in case I cock this up. And sit on that pest while you're at it.'

Everyone immediately hustles as far away as they possibly can, Sanna still flexing her fingers.

The bus is groaning louder now as the stain continues to spread. Iris looks around at the damage, and for a moment Saskia sees what might have been tears in her eyes. Then Iris blinks and they're gone. Saskia thinks that's the only chink in her armour, but then Iris leans in and her words are a perfect, shimmering blue. 'I'd be lost without her you know. Completely lost. That's why she wants to take her away from me, I suppose.'

'Do you... do you think I'm the last one?'

'The last bomb? Let's hope so, dearie. Let's hope so.' Iris indicates for Saskia to sit. 'So here's what I think's going on. I think these bombs aren't the usual kind. For a start, we're still alive – plus point. For seconds, you saw how the people looked when they... Kind of...' Her hand flails, searching for the right word. 'Like they'd been... erased. Re-edited. Right out of the story.' She looks around at the wreckage again. All her decorations, everything that made the bus distinctive was now hanging in rags or completely destroyed.

'You think this is a story?'

'Well, at the moment it feels a bit like a bloody Wikipedia entry and Little Miss Dynamite's one of those humourless sods that deletes articles they don't like.' Iris winces again. Saskia looks down at her hand. She wonders if Iris usually gets hurt as badly as this, and something tells her she probably doesn't.

'I don't understand.' Saskia has never been good with metaphors.

'It's alright,' Iris says. She heaves a huge sigh, re-gathering her glamour. Then she smiles and the tornado returns; albeit weaker. 'The thing about rewriting stories is that it's a two-way street. Your bomb in there will try to rewrite you given the right trigger. I think we can make it do the opposite... if we just choose the right words.'

'The right *coloured* words?'

'Yes! Exactly!' Iris' enthusiasm is green and sparkling. 'Now what I need you to do is tell me about the bomb. How it feels. And whatever you do, don't lie to me, OK?'

Saskia nods. 'You too,' she says.

Iris stares deep into her eyes: 'Where's the ticking coming from, pet?' Her voice has changed. Saskia knows a fancy name for this colour: vermilion.

'The ticking's inside my eye,' she says. 'This one.' She raises a finger and places it carefully over her right eye. Oddly, her own words have a colour now, a deep sunflower yellow.

'Does anything happen if I speak any closer to your eye?' says Iris.

'Yes. Ticking gets louder.' Words a richer yellow. Saskia doesn't know why; possibly because she's afraid. 'And it feels like it's... flexing.'

'What do you mean?' Deep vermilion, loud in her eye.

'Like it's put down... roots in me. Like a plant. I can feel it here.' Saskia holds her hand up to her cheek. 'And it's spreading.'

'But still... centred up here, am I right?' Iris' finger gently reaches out and rests on Saskia's eyelid.

Saskia does her best to keep her words as yellow as possible. 'That's right.' A beat. 'Are you sure you should be touching my eye?'

'It's not that type of bomb. It won't go off.'

'So why are you touching me?'

'Does that have a colour too?'

'No. But it hurts.'

Immediately Iris takes her finger away. 'Sorry, love.'

'It's OK. I always hurt when people touch me.'

'I promise I won't do it again. There's no need. Now...' The quality of Iris' voice changes again, becoming deeper. Saskia watches as her words take on a new quality. They become more tangible now, the colours thicker.

'I need you to tell me your name,' says Iris.

'I will,' says Saskia. 'But I need you to tell me something first.'

'What's that?'

'Why did you pick us all up on your bus today?'

There's a long pause. Then Iris leans forward again and whispers. 'I get lonely, love. Really lonely. I just like to have people around me, even if it's only for a little while.'

Saskia nods, understanding. 'Thank you. My name's Saskia,' she whispers. She can't see what colour her response is. Her vision is full of deep vibrating mahogany.

'Saskia, I'm going to tell you a story about the bomb in your eye. I need you to listen very carefully, alright?'

'OK.'

'The bomb in your eye isn't made of anything solid. What you feel moving around in there is like code in a computer. A code that responds to words. So if we can find the right words, we should be able to winkle it out.'

'OK.'

'I need you to picture the bomb in your eye, Saskia. Think about it like the centre of a spider's web. Can you do that for me?'

'No.'

'Why?'

'I'm not very good with metaphors.'

'Right.' Iris frowns at her. She clears her throat and then turns around to the people at the back of the bus. 'Oi! Tracksuit boys! Get down here!' Reluctantly, the tracksuit twins shuffle down the aisle. 'It's your lucky day, boys. I'm going to do a little singing, and I need your help. You, matey, are going to do a little drumming for me.' She beats out a slow rhythm on the back of her chair, and the first tracksuit guy hesitantly begins to imitate her. 'Good. Keep that up. Now you, sonny Jim are going to sing back-up.'

'Can we swap?'

'Don't worry, it's an easy one. Nice and slow. Like those bald little monks you see on the telly.'

Saskia is having trouble following all this, the competing overflow of word colours beginning to overwhelm her senses. She can feel the bomb spreading through her system, spring-loaded beneath her skin, just waiting for the smallest lie to set it off. She carefully feels around on the floor and lies down, curling up into a ball. Her loaded eye remains fixed on Iris, but the rest of her begins trying to raise the drawbridge, filtering the colours, noise and confusion as best she can.

She doesn't hear the singing start. It simply seems to drift in gradually, like a mist of colour raining down towards her face. Somewhere behind the colours are the steady slapping sound of hands drumming on a cheap vinyl seat, married with somebody humming low in their throat. Then words come spiralling down through the colour-stream, words of ivory and bone and eggshell, building sentences and structures in front of her. They don't make literal sense exactly – she knows that because she doesn't understand them – but she can feel them passing through the wet surface of her eyelid and onto the throbbing bomb beneath. Sometimes Saskia catches a lyric here and there, sometimes she's sure Iris is just chanting numbers, but as the words burrow behind her eye, the concept of what they're doing is stunningly clear; like the transmission of a picture from one mind to another.

And then, Saskia feels the knot of the bomb slipping out of her. It was like the words of eggshell, bone and ivory were lifting it clear, with all the delicacy of a surgeon's forceps. But then something snags, almost as if the bomb is caught on an eyelash. Saskia turns her head to look more directly at Iris. She can perceive the bomb, twisting and out of focus just on the event horizon of her vision, surrounded by a vortex of words. It's a mass of blue and red cords twisted around a kernel of grey, and beyond that is Iris' face, her song holding the bomb in equilibrium.

'Saskia.' For a moment she doesn't even recognise her own name. 'I'm going to ask you a question and I need to you answer it truthfully, OK?'

'I... OK.'

'Right. Now sweetie, I need you to tell me... are you pleased you got on my bus today?'

'No.'

The answer is out with no hesitation at all. Saskia sees the pain of it splash across Iris' face. The bomb spins in the backwash of the word, the blue cords seeming to glow in sympathy with Iris' pain.

'Thanks, love. That's what I needed to hear.'

The bomb is spinning faster now. Saskia can just make out the red cords threading around its circumference; the blue ones running up towards the poles. They're so tangled, so complicated that she has no idea how Iris is going to disentangle them. They pulse in time with the music, and Saskia becomes so fascinated that she doesn't see Iris' reaching word-fingers until they're almost touching it. Saskia's dimly aware of her turning to say something to the tracksuit twins, of the music changing ever-so-slightly...

Then everything turns a soft green.

The word-fingers deftly cut the blue cords, somehow missing the red ones entirely.

As if shedding a tear, Saskia feels the bomb fall away from her eyelash.

In the wash of green song, the bomb floats up until it's level with Iris' face. Saskia sees that its core has changed colour now, Iris' words having rewritten its fundamentals. Re-edited it.

Iris reaches out with her hand, cupping the bomb in her palm. Flicks her wrist.

The bomb explodes.

Everyone's eyes fill with eggshell, bone and ivory.

When they open them again, the gun-metal stain has disappeared. There are still extensive bald patches all over the bus, but the nasty infection of ordinariness has been banished. Iris stands and brushes her cardigan down. The tracksuit twins are still busking away, and she gives them a little pat to let them know it's alright to stop.

'Thank you,' says Saskia, still on the floor. 'I wasn't expecting that to work.'

'To be honest, lovie,' says Iris. 'I wasn't sure it would either. But thanks for the thanks.' She turns toward the front of the bus. 'Donald!' she yells. 'We can slow down now, hon. Bring her in for a landing.'

'Is everything safe now?' asks the first tracksuit guy.

Iris peers down at Sanna, still buried beneath a pile of petrified passengers. Sheepishly they stand up to give her a closer look. Sanna's face is blank and drooling. Saskia can see clear nothing-y sounds falling from her mouth. She's never seen that before.

'It will be, once I've taken care of her,' says Iris. 'Don't worry, I think that's something I should be able to take from here. She won't give me any trouble.'

Saskia watches Iris as she stands next to the broken window, the wind rushing through her hair. She looks exhausted, and her hand - the one that Saskia suspects is broken - rests on one of the bus' scarred patches. When Donald finally pulls the bus over to the side of the road, Iris sits down and rests her head against the scar. She smiles at the passengers as they troop off and begin telling the police what has happened, but Saskia knows it isn't a real smile. Smiles don't have colours, but she's learned to tell the difference with Iris. She also knows it will be ages before the police finish with everyone outside, so she decides to sit next to the old woman and keep her company. Blue and red lights fill up the bus, while outside busy-sounding voices demand rational explanations.

But the only thing the police can get out of anyone is pure vermilion.

Dog Days of Summer
Roy Gill

Summer 1984

Andrew was bored. The sticky weather had glued his t-shirt to his skin, and his head throbbed. He longed for the cool sanctuary of the house, the quiet escape of his books, but his mother had chased him outdoors.

'Far too nice a day to be inside reading,' she admonished, scooting him from the comfy chair in the room that had been his Great Uncle Edward's study. 'Go and be healthy. Sunshine is good for you. Play!'

Reluctantly he had gathered up a handful of toys, and gone out into the baking inferno of the back garden. After a period of mind-numbing idleness, he set to clearing a herd of scurrying woodlice, and was busily recreating Luke Skywalker's rescue from the screeching Sand People in the desert wastes of Tatooine, when his mother let out a war-like cry of her own.

'No, no, no! Much too loud! How am I to study if you make a noise like that?'

He stuck his head out the sand-pit. 'Maybe I could go back inside?' he said. 'And play there?'

'Nice try, kiddo. Just turn the volume down.'

Collecting his figures, and the screwdriver he'd been waving about as makeshift lightsabre, Andrew moved to the far end of the garden.

There was an apple tree there that afforded some shade, and behind it a dilapidated wooden fence. A hole had appeared in the bottom some months ago, the corners of the wood gnawed through by sharp teeth.

At first the gap had been the size of a hedgehog or small rabbit. Next it was big enough for a fat cat or badger. By the time Andrew's mum had taken notice, it was large enough to admit a medium-sized dog.

'Must be a fox,' she had said. 'There's something wild trying to get in at any rate.'

'Maybe it's a wolf,' Andrew had offered.

'A wolf?'

'Like in olden times, in winter. It's hungry so it's come in from the woods, and now it's looking for food. It's hunting...'

'The things you say.' His Mum had popped a tear in some parcel tape with her nails. 'Sometimes

I think you're getting too old for these fairy stories and fantasies. Here, hold this while I stick it –'

A thick square of cardboard labelled 'Fine Fayre Frozen Peas' soon covered the gap, and Mum stood back to admire her handiwork.

'It's a bodge job, but it'll do. No sense in paying money to fix it.'

'There isn't?'

'No, Andrew. There's not. I've told you before. They're going to be building over all of this soon– all that mess of mud and trees will go, and they'll build a brand new estate instead. Lots of new families will move in. New children for you to play with! You'd like that, wouldn't you?'

Andrew shook his head.

'Well, it's gonna happen, kiddo. And they won't want this damp old dump in the middle of it. They'll pay me good money to buy it and tear it down. Then we can have some place smart and new.'

'They're going to tear down Great Uncle Edward's house?'

'The sooner the better. Why d'you think I took this pile on?'

'But I *like* living here. I like all the things he left. His gramophone. His books. Those funny clockwork statues that go marching about…'

His mum had given him a sharp look. 'The sooner they start building the better.'

Ever since that day, Andrew made regular trips to the fence, listening for the sound of diggers, and squinting through the little gaps in the slats, waiting for a flash of yellow jacket or hard hat.

So far, there hadn't been any sign at all.

He sat himself cross-legged on the earth, as far out the sun as possible, and glared back down the garden.

His mum had brought out one of the old stripy, slouchy deckchairs and was peering through her sunglasses at a textbook.

It was alright for her to read. It was so *unfair*.

He leant back on the fence – and gave a yelp.

The old pulpy wood that touched his back was not just damp, it was properly cold. He spun round, ran his hand across the surface. His fingers tingled. Sticking his eye to the nearest knothole, he looked through. The woods beyond were white, bright and sparkling in the sunshine.

No, that couldn't be right... He rubbed his eyes and looked again, but it was no illusion.

Moving swiftly to the patched-over corner, he picked at the thick tape that held the cardboard in place. Months in the garden had turned it black with mould, stripping away its sticky properties. With a soggy pop, the card pulled back, and Andrew ducked his head through.

Snow hung heavy on the trees and carpeted the ground. A ditch filled with rainwater had frozen over, and a clutter of beer cans glittered with frost, like scattered Christmas decorations. He stuck out his hand – held it in the cool air.

It's like Narnia! I've only gone and found the way to Narnia... His heart thumped in his chest.

Maybe he had just opened a cardboard-flap cut out of a box of frozen peas – not clambered through an old wardrobe - but then this *was* the eighties. On *Tomorrow's World*, Judith Hann kept promising the future: soon we'd all be listening to small shiny records called CDs, and be able to take a holiday on the space shuttle…

Perhaps magic doors had been updated too?

He glanced back down the garden. His mum's paperback lay flat on her face as an improvised sunshade. Beneath the crinkled pages, she was snoring and twitching in the heat.

Moving quietly, Andrew bent down, and slipped through the hole.

The snow crunched, pushing its way through the holes in his sandals and chilling his feet. He fought a sudden urge to rush to the nearest tree and *lick* one of the branches: it looked so white and perfect, like ice cream. After the swelter of the garden, it was blissfully cold.

'Little boy? I say, little boy? Could you assist me?'

The voice was high and imperious – and seemed to be coming from a nearby bush. The lower branches shook, dislodging blobby clumps of snow.

A string of expletives caused Andrew's eyes to widen in surprise for the second time, then the voice seemed to pull itself together. 'I'm over here, little boy. Can't you see me?'

A hand waved feebly, and Andrew saw there was a little old woman lying on the ground, wrapped in a cream-coloured shawl, her white upswept hair blending perfectly with the snow. She raised her head, revealing a wrinkled shrewish face with bright intelligent eyes.

'What are you doing in that bush?' Andrew said.

'I should have thought that evident,' said the old woman crossly. 'I'm trying to get out.'

Andrew shifted, awkwardly. 'So what's stopping you?'

'My foot is trapped. Oh for goodness sake, child. Stop lollygagging, and come and help.'

Cautiously, Andrew moved closer.

None of this made sense. If the world beyond the fence really had become some sort of Narnia-wonderland, he might've expected to run into a parcel-carrying faun or a terrifying White Queen, not some bad-tempered old woman.

She was probably one of the mysterious neighbours from down the road, he decided, none of whom his mum ever spoke to. *Yes, that was it!* The old dear had gone for a walk in the woods, and slipped. Old people were always doing that, falling on ice…

…in the middle of August.

'Look,' he said reasonably, 'if I do help, you're not going to turn out to be an evil witch or something, and come out and curse me, are you?'

'I'm not evil, merely rather grumpy,' the old woman said. 'And I've already used up most of my curse words this morning.' She paused, composed her withered features into a smile, and spoke more gently. 'Little boy… You can trust me, you know. I'm not really that fearsome.'

Her blue eyes met Andrew's, and he found he did trust her, rather. She reminded him a little of

Miss Marple, on Sunday evening telly. He could just imagine her waffling on about cucumber sandwiches, pretending to be old and dopey, while secretly analysing everything.

'Ok... What do I do?'

'Claw your way into the undergrowth, dear, and see if you can find a way of releasing me.'

Andrew fought his way through the branches, shuddering as the snow he dislodged slithered down the back of his neck. Nestling under the leaves, he found what looked like a scale model of a red double-decker bus. The old woman's foot, clad in a thick black stocking, was tightly wedged inside the little concertina-doors.

Andrew pulled himself back out of the bush as fast as he could.

'How – how did that happen? You were taking your toy bus for a walk, and you fell over and...' He tailed off.

'It's very simple. I was trying to adjust the dimensional, um, *doobray*, and I may have bodged it a little... I only just made it out before the exterior size re-allocated. Well, most of me got out, at least.' The old woman grimaced. 'That's what's caused this odd snap of weather. The energy has to come from somewhere.'

'It's winter in the woods,' Andrew said slowly, 'because your bus changed size?'

'A very cogent summary.'

Andrew lifted a branch and stared again at the bus. It was a surprisingly perfect model - if that's what it was - about a metre tall, with amazing amounts of detail. There were tiny splatters of mud on the wheels, and the sides were decorated with billposters advertising the Notting Hill Carnival. The pink curtains round the windows were a bit odd though…

'How big should it be, really?'

The old woman's eyes narrowed. 'Don't be obtuse, child. It should be bus-sized, of course.'

'And then it shrunk?'

'With indecent rapidity. The old girl seems troubled… We were tracking some unusual visitors to your area, and I think they disturbed her.' She lowered her voice to a confidential whisper. 'Smaller things are trickier to hunt!'

'This is completely mad,' said Andrew.

'No madder than my usual escapades, I assure you. Now, if you would, could you see about freeing me? I've been wriggling and wiggling all morning, and I'm quite worn out.'

He hunkered back down under the bush, and peered into driver's cabin. Alongside the steering wheel he could see rows of multi-coloured lights, winking on and off, and a tangle of wires and gizmos. Beyond, in the main body of the bus, there were loads of little tables, chintzy lamps and chairs, and tiny scattered books, almost as if someone had taken the contents of a doll's house and shoved them in, higgledy-piggledy.

'It doesn't even look like a proper bus inside.'

'Oh child! Set me free, and I'll explain everything. Well, nearly everything. At my age, I've forgotten half the stuff I used to know, and most of the stuff I will know…'

The old woman chuntered on, while Andrew examined further. Her foot was twisted at an odd angle, the heel wedged up against the bus's ceiling, the toes pointing towards the steering wheel. It reminded him a little of that bit in *Alice* where an overdose of 'Eat Me!' cakes made the girl too big to escape a particular room.

He took hold of the old woman's ankle, and gave it an experimental wiggle. This triggered a yelp and a cry of 'Monstrous urchin!'

'I am trying to help, you know,' he said. 'But it's looking pretty jammed.'

'Then I'll just have to lie here till the wolves get me.'

'Wolves?' Andrew glanced around the frosty woodland, and for the first time, he shivered. 'I used to pretend there were wolves out here, gnawing through the fence, trying to get in… But it was a joke, really. A game.'

'It's no game, believe me.' She tugged at her shawl, pulling it closer. 'At least it'll be quick. Maybe if I'm lucky, they'll start with my legs and gnaw me free. Although heaven knows it'll take long enough to organise a new pair…'

She started another ramble, and Andrew forced his attention back to the problem at hand. She was definitely stuck… unless a sudden shock could dislodge her? A quick sharp poke in her calf, and the old biddy would jump, hopefully pulling her foot free in the process. He felt in his pocket, and took out the screwdriver he'd been playing with in the garden.

It had one of those cross-hatched tips – it could certainly give someone a nasty jab…

Dare he do it? He brought it closer to her leg, weighing up his options.

In the driver's cab, something moved abruptly – and the whole miniature bus *thrummed* and shifted.

The old woman felt the vibration and called out anxiously, 'What ever did you do, child?'

'I'm not sure.' Andrew brought his face to the driver's window. In the middle of the cat's cradle of wires that hung near the steering wheel he could just see a sort of glowing crystal attached by a couple of crocodile clips. As he brought the screwdriver closer, the clips moved, and the bus thrummed again, much louder this time. The screwdriver tip must be magnetised, he realised, probably to help with some fiddly DIY.

'Your size-changing thingy,' he said. 'Is it a sort of shiny crystal?'

'I suppose you could call it that… You can't reach it, can you?'

'Not quite.' He tried another pass of the screwdriver, causing the clips to twitch in response once more. 'I can twiddle the bits attached to it though. Like magic!'

'Oh!' The old woman considered. 'Well, disconnecting the etheric solenoids will either solve the problem entirely – or cause the most colossal explosion. Or would that be implosion? I've never been entirely sure…'

'What should I do?'

'What I always do in these situations.' For the first time since he'd met her, the old woman sounded positively gleeful. 'You must go at the problem *full tilt*, and to hell with the consequences!'

'Well… if you say so.'

'I do. Most emphatically!'

Andrew bit his lip, and moved the screwdriver sharply upwards. The clips shot off with a metallic *ping*, and the crystal dropped to the floor. There was the most appalling grinding, tearing sound.

All of a sudden, the bus began to *grow*…

'And where exactly have you been?' His mother's face was flushed and red. 'I was *this* close to calling the police, Andrew. This close! Where were you?'

'On board the bus.'

'What bus? What are you talking about? There are no buses anywhere near here. Andrew, what have you been up to?'

'I rescued an old lady who had her foot trapped. Then her bus grew big, and she invited me in for lemonade and seed cake, but it wasn't very nice –'

'Oh Andrew…' His mother's expression turned rapidly from anger to concern. She put her hand to his forehead. 'I thought so. You've got a temperature. Sunstroke, it must be. I can't take my eyes off you for a second, can I?'

Andrew opened his mouth to protest, but his mum shushed him. 'Not another word! Inside! I'll fetch you some ice cream or some orange juice. Something cooling, anyway.'

She ushered him towards the back door. In an odd way, he *did* feel kind of queasy – he wasn't sure if it was the nasty dry cake the old woman had given him, or the sudden burst of tropical heat as the bus had stretched itself back to normal size.

They'd sat inside, him and the old lady, watching the melt-water stream down the windscreen and the snow roll off the branches.

'A clever trick of yours,' she had remarked, 'using that magnetic screwdriver. I shall have to remember that.'

'It's my Mum's. I only had it with me because I was pretending it was a lightsabre.' Andrew had paused. 'She doesn't like it when I do that. She's so practical. She says I'm not like her at all.'

'Practicality is very over-rated.' The old woman gave him a sympathetic smile. 'Besides, you rescued me, didn't you?'

'S'pose.'

He slid down from the high stool by the bar alcove, and went to stare out the window at the swampy woodland beyond. 'The snow's nearly all gone,' he said sadly. 'But I don't know how you're going to get out. The road's the other side of the wood, and you've got all these trees in the way...'

'Don't you worry about that. This old bus can go anywhere! I'll be gone like a summer breeze...' The old woman looked up from a bleeping flashing pocket-watch affair she was stuffing haphazardly into a locker. 'The creatures I was tracking seem to have moved on too. But I'd keep an eye out for them, if I were you. Their sort has a nasty habit of coming round again, every seven years.'

'Seven years!'

'Pure affectation on their part.'

'I'll be fifteen… nearly sixteen.' Andrew boggled.

'Age comes to us all, dear. I'm Iris, by the way.' The old woman laughed. 'What an unseasonal adventure! I suspect I'll be the last Iris you'll see this summer.'

Andrew looked at her blankly.

'Just my little joke.' She shooed him towards the folding doors. 'The bus will remember the help you gave us. Once a passenger – always a passenger!'

'Once a passenger, always a passenger,' said Andrew vaguely.

'What was that?' His mum gave him a sharp look.

'Once a passenger, always a passenger. On the bus… It's what Iris told me.' He shoved his hands in his pockets. 'Knew you'd never believe me.'

'Indoors and upstairs this minute!' His mum glanced back towards the fence at the end of the garden, and frowned. 'I am going to have to get that hole properly fixed after all.'

Summer 1991

Andrew's mum had been bashing away on her typewriter for months, working on her thesis. There'd be long, long periods of silence, then a cacophony of thumps, followed by a cry of 'Shit!' and the agonised squeal of paper being torn from the roller.

Any noise at all - except when made by her - was said to be disturbing, and was strictly forbidden.

Andrew had learned to love his headphones.

Now the hazy, dreamy days of summer had arrived, she'd moved outdoors. She sat under a vast white sunhat, typewriter balanced on a folding card table. As usual, he was not allowed to stay in the house as that was 'unhealthy'.

He'd offered to cut the grass, thinking it would appease her.

'Let it grow. What do I care?' she snarled, glaring up at the neighbours' houses. The new-builds had been there five years now, and she still resented their presence, pressing in around Great Uncle Edwards's gently crumbling legacy. 'Anything's better than the noise of that bloody mower.'

The grass grew longer as the summer pressed on, until the legs of her card table were almost hidden, and the clack of her keys merged with the drone of the insects…

Andrew took his Walkman up Lupin Hill, avoiding the neat gravel steps and heading up the rougher side.

When he'd been a kid, they told him not to come here. *Stranger Danger*, he supposed. *A Bad Man might look at you. Show you puppies.* Or maybe it was because of the time he'd gone wandering off and talked to some mad old bag lady, and come home running a fever. He didn't remember.

Today, the hillside blazed in the baking sun, and Andrew lay on the grass, basking, playing his Pet Shop Boys tape over and over. They sang about London, and the exciting things that happened there. *They were never being boring, because they were never being bored.*

Not like round here.

At least he was unlikely to run into anyone – none of the boys from school came up here during the day. They were too busy hanging out in Halfords, lurking round the precinct, leering at the girls. At night Andrew would sometimes hear their whoops and shouts as they huddled round the campfires they built – the sound would carry all the way down the hill to his bedroom. He'd plug his ears and he'd hate them – half for keeping him awake, half for never inviting him to join in.

Jerks.

He listened to his tape until it went quiet, even with the volume dial up full. He listened as it ran slow. Then he took out the batteries and propped them on a stone in the sun. Scott had told him that could bring them back to life.

Zombie batteries! Imagine that.

Andrew still resented Scott's holiday, off staying with his no-good dad in Spain. Scott's father had a slot machine business, meaning Scott got all the records left over from jukeboxes at the end of their run. That's how Andrew had met him. Scott had been down the market, flogging his scratchy old 7" singles with the strange cut-out centres, and Andrew had bought some. The Smiths, Kirsty MacColl, Voice of the Beehive…

Now Scott would put them to one side: all the weird songs, he'd keep them for Andrew. Sometimes he'd just give them to him.

'Must be soft or something,' he'd say, as he passed the records over.

Andrew blushed at the memory.

God, but this summer was dragging on…

Something metallic and scalding hot dropped into his hand. He gave a shout of alarm, and flung whatever it was away. His eyes flew open.

A boy with an outrageous shock of red hair towered over him.

Andrew sat up swiftly. 'Whad'ya do that for?'

'Your little tin treats seemed cooked to me.' The boy gave a squint-mouthed grin, and pointed at the two batteries where they'd landed on the grass.

Andrew blew on his hand and glowered. 'You mad git – you've burnt me.'

'Don't you want them?'

'Why would I? They're spent. No juice left.'

'Can I have them?'

Andrew shrugged, watching the newcomer warily as he put the batteries away in a leather pouch hung round his neck. His outfit was bizarre to say the least: hiking boots and long socks coupled with a tight formal jacket and trousers, and loads of bags and bundles strung around him. It reminded Andrew of the time he'd been cajoled into a scavenger hunt. You had to find all sorts of random things, put them on, and make it to the finish line.

'Are you winning?'

'What?'

'Have you got everything you need?'

'Not yet.'

The boy stared at him directly, and Andrew looked away.

'Good luck with your race, anyway'

'My what?'

'The scavenger hunt.'

'Scavenger. Yes. That's me.' The boy shifted closer. 'My mates have got a party going on, through the woods. Feel like coming?'

Andrew gave the boy a lofty look, as if he received such invitations all the time. 'Might be ok, I guess. Is it in the new estate?'

'Yeah, it's in 'new state'.' The boy pronounced the words with care. 'It'll be great. There'll be food and dancing and feasting and shouting. And lots of people.'

'Well, maybe later on,' said Andrew, airily. 'Depending on how things go.'

'Stuff later,' said the boy. 'We're going now.'

He reached down, grabbed Andrew roughly by the hand, and pulled him to his feet.

'Right now?'

'Oh yeah. It'll be *fun*.'

Andrew's heart leapt.

Andrew knew they'd built houses all round Lupin Hill, leaving just the bit in the middle that was too steep and boggy. There was nowhere you could stand and not see buildings of some sort through the trees…

But the further he walked with the red-haired boy, the further the woods seemed to stretch.

He could see other people too, some he recognised: Tom Hargreaves, who he'd usually try to avoid at school, gave him a vague smile. Others were total strangers: all walking hand-in-hand with redheads dressed in rag-tag clothes. Every so often, his friend – or was it his warder? – would stop, tilt back his head, and let out a whoop. The others like him would pause and holler in response, before moving on.

And still the forest seemed to grow…

'Where are we going? I don't recognise *any* of this.'

'Through the woods. That's where. That's where it always is.' The boy stopped, and gave another loud cry. From deeper in the forest, other voices howled back.

'See? We're nearly there, aren't we?'

The clearing was the size of a football pitch, a huge fire blazing at its centre. Over to one side, by the edge of the trees, a large structure shrouded in tarpaulin had been daubed over with graffiti: right at the top, a pair of green eyes seemed to watch the people gathered for the party, as they sat round in groups, laughing, drinking and eating.

At least, thought Andrew, *some* of them were laughing – mainly the lads in the rag-tag clothes. The others – the people more like him – appeared to be a bit dazed.

A woman carrying a pair of bongos sat down next to him. She was wearing a psychedelic dress with red and green swirls, and huge Jackie O glasses. At first, Andrew thought she must be with the rag-tag people — but she looked too old, more like she was in her early thirties.

She swept some of her honey blonde hair out her face, lifted her dark glasses, and hissed, 'I don't want to put the wind up you, babe, but you might want to make a move before the feast is over. When you run with the wolves, you might get bitten, you dig?'

Andrew frowned. 'I have no idea what you're talking about.'

'I said, *you wanna skadoodle before the fire burns down.* That's when things turn - ' She stuck her fingers in her mouth and pulled back the corners, exposing her teeth.

'No, I've still no clue –'

Abruptly, the woman abandoned the conversation, and started playing her bongos, beating out a rather expert bossa-nova.

The red-haired boy ambled over, and dropped easily into a squat between Andrew and the woman. 'Everything good?'

'Cool, man,' said the woman, not breaking the rhythm.

Andrew nodded lazily. He had an agreeable woozy feeling in his head from the warmth of the fire, and the strange drinks people kept bringing him. If this was a party, he should go to more of them.

'I brought you some meat.' The boy handed Andrew a blackened joint with a bone sticking out, and encouraged him to tuck in. 'You like?'

'Yeah, it's great. Real, um, *meaty.*'

'Lots more later.' The boy got to his feet and headed back to the fire.

'Ever get the spooky feeling these guys aren't from round here?' The woman let her bongo rhythm slow dramatically. 'You've heard of the dog star, right? Sirius?'

'You're telling me that's where they're from?'

'That'd be convenient, wouldn't it? Nice and rounded?' The woman rolled her eyes. 'No, doofus, they're from a moon near by.'

'Oh, go away…'

'Don't believe me?' The woman grabbed his arm. 'Look up!'

Andrew tilted back his gently-spinning head and stared. Night was creeping in, and the dark blue sky shone with stars – and also three giant, bright purple planets.

Abruptly, he felt very sober.

'They've got a teleport lodestone buried here. Once every seven years it *zoops*, joins their home forest to yours, and they go a-hunting and a-scavenging.'

'What for?'

'The things they need, Daddy-O.' She added a *dum-de-dum-dum-dum!* on her bongos for emphasis.

'And you're trying to stop them?'

'Stop them? It's a *party*, baby, why would I wanna do that?' The woman spoke loudly as a group of revellers rolled past. She lowered her voice and continued. 'I just needed to park the bus on top of the lodestone for a while, give its galactic batteries a top-up. That's what I was aiming for back in the eighties – or was it forward in the eighties?'

Old memories began to stir in Andrew, about a forgotten summer when he was a kid, and a winter that wasn't, and a mad old lady with a magical double-decker. 'Iris?'

'Got it in one.'

'And your bus is here too?'

'Under the tarpaulin.' She gestured to the covered edifice at the edge of the clearing. 'I dunno… Park something someplace long enough, and loonies will either scrawl on it, or start worshipping it. Don't even talk to me about Stonehenge.'

Andrew was trying to reconcile this psychedelic sixties refugee with the formal, irritable old woman he'd met before. 'You're so *different.*'

'What can I say, Screwdriver Boy? You gotta move with the times.'

'You know it's the nineties, right?'

'I didn't say you have to move in the same direction, did I? Now, let's get a shift on before these wolves get snappy…'

Later, on the bus - as Iris steered them home through the strange, roiling, multi-coloured corridors of eternity, singing along loudly and tunelessly to one of Andrew's tapes - he said: 'Iris, do you really think they were going to eat me?'

'Oh my darling, darling boy. So innocent!' She leant over from her position at the wheel, and kissed his shoulder. 'Let's just say that was one possibility, you dig?'

Summer 1998

Coming home was odd, Andrew reflected. The houses and buildings looked the same but different, as if someone had crept in and subtly changed them in his absence – moving things half a metre to the left, perhaps, or sneaking in an extra dusty window. He'd been away up in Stirling for nearly four years, his visits home increasingly erratic. But all that was over now; he had a piece of paper with a First Class degree in English Studies – and absolutely no idea what to do with it.

His shoulders felt heavy, and not just from the weight of the rucksack full of books and unwashed clothes. There was going to have to be a *conversation* with his formidable mother, and he wasn't looking forward to that at all.

As he walked up the street to Great Uncle Edward's house – still standing, but the roof a little more saggy – he noticed a woman camped out on the doorstep. She was in late-middle age with a worn but friendly face, dressed in a leopardskin-print jacket, with a baggy, shapeless hat. A small stuffed Panda toy nestled in her lap.

He slid the rucksack off his back, and sat down beside her. 'Iris. It's been a long time.'

'Eee, you're getting better at this, lovey! Sit down and have a ciggie with us.'

'The bus parked round the corner may have been a bit of a clue. It really is confusing, though. Every time we meet you're different.'

'While you stay the same? Look at you – you big strong thing! Can't believe you're the same lad that helped get me foot out the bus.'

'Good point. Well made.' He smiled. She seemed unlike the previous Irises, more dowdy perhaps, but warmer too.

She drew on her ciggie. 'I was right daft back then. Skittering about time and space all on my own. I have a stout travelling companion now, to help get me out of scrapes!'

'Less of the stout!' growled a fruity voice.

Andrew stared at the stuffed panda, then shook his head.

Iris regarded him critically. 'Oh love… you look right down in the dumps! What's the matter? You should have the world at your feet, smart young thing like you.'

'I dunno… It's just…'

'Unhappy in love, pet? Is he bad to you?'

'No, he's not! It's just it's really hard to meet up these days, and Scott's moving away soon, and…' He stopped. 'How did you know?'

'Yer Auntie Iris always knows.' She patted his arm gently. 'That old bus of mine, it doesn't just travel in time, it travels about in stories too. Good ones, bad ones; new ones, old ones; right shlocky mardy ones…'

'Planet of the Werewolves, and the Magic Kingdom of Snow?'

'That and all.' Iris nodded. 'Some end happy, and some make you cry, and some just stop - right at the bit you want to know more. Life's like that! You don't get to play out the tidy endings too often. But if there's one thing I've learned, if you come up against a problem…'

'Take it at full tilt? And to hell with the consequences?'

'You've got it, chuck. Every time.'

Andrew contemplated. 'Are we in a story now, Iris?' And if so which one? *Beautiful Thing*? *New Boy*? *Marked for Life*? He glanced at the crumbling house. *The Addams Family*?

'Oh love… We're always in a story.'

The door behind them opened, causing them both to turn round.

'Andrew, you're smoking! On the doorstep! Didn't I bring you up better?' His Mum did not look pleased.

'Mum, it's just one. It's not a habit, honest, and it's not important. I've got something to say–' he began, but her attention had shifted to Iris.

'YOU! I might've known!'

Iris pulled herself to her feet, a little unsteadily, the toy bear dropping to the ground. 'Oh, here we go… Sensible Flora! Always thinks she knows best!'

The two women, arms crossed firmly over their chests, stood and glared at each other.

'Mum! Iris! What's going on?'

'Ask her!'

'No, petal. You ask her! And while you're at it, ask her what she's done to this place?'

A small furry hand poked its way gently into Andrew's, distracting him from the confrontation. He glanced down, and saw Iris' panda was sitting on the step beside him.

'Well, I don't know about you, old boy, but I'm parched. These dog days of summer are perilously hot. Tempers get frayed.' Two beady black eyes blinked at him. 'Fancy a drink?'